one
more
time

Emily S. Morris grew up a military brat and has lived in such exciting places as Alaska, Hawaii, and Delaware. Like her characters, Lucy and Nicky, she is a 1990's graduate of Dover High who spent *a lot* of time at the beach. After earning a Master's degree in Screenwriting, she began a career as a novelist. She lives in Ohio with her family.

For more about Emily and her work, please visit her website: www.emilywritesromance.com

one more time

Emily S. Morris

ONE PLACE. MANY STORIES

HQ
An imprint of HarperCollins*Publishers* Ltd
1 London Bridge Street
London SE1 9GF

www.harpercollins.co.uk

HarperCollins*Publishers*
Macken House, 39/40 Mayor Street Upper
Dublin 1, D01 C9W8, Ireland

This edition 2025

1
First published in Great Britain by HQ,
an imprint of HarperCollins*Publishers* Ltd 2025

Copyright © Will-o'-the-Wisp Holdings LLC 2025

Emily S. Morris asserts the moral right to be identified as the author of this work.
A catalogue record for this book is available from the British Library.

ISBN: 978-0-00-876960-4

Set in Sabon LT Std by HarperCollins*Publishers* India

This novel is entirely a work of fiction. The names, characters and incidents
portrayed in it are the work of the author's imagination. Any resemblance to
actual persons, living or dead, events or localities is entirely coincidental.

All rights reserved. No part of this publication may be reproduced, stored
in a retrieval system, or transmitted, in any form or by any means,
electronic, mechanical, photocopying, recording or otherwise,
without the prior written permission of the publishers.

Without limiting the author's and publisher's exclusive rights, any unauthorised
use of this publication to train generative artificial intelligence (AI) technologies
is expressly prohibited. HarperCollins also exercise their rights under Article
4(3) of the Digital Single Market Directive 2019/790 and expressly reserve
this publication from the text and data mining exception.

Printed and bound in the UK using 100%
Renewable Electricity at CPI Group (UK) Ltd

For more information visit: www.harpercollins.co.uk/green

For my boys,
This is what I was doing while you were at school.
(Don't read it till you're eighteen.)

CHAPTER ONE

LUCY

There comes a time in every woman's life when she finds herself stumbling through the hallway of a five-star hotel juggling a purse, a bouquet of flowers, and a bag full of penises.

At least, that's what Lucy McManis told herself as she rummaged through the dark, cluttered abyss that was her handbag. Her hands were full, her feet hurt, and sweat from the 107-degree day was rapidly crusting over her skin in the frigid air of the Lusso Resort and Casino, Las Vegas. All Lucy wanted to do was sit down with an icy cocktail. First, though, she had to find her keycard.

She moved her fingers over the mysterious flakes and crumbs that lingered, imperturbable, at the bottom of her purse and wondered if her current predicament was just another one of those milestones that no one had told her about. Like the one where her neck developed a subtle wobble of its own, with no correlation to the movement of her head. Or, the new one where her feet swelled up simply by looking at a pair of three-inch heels. Bag of dicks – just another signpost on that glorious adventure known as womanhood.

The thought, dubious though it was, gave Lucy much-needed comfort. The angry moan of craft paper losing its battle with physics, however, did not.

When the thin twine handle of the shopping bag gave slightly beneath her fingers, Lucy's other hand skittered more frantically among the months-old drugstore receipts, multiple hair combs, and a squishy round thing that was hopefully a promotional stress ball.

She'd used the damn keycard to get the elevator to move. Where had it gone?

She grumbled an incomprehensible string of curses, recalling a time when hotel keys were made of metal and big chunks of plastic and reliably sunk to the bottom of lakes, car trunks, and handbags under the weight of their own ostentation. The good old days.

Lucy plunged her face into the gaping maw of her leather bag in a last-ditch effort to find her golden plastic salvation. It only took a moment for the decision to pay itself forward. And it wasn't with a hotel room keycard.

She felt the collision first on her forehead, which smashed into something warm and solid. Next was her foot, twisting awkwardly over a lump on the floor. Her arm flattened against her body with a thunk that made her gasp. The flower bouquet slipped from her fingers and tumbled away, a very pretty pink bouncing ball. Finally, and possibly most lethal (at least to her pride), came the loud rip of flimsy brown paper.

The shopping bag didn't just tear, though. No. It exploded. Like a pornographic piñata. Dildos, headbands with bobbing penises, and dick-shaped lollipops flew through the air and scattered from one side of the wide hallway to the other, glimmering like the world's rudest confetti on the thick chocolate brown carpet.

Glimpsing a pair of black Vans in her peripheral vision, Lucy realized that what she'd crashed into was a man. A rather large man by the sturdy feel of him.

'Gah! So sorry!' Lucy bellowed as she tried to mitigate the disaster and stay upright.

She bent over to scoop up the fugitive phalluses as quickly as possible, as though speed could help anyone unsee the abundance of pink, purple and inexplicably green disembodied cocks dotting the hallway.

It was an exercise in futility. The plastic wrappings were too glossy, the silicone too slippery.

'Man, that's a lot of dicks,' came an amused rumble from above her.

Lucy grudgingly accepted defeat and rose to her full height, staring down at the X-rated mess. She huffed, 'So, so many.'

As Lucy contemplated the logistics of fitting roughly one million penises into her smallish purse, the man spoke again. 'Lucy Rollins?'

The smooth timbre of his voice sent goose bumps marching down her arms. The fact that he had spoken her name, her *old* name, had her heart jumping out of her chest.

She looked up, meeting his eyes immediately. The deep green color she found there had her clutching the wall for support. That color had lived in her memory, had been burned into her gray matter like a brand. His were the only eyes she had ever seen with that particular depth of loden, earthy and warm. He was the sexiest man she'd ever laid eyes on. The sexiest man she'd ever known. The most delicious human who had ever touched her. And he had touched her. Years . . . decades . . . a lifetime ago.

'Nicky Broome,' she breathed.

'Oh my God,' Nicky said. 'It's you. It's really you.'

CHAPTER TWO

NICKY

'Hi,' she breathed. Barely a whisper. Really more of a sigh.

'Hi,' he replied. He was glad she'd spoken first with something easy to reply to, because his instinct was to word-vomit all over her with inappropriate familiarity.

I've wanted to see you forever. Where have you been? I thought I'd never see you again. Where did you go? Why has it been so damn long? Holy shit. Holy shit!

Lucy looked so much the same. There had been no moment of pause, no stutter of his brain to come up with the name to go with the familiar face. It had been years, far more than he had any desire to calculate. Still, he recognized her.

Her hair was a darker brown, shorter. Cut in a sharp bob to her chin, with bangs that dusted the top of perfectly arched eyebrows. She was older, of course. They were both older. But it was *her*. It was Lucy. He'd have known her anywhere.

Nicky realized that silence had opened up between them like a fissure while he'd been musing.

'You look the same,' he blurted, like a doofus.

'You don't,' she said, her eyes flicking to the thick tangle of tattoos on his arms.

'How are you?' Nicky asked, unwilling to shift his eyes from her face for fear she might vanish.

'Well . . .' She chuckled, waving her hands to indicate the truly staggering number of dicks all over the hall. 'I've been better.'

Nicky tutted his own amusement back at her, partly because of the situation. But also, because he had spotted her left hand and there was no ring there. It felt like a victory.

'Headed back to your room for some alone time?' he quipped, grinning.

Lucy laughed, then. A big, unfettered belly laugh, with her eyes closed and her head tilted back. It stole the breath clean out of his lungs.

'No,' she tutted. With a flirtatious tilt of the head and a very mischievous gleam in her eye, she added, 'These aren't *all* for me.'

Nicky felt his stomach flip. Do actual somersaults. He was a grown man, well into his forties. He was a successful person, had been around so many blocks it was hard to remember them all anymore. Still, his stomach fluttered like he was a teenager.

Lucy cleared her throat and shook her head as though clearing out cobwebs, or trying to adjust to the same sudden shift in reality that he couldn't quite grasp himself.

She looked down at the mess on the floor. 'I should, uh, get this sorted.' She bent over and began collecting the penis-pops by the sticks, giving him a perfect view of her ass in a pair of shorts tight-fitting enough to identify the outline of a credit card in her back pocket. He inhaled sharply.

'Wait,' he tried. 'I have a solution. Don't move.'

Lucy stood back up and eyed him, curiosity playing all over her features. Her face had softened, maybe, from how it had been. But it was still her. Lucy-goddamn-Rollins. In the flesh.

'I mean it,' he added. 'You're not going anywhere, right?'

'Nope,' she replied.

Nicky shuffled backward down the hall, digging in his pocket for his keycard while keeping her in his line of sight. 'Just be a sec.'

He found his card and his door, then popped in as fast as his feet would carry him. In the suite's hall closet, he grabbed a canvas bag marked with the hotel's name and instructions for laundry collection. He raced back to the hallway, expelling an audible sigh of relief when he found her still there, leaning against the wall trying to un-mash the flowers.

Nicky hustled over, and began tossing the porno party decorations into the laundry sack. Lucy joined, and in moments they had the whole place dick-free.

'Thank you,' she said.

'You're welcome.'

For a moment, they just stared at each other. Gaped in

perfect silence as a gentle puff of air conditioning rustled Lucy's hair.

There were so many things he wanted to say. Things he *needed* to say. But Nicky's mind could only spin as it tried to catch up. He'd just been heading out for a meeting and there she was. Just thinking about contracts and business obligations and *boom*. He was so fully stunned; he didn't know what to do with himself.

Lucy broke first, looking away and mumbling, 'Well, I'm just down the hallway, so . . .'

'Can I walk you?' Nicky asked.

She hesitated, just long enough for a spark of nervousness to zap him in the chest.

'Okay,' she replied, finally. Then she started digging around in her handbag again.

'Are you here for a convention?' he asked, holding up the laundry bag and raising an eyebrow.

'That sounds like fun, but no. I'm here for a wedding.' She waggled the hot pink bouquet.

'Oh.' *Fuck*.

'Not mine,' she clarified.

'Oh.' *Thank God*.

'This is me,' she said, stopping. 'But I still can't find my keycard.'

'Um, could it be . . .' He pointed to her back pocket.

Her hand slipped into the back pocket of her shorts.

When she pulled out the golden keycard, she looked between it and Nicky, her eyes scrunched up in confusion. 'How did you . . . ?'

'Lucky guess?'

A sly smile crept across her lips. 'Lucky?'

'Yep,' he replied, with a sly grin of his own.

She turned to flash the card over the lock-pad.

Nicky blurted, 'I'd really love to catch up. Dinner, maybe?' He tried not to sound desperate. Really, he did.

She looked down at the flowers in her hand. Exhaled slowly. Nicky could feel the 'no' coming. Hated it.

'Drinks?' he offered.

Her eyes snagged on his. He tried to read her thoughts in their variegated shades of blue.

'Yeah, okay,' she replied with a little smile. It was really no more than half a smile, but he'd take it.

'Great. I'll pick you up here at seven.'

'Seven-thirty?'

'Sure. Seven-thirty.'

She swiped the keycard over the pad, and the lock clicked open.

'It's really good to see you.' Nicky handed her the canvas sack and brushed a finger along the back of her hand as she took it. 'I'll see you later?' It sounded much more like a question than he'd intended.

'Yeah, Nicky. I'll see you later,' she replied quietly.

CHAPTER THREE

LUCY

Lucy stepped into the suite and leaned her back against the door as it closed. She wasn't sure how she'd made it down the hallway. Her legs felt like rubber bands. She didn't know if they were about to noodle to the ground or snap back and set her running. Her heart was pounding out a death metal song against her ribcage. The things she'd been carrying all plunked to the ground, except for the shredded remnants of the paper bag. It skittered across the marble entryway ahead of her like it had a mind of its own.

She'd acted like a maniac, right? She'd been silent and weird. She should have just casually said, 'Oh, wow! Good to see you. How've you been for the last lifetime?' And then flipped her hair or put her hand on her hip or something. No big deal. Casual.

The thing was, when she'd seen Nicky Broome up close for the first time in a trillion years, it hadn't felt casual. Not at all. It felt like getting hit by a truck.

'Hey!' came the bright, cheerful voice of Chloe from the living room. Lucy heard the soft clack of her daughter's footsteps. 'Mom!' Chloe stepped over the paper bag and headed right for Lucy. 'Are you okay? What happened? You're pale as a sheet.'

Oh, you know, exploded a bag of dicks all over a ridiculously hot, world-famous rock star. Pretty sure he was checking out my ass. Made a date (or something) with him later. Just your average Sunday.

'Nothing happened,' Lucy sighed. 'I'm fine. It's just hot out there.'

If there's one thing that Lucy had mastered in her twenty-one years of motherhood it was delivering a gentle lie. She was damn good at it.

'Oh, I know,' Chloe said, lifting the bags from the floor. 'July is a dumb time to be in Vegas. Even Chandler's beginning to see it now.'

The mention of her daughter's groom brought Lucy back to reality. The reminder that there were things to be done, items to tick off the list, made her feel more solid again. She pushed herself off the door and shuffled behind Chloe into the kitchen area of their absurdly enormous suite.

'Where's the stuff?' Chloe asked with impish glee.

'The big bag,' Lucy replied.

Chloe squealed when she looked inside the canvas sack. 'Amazing! Wish I could have gone with you!'

'How were Mr. and Mrs. Heylen?' Lucy asked.

'Grumpy. Tired. Said about three words,' Chloe lamented.

'So, totally normal, then?'

'More normal than normal. So damn normal it's actually painful. How they ended up with Chandler and Mason for kids I will never understand. They're so conventional and boring. Like, *clinically* boring.'

'Pretty sure I'm the wrong kind of doctor, but I'm going to go out on a limb here and say "boring" isn't a legitimate medical diagnosis.'

'Yet, they are that boring. And I know they still think I'm a basket case. But what can you do?'

'You've finally given up on trying to convince them you're average?' Lucy teased, placing the flower bouquet in the kitchen's full-sized refrigerator.

Chloe beamed at her, and it gave Lucy such an ache of love and wonder that she actually clutched her chest.

'I'm so grateful to have you,' Chloe said, racing to Lucy's side and squeezing her tight.

'Not half as grateful as I am,' Lucy replied, kissing the top of her daughter's soft chestnut hair.

Maybe weddings were like this. Typical weddings, that is. She'd gotten more hugs from Chloe in the previous six months than she had in the six years before the engagement. Lucy didn't remember so many hugs when she'd married Brandon, Chloe's father. Then again, Lucy's parents were the prototype from which all Mr. and Mrs. Heylens had been cast.

Ugh, that thought had her drifting back to her childhood. From there, it was only a quick loop and a left back to Nicky Broome.

'What time are you headed out to pick up the girls,

again?' Lucy asked nonchalantly as Chloe hefted the sack of penises toward her bedroom.

'I'm going to the airport to meet Hannah and Gabby around seven, Alexis and Francesca arrive at eight-ish if their layovers work and they can catch the second leg to Vegas. Then, once we're all together, we'll do a late dinner at Spago in the Bellagio.'

'Sounds fun,' Lucy replied. *Sounds perfect.*

'You could come with, you know. Daddy's assistant is making all the arrangements and throwing that Wall Street cash around. He could add you to the reservation.'

'No way! You have fun with your friends.'

'You're sure?' Chloe asked.

'Totally sure. I'm just going to take a long, hot bath in that swimming pool I've got in there, have a nap, and get some room service or something.' *Or something. Like figure out what to wear for drinks with a Grammy winner. Maybe there's a YouTube tutorial?*

*

The sweet sounds of Donny Hathaway's voice trilled from the integrated Bluetooth audio system in the bathroom. (The whole suite was wired for sound, because of course it was.) Lucy hummed along as she sank into the steaming bubbles of the Olympic-sized bathtub in her private en suite and conceded that allowing her ex-husband to pay for everything had been the right decision.

There had been a moment when Lucy had wanted

to split the cost of the wedding with him. She'd been thinking 'equal parents, equal cost' or something similarly boneheaded and noble at the time. But when Chloe had announced that she wanted a destination wedding, Lucy raised her white flag. She'd let the millionaire have this one.

For years, Lucy's ex-husband wielded his money like a weapon to win Chloe's love. As though their daughter was a prize they were fighting over. It was a competition Lucy had never signed up for and had no hope of winning. How could a college professor in Ohio compete with a Manhattan hedge fund manager? Ridiculous. Lucy's refusal to play hadn't discouraged Brandon, though. There were outlandish summer vacations. Birthday presents that cost more than Lucy's car. (On her sixteenth, it had been an actual car that cost almost as much as Lucy's *house*.) There were offers of a British boarding school, then Ivy League university. While Chloe decided to go to public school and enroll in the university Lucy taught at instead, it still felt like Brandon was winning somehow.

He was an expert at filling the empty hole left by his absence with buckets of cold hard cash. It was typical finance-bro stuff – minimum effort, maximum result. But, especially in Chloe's teen years, the strategy had been effective. Teenagers are ruthless but simple creatures, and Chloe absolutely J'adored her Dior.

In weak moments, like while doing the three hundredth load of laundry or rumbling along in a yellow bus on a school field trip, the whole thing made Lucy bitter. It had taken a lot of years (and eye-rolling) but as Lucy sipped champagne in a sea of soft, foamy comfort, she thought she might finally be over it. Lucy may refuse to drive her daughter's G-Wagon, but she was sure as hell going to enjoy the penthouse suite at the Lusso.

'I'm off!' Chloe screamed through the door.

'Okay, have fun!' Lucy yelled back.

'Don't wait up for me!'

'I won't!'

Lucy had her own Vegas craziness to deal with. And his name was Nicky Broome.

CHAPTER FOUR

LUCY

The knock came at exactly 7:30, like he'd been waiting outside the door for the precise time they'd arranged before making his move. Lucy knew it was exactly 7:30, because she had been sitting on the sofa nervously tapping her foot while staring at her phone as the 29 had switched to 30.

She thought she was ready. She was dressed, that much was true, but as she opened the door and saw Nicky Broome waiting for her, Lucy knew with one-hundred-percent certainty that she was not *ready*.

Nicky Broome just casually standing in a doorway was a damn marvel. It was an expensive cologne ad. A work of art. A fucking Times Square billboard.

He was tall and broad, but not in a gym-rat way. He was lean, elegant. He wore a black Henley, sleeves pushed up to his elbows. Dark jeans. Simple, really. Nothing special. Except the walls of the Lusso's penthouse floor were gold-leafed and the light from the sconces was warm and dim. It made his skin seem lit from within.

The colorful tattoos on his arms rippled with the movement of muscles and sinew beneath as he shoved his hands in his pockets. And for a second – less time than it took her to exhale a wistful sigh – he looked like himself. His old self. The boy Lucy used to know. She had to close her eyes against the slap of pure nostalgia that threatened to knock her over.

When she opened her eyes again, Nicky's artfully messy brown hair had flopped over his forehead. He smiled and she noticed that he was freshly shaven. The idea that he might have shaved for her made her heart skip and her cheeks heat.

'Hi,' he said. 'You look great.'

'You too,' Lucy replied.

Nicky leaned forward just as Lucy was pulling the door open. Maybe he was moving to kiss her cheek? Or maybe it was some sort of famous-guy air-kiss situation? Either way, with Lucy backing up to open the door, it ended up being more of a stumble over the threshold.

Instinctively, Lucy grabbed his shoulder to keep him from falling.

It took about a nanosecond for her brain to catch up, which was when she transitioned from a protective grab to an epically awkward half-hug of his bicep.

Wow, killing it so far.

'Still up for drinks?' Nicky half-chuckled, with a sweet smile that told her he was going to ignore her graceless bumbling.

'Sure,' she replied, dropping his arm like it was radioactive and trying to keep her cringe strictly internal.

Lucy took her clutch from the entry table, closed the door behind her, and fell into step at Nicky's side.

As they started down the hallway, the damn thing seemed to elongate. Like a horror movie. The elevator somehow got farther away the more they progressed. Maybe it was a function of the implacable silence stretching between them. Or perhaps it was the constant refrain of 'what is happening to my life right now?' that was pounding in her skull like bad techno at a rave. Either way, by the time they finally reached the elevator and Nicky pushed the down button, the tension between them had expanded and sucked up all the oxygen in Las Vegas.

The silence was a weight pressing on Lucy's chest. She wouldn't last ten more minutes like that, let alone however long drinks with a rock star might take. (They were all champion drinkers, weren't they?)

She turned to him. 'If it's going to be too weird—'

Only to catch the end of whatever he was saying at the same time, something like '. . . don't want it to be awkward.'

They laughed at their overlap.

'You first,' he said.

Lucy grimaced. 'It feels weird, right? Does it feel weird?'

He sighed. 'I wouldn't say weird. It's just been a long time.'

Twenty-eight years. It had been *twenty-eight* years.

The elevator doors opened before them. Nicky stuck his hand in the door to keep them open.

He blurted, 'It's me. I'm nervous. I need to not be so nervous.'

Excuse me?

'*You're* nervous?' Lucy grumbled. 'Are you kidding? I'm standing here with the lead singer of Super. How do you think *I* feel?'

'Okay, right,' he said, taking a deep breath. 'Let's pretend like we're just a couple of people who knew each other in high school.'

'Yeah, okay. But I was a hundred-percent nervous around you in high school, too.'

'You were not,' he rebuffed, incredulous.

'Seriously? Everybody was nervous around you. You were Nicky-fucking-Broome, hottest guy in high school, probably the hottest guy in the state. And you were so ridiculously *cool*.'

'Me?' he asked, as though truly shocked.

Lucy looked to the heavens for assistance, but found only a garish exit sign. 'Oh, my God. Yes, *you*.'

Nicky stepped into the elevator and held the open button until Lucy had safely followed.

'I would not have called myself the hottest guy in school,' Nicky grumbled. 'Definitely not the coolest.'

'Nicky Broome,' Lucy admonished, 'you brought a twenty-one-year-old girl – sorry, woman – to prom.'

He shrugged. 'I knew her from work.'

'She had tattoos.'

'Well—'

'And a tongue piercing.'

'I mean—'

Lucy could not be stopped. 'And rocked that pink leather minidress like she was on MTV. It was so much like Molly Ringwald's prom dress from *Pretty in Pink* and yet was so damn tight. She wasn't wearing anything under it, right? God, I've always wondered about that. I'm right, aren't I?'

Nicky looked at the floor, trying but failing to hold back a smirk. That answer was good enough for Lucy.

'I knew it! Ugh, that dress was the perfect level of subversive. I was so jealous of that dress. What was her name? She was a legend.'

Nicky laughed. 'Her name was Heather.'

'Of course, her name was Heather. The perfect name for her.'

'What about you?' Nicky asked as the elevator descended.

'What about me?'

'You were the cool one,' he said without a trace of sarcasm.

Lucy was dumfounded. 'Uh, no. I was a complete nerd in high school. Utterly forgettable.'

'Lies,' Nicky said plainly. 'With all those cut-up concert tees and the Doc Martens and those fucking hair buns? What do they call those things by the way?'

'Space buns,' Lucy offered.

Nicky groaned like they had driven him crazy – in a good way. '*Space buns*,' he mused softly.

Lucy laughed. 'Yep, add some time at Comic-Con and you've just spelled out the FBI's 1994 guide to identifying a geek.'

'Bullshit.'

Lucy snort-laughed. 'Well, I definitely call bullshit on you. You *had* to know. You had to! Girls actually stopped midstride in the hallways to gawk at you.' She knew. She had occasionally been one of them.

'Is that what they were doing?' he asked.

God, teenagers were stupid. If proof were ever necessary, here it was.

'Wow,' Lucy mused. 'You have just completely altered everything I thought I knew about high school.'

He shrugged. 'I always felt like an outsider.'

Nicky looked at her then with a sort of vulnerability, a kind of tenderness that made her skin prickle.

'Same,' Lucy breathed.

The elevator doors opened and broke the moment. Nicky made a point to pull the sleeves of his Henley down to his wrists.

'This way,' Nicky said. He guided her forward with the mere hint of a touch at her lower back. It was a graze. A whisper. Barely there. Still, Lucy's body lit up like the Strip – all blinking neon and blinding incandescence.

Holy shit.

Nicky led her through a busy atrium, then a bank of slot machines lined up like soldiers awaiting inspection. Only one was occupied. By a woman wearing heavy eyeliner and a shirt with daisies printed all over it. Her head turned from the flashing dollar signs on the screen in front of her. As soon as her eyes landed on Nicky, she did a double take. An actual double take, with a confused furrow forming over her brow as her jaw hit the floor.

Same, honey. Same.

Nicky stopped them at a restaurant called Gioco situated between the poker room and poker *slots* room.

He stepped to the hostess stand, where no name was asked, and none was given.

Instead, the bespectacled hostess greeted them with: 'Welcome. Please follow me, Mr. Broome.'

The hostess guided them through a large dining area dripping in coffee-colored velvet and bronze lighting. To her credit, the young woman gaped slack-jawed at Nicky only three times on the short trip. Lucy admired the girl's self-control.

She left them at a rounded banquette nestled in a private nook. It was more velvet, more bronze, more opulence. Shielded from the rest of the space by a thick curtain, the room felt close, comfortable, and seductive. Impossibly sexy.

Lucy slid herself into the booth and picked up her menu. No prices, just detailed descriptions, and a bunch of liquor brands she'd never heard of.

Almost immediately, their server appeared. Just as quickly, the man tried not to choke when he recognized Nicky.

'What can I get for you, miss?'

The 'miss' was a nice touch, since she most certainly qualified as 'ma'am.'

'I'll have an Old Fashioned, please. Heavy on the cherries,' Lucy said.

'Certainly,' the server replied.

'And you know what?' Lucy added. 'Make it a double.'

'Of course.'

Nicky said, 'Modelo, draft. Please.'

'It would be my pleasure,' the man replied before disappearing.

As silence once again stretched out between them, Nicky's eyes bounced around Lucy's face.

She suddenly felt acutely self-conscious, as though every one of the twenty-eight years since she'd last sat across from him had dropped on her face all at once. She knew that there were lines where there hadn't been before, freckles and marks that remained stubbornly unresponsive to decades of dedication to anti-aging creams and potions. She was closer to fifty than forty. She knew this. It wasn't a secret or anything she was usually bothered by.

'So,' Lucy said, privately reaching deep to find the self-confidence she'd somehow mislaid between her hotel room and the restaurant.

'So,' Nicky parroted.

Lucy couldn't find the patience required for small talk. Instead, she blurted, 'So, this international rock-star thing. What's that like?'

Nicky chuckled. 'Not going in soft. Okay, I appreciate that.' He idly fingered the flickering electronic votive in the middle of the table, staring at it with a faraway look. 'Uh, right now it's good. Sometimes it's amazing. Other times . . . terrible.'

'Gloriously vague,' Lucy said, smiling.

'I don't know how to quantify it. Music is more than a job, I guess. More even than a career.' He paused for a moment, thinking. Looked up to her and added, 'I don't want to get all woo-woo on you here. I try to save all my crazy up for the second date.'

Shit on a stick. Is this a fucking date?

Lucy glossed right over the slightly terrifying implication of his comment and said, 'I work at a liberal arts university, woo-woo is my bread and butter.'

'Okay, how do I explain it?' he asked, gazing at her as though she might have an answer. 'Music is part of everything I do. Every day. It's how I move through the world. It's an internal soundtrack, and the ambient noise of life all around. So, to call it work, like this thing that I do and then stop doing seems . . .' His voice trailed off, like he was searching for the right word.

'Insufficient?' she offered.

'Exactly,' he said. 'Insufficient. What about you? What's your work like?'

'Not as exciting as yours,' she replied. 'I'm a college professor. Well, associate professor, but I'm up for tenure this year.'

'Something in music?'

'Sort of, but not— Wait, why would you think that?'

'You really seemed to love it.'

The fact that he remembered that about her – and the space buns, of all things – sent a warm, fuzzy feeling coursing through her limbs. 'I did.' She corrected, 'I *do*. But technically my area is American Cultural Studies. Which is just a fancy way of saying pop culture, TV, movies, music. All of it. I mostly focus on the second half of the twentieth century.'

'College sounds like a lot more fun than I was led to believe.'

'Well, technically, what I teach is history now.'

'Jesus,' he griped.

'Right?' Lucy replied. 'It's a trip. The students this coming year in my 101 classes were born in 2005.'

'*What?*' he bellowed, astonished.

'Uh-huh.' Lucy didn't feel her age often, but when she looked at the birth years of her students it really hit her.

Nicky shook his head. 'It's like one minute you're still dreaming up ways to have everything you want and the next you're googling "how do I reduce my cholesterol?"'

'It happened overnight,' Lucy added.

'Yes! When was it for you?'

Lucy took a moment to think about it. 'Forty, I guess.'

'Me too.'

'Fucking sucks,' Lucy concluded.

'It really does.'

The server returned with their drinks, popping in and out like a phantom.

Lucy took a glug of her Old Fashioned. Delicious. Perfect.

Nicky rucked his sleeves back up to his elbows and sipped his beer. Lucy tried to breathe and not to stare at his tattoos. Failed miserably.

On his forearm was something that looked like it might be a blue narwhal. Delicately inked words that started on his forearm did a little twist up around his elbow and higher, disappearing under his shirtsleeve. Lucy had a sudden vision of charting Nicky's skin, exploring every last splash of ink and recording it like some kind of sexed-up tattoo cartographer. She couldn't be the only one, though. Not when it came to Nicky Broome. There was probably a website dedicated to it somewhere. She'd look it up later.

Nicky leaned over his elbows on the table. 'Okay, it's time.'

Lucy's heart thumped uncomfortably. She knew they would have to talk about it at some point, but she wasn't ready. Hedging, she asked, 'Time for what?'

'First, what's your poison? Apple Music? Amazon? Maybe Spotify? Tidal?'

Oh, thank God. She took another sip as she waited for her heart rate to settle out of cardiac arrest territory.

'Spotify,' she said finally.

'Me too. Okay, let's see it,' Nicky said, beckoning with his hand.

'I don't know. That's kind of personal,' Lucy teased.

'Come on,' he teased right back. He held up his phone and waggled it in front of her. 'I'll show you mine.'

How could anyone resist that?

'Fine,' she said, 'but don't go moving things around.'

'Promise.' He mimed crossing his heart.

Lucy retrieved her phone from her little evening clutch on the seat beside her. She unlocked the phone and clicked to open the app. She slipped it into Nicky's waiting hand, just as he did the same.

She scrolled through his playlists. They had names like *Blah* and *Orange* and *Wishbone*, so she just picked one at random.

'What'd you get?' he asked.

'Marshmallow?'

'That's a good one. For workouts.'

Lucy took a deeper look at the list and grinned. 'Yeah, I see what kind of workout you're getting.'

'What's that supposed to mean?'

'These are all sex songs,' Lucy replied plainly.

'They are not!' he exclaimed, with a teasing smile.

'Uh, you have "Pour Some Sugar on Me" in here.'

'One song!'

Lucy flicked down the list, laughing as she went. '"Tush," "Crazy on You," "Give Me All Your Lovin'," "You Shook Me All Night Long," "Whole Lotta Love"? Shall I continue?'

'Okay, okay,' he griped.

Lucy dug further into his lists.

'Oh, Nicky!' she gasped.

'What?'

'This playlist called Furniture. The Smithereens?'

'What's wrong with The Smithereens?'

'The best thing about The Smithereens is their name.'

Nicky's mouth dropped open. '"Blood and Roses"? "A Girl Like You"?'

Lucy shook her head. *Nope. Not going to convince me.*

'Okay, no Smithereens. Interesting.' He looked back

down at her playlists and said, 'What made you want to go into teaching?'

Good question. One she'd asked herself plenty.

She tried, 'It wasn't teaching so much; it was academia in general, I guess. I got to college and it felt like, I don't know, a warm hug.' It sounded dumb, but Lucy remembered the feeling of peace and stability that had enveloped her at college. At eighteen, it had felt like the best kind of drug. She continued, 'It was comfortable. Nice. Don't get me wrong, there's plenty of backstabbing and underhanded garbage like in every workplace, but it's just so . . . *cozy*. I don't know how else to put it. The campus and the old buildings and the library. The students who mostly don't want to drink themselves to early cirrhosis. The dedication to thinking. Valuing thought and experimentation and ideas. It appeals to me in a way few other things do.'

Nicky hummed his understanding, but also stared at her lips and clutched her phone like he was trying to Hulk-smash it with his grip.

'Did you ever go?' Lucy asked. 'To college?'

'Nope,' he replied.

'Well, it's where I'm the happiest, I guess,' Lucy finished. Maybe that was still true. Probably. She looked down at Nicky's phone again, flipped to a different playlist. 'Whoa, whoa, whoa. Wait just one minute. There is an awful lot of David Lee Roth in here and almost no Sammy Hagar. Are you—' She feigned a look of shock and horror. 'Are you Team David?'

'Oh, shit,' he played right along. 'You're a Sammy lover?'

'Of course!' she replied. 'As though David Lee Roth could compete. Ha! Impossible.'

'Ouch,' he said pressing a hand over his chest dramatically. 'It hurts.'

She laughed at the histrionics, and Nicky winked at her.

Lucy felt that wink in her panties, and got the distinct impression that yeah, she was probably on a fucking date. And it was also very likely that she was in deep, deep trouble.

CHAPTER FIVE

NICKY

Drinks turned into dinner. A leisurely thing involving a bottle of wine and steaks for savoring slowly. One tiny, minute-dragging nibble at a time.

Nicky had watched transfixed through the first course as the wine had warmed Lucy's skin and exaggerated her expressions. Not that she was sloppy, just *more*. A concentrated, lit-up Lucy.

She wore a silk tank top something-or-other that looked like it would slide down her arms and spill to the floor with a mere flick of his wrist. She kept tucking her hair behind her ear and running her tongue across her bottom lip. He tried to memorize it, so he could play it back later, over and over again.

'So, Las Vegas,' she said, cutting her steak. 'Are you here for business or pleasure?'

Both, now. He hoped.

She added hastily, 'Or, wait . . . do you live here?'

'In the hotel?'

'Well, I don't know,' she said. 'Rock stars can be eccentric and peculiar.'

He hated how she kept calling him a rock star. The way she said it hit him like an insult. She made it sound like he was from another planet or something.

'I'm here for business.'

'Concert? Recording?'

'I'm afraid I'm not at liberty to say,' he replied.

Shit, maybe he *was* from another planet.

'Ooh, mysterious.'

Nicky leaned over the table and whispered, 'Super's doing a residency here in eighteen months or so. We haven't announced it yet.'

'That's exciting! Like Wayne Newton!' she exclaimed with that damn mischievous twinkle in her eye that made his heart thump hard.

'Uh,' he played along, 'more like Elvis.'

'Or maybe Engelbert Humperdinck?' she asked, trying really hard not to giggle.

'Aerosmith.'

'Liberace?'

'Maybe, Elton John.'

She tilted her head and squinted her eyes as though assessing him, 'Oh, so more like The Osmonds, you're saying?'

'You're killing me, Lucy Rollins,' Nicky said, grinning like a damn fool.

'Man, I haven't been called that in ages,' she said wistfully, staring down at her plate.

'What are you now?'

'McManis. After I divorced my first husband, I kept it so that my daughter and I would have the same last name.'

Finally, they were getting to the good stuff.

'What's your daughter like?' he asked.

'Chloe is twenty-one, beautiful. Funny. Brilliant. Madly in love. I'm here for her wedding. After the honeymoon they're moving to Boston where she'll start a program in clinical psychology at BU.'

'Wow,' Nicky marveled.

'Do you have any kids?' Lucy asked, before taking a bite of teeny fancy carrots.

'Two. Twins, with my first wife. Wade and Conner. They're twenty-five. Wade's in New York, an architect. Conner's a musician. In LA.'

'Wow,' she echoed.

They gazed at each other, and Nicky knew what she was feeling. He could feel it, too. So much time had passed. Time enough for children to be born and grow and become adults. Was it too much time? Were there too many minutes between them? Between what had been and what *could* have been?

Nicky took a deep breath trying to steady his thoughts and bring them back to the moment.

'So, you said *first* husband . . .'

'Shit,' she replied with a grimace. 'I was sort of hoping you might not catch that.'

'Come on, how many?' he joked.

She sheepishly held up three fingers.

'Same for me,' he said.

'Really?'

'Yeah,' said Nicky. 'Currently none, for the record.'

She nodded. 'Same.' *Thank God.*

He added, 'There were two that were official. Then another one that . . . Well, let's just say there were NDAs involved and technically – according to the law – it didn't actually happen. But don't ask, I can't tell you who. She's famous.' Man, he enjoyed playing with her.

'Oh, now you have to tell me!'

'NDAs, remember?' he taunted, unable to withhold his grin.

'Twenty questions? Very vague?'

He shook his head.

'I'll get it out of you. I can be very persuasive when I want to be,' she teased.

He had no doubt of that. None at all.

After Nicky paid and they left the restaurant, he still hadn't had enough. There were still questions he hadn't figured out how to ask her. Things he'd wanted to say for decades that he still didn't have the courage to voice. He needed more time.

In a bid to keep people at bay, Nicky yanked the sleeves of his shirt back down over his wrists and pulled a black ballcap from his back pocket. He pulled it down low over his eyes. The tats and the face tended to give him away.

'What's this?' Lucy said, looking him over. Then her ridiculously blue eyes flashed with understanding. 'Ah, incognito mode.' She smiled.

Nicky rolled his eyes. 'Yeah, something like that.' Jesus, he really was from a different planet. Thing was, normal was always just right there. On the other side of his ballcap. On the other side of the cameras everybody had in their pockets these days. So close, but always just out of reach.

As they walked on, Nicky leaned into her, both to be heard over the jangling and bleeping of the ever-present slot machines, and to get a better dose of her. He took a moment to inhale deeply, like a creeper. He was so close that he could smell the dessert coffee on her breath, and beyond it to something spicy and floral, skin-warmed and deep.

'Want to take a walk?' he asked finally.

'Outside?'

'Inside? Around the resort?'

She leaned into him, resting a hand on his forearm. He felt her breath on his ear, trailing down his neck. It sent a shiver of pure pleasure straight to his cock.

Jesus.

Nicky couldn't remember the last time he'd had such a strong reaction to a woman. *Maybe never?*

'Sure,' she breathed.

They ambled around the casino floor, people watching. He only caught three or four people staring at *him* then turning excitedly to the person beside them. There would probably be some fuzzy pictures floating around the internet after this, but he didn't care. As long as people didn't intrude.

Nicky took Lucy's hand to guide her around a drunk guy who was very excited about winning a hand of blackjack and then just never let it go.

Their walk was just as silent as the one they'd taken earlier. This time, though, the heaviness between them wasn't awkwardness, it was only the weight of their intertwined hands. The quiet wasn't a burden, more like potential than apprehension. It wasn't much, but he'd take it.

They meandered without any real direction for a length of time Nicky couldn't quantify. He had no desire to look at his phone, felt no urge to measure the experience.

Eventually they settled into idle chatter, then to conversation. They walked and they talked. He made her laugh a few times.

She was still so damn smart and quick, and so fucking pretty. And she was really *there*. Lucy. The girl who had lived for so long in his memory and his dreams.

Somehow, in the formless haze that is casino time, they landed at Lucy's end of the fortieth floor. At her door, she pulled the hotel keycard from her clutch with a flourish.

'I've got it now,' she said, as a triumphant smile tried to make it to her eyes.

She held the card over the keypad, and the lock clicked open with a sound that echoed in Nicky's brain.

He braced his hands on either side of the doorframe to keep himself from reaching for her body, her curves, those infuriatingly silky little straps that held her top up.

She turned to face him and exhaled a ragged breath. 'You want to come in?'

'So much,' he moaned. 'But I try not to make the same mistakes twice.'

A flash of confusion and hurt passed over her blue eyes. 'Okay.' She turned quickly back to the door.

Nicky scrambled, 'No, shit! That's not what I meant.'

Lucy turned back to face him, and a wisp of hair slipped over her mouth. He dragged his index finger slowly across her lips and pushed her hair back over her ear. 'I don't want it to be like last time. I don't want to . . . rush with you.'

Her eyes searched his face, her cheek tilting ever so slightly toward the hand that he couldn't bring himself to move from her jaw.

Nicky leaned in close, brushing his lips against her ear. Her body shivered, and he felt it everywhere. 'Let's do this again. Tomorrow.'

'I'm busy,' she whispered.

Nicky groaned and rested his forehead against hers.

She finished, 'Until five.'

'I'll be here at five-oh-five.'

She chuckled.

'Five-fifteen?' he begged.

'Five-fifteen,' she echoed.

Nicky pressed a kiss to Lucy's cheek, soft and slow. He breathed her in one more time and then, with a level of self-control he'd never employed before in his entire life, he backed away.

'Thank you for dinner,' she said, gripping the door handle with white-knuckled intensity.

'Thank you for joining me. See you tomorrow?' He really had to practice saying that so it didn't sound like an open-ended question.

'Five-fifteen,' she replied.

Lucy slipped inside her suite, and the door snapped closed.

Almost immediately, Nicky regretted his newfound discipline and the chivalrous nonsense that had generated it. He shoved his hands in the pockets of his jeans to keep from knocking on the door and taking it all back, from blurting all the questions that had formed over the previous hours. And then kissing her senseless. Maybe not in that order.

But it would be better this way. What was left of his higher reasoning knew it was true. He'd completely fucked things up the first time around with Lucy and really didn't want to do that again. Didn't make it any easier, though.

As he shuffled back down the hallway, Nicky's mind turned back to the one thing that had grated at him that night. Her damn Spotify. It had been a kick to the gut.

Her playlists were good. He respected them. She seemed to be into the blues and soul now. There were some all-girl bands he didn't listen to enough. The only problem was that his own music was conspicuously absent.

There had been plenty of Pearl Jam. An ungodly amount of Foo Fighters. Nirvana, Queens of the Stone Age, Rage Against the Machine, The Black Keys, Pixies, The Hives, even Maroon-Fucking-5. Not a single Super song. Not even 'The Breathing Room.'

Nicky knew for a fact that it alone had something like eight-hundred-million streams on the platform. Was it possible that not even one of those had been her? The idea made his fists clench.

If he could just think of a way to ask her about it that didn't make him sound like an asshat. Unfortunately, 'hey, what'd you think of that big hit I wrote?' was flat-out douchey no matter how many winks and smiles you added. (Ask him how he knew.)

What Nicky really wanted was for her to bring it up. He needed her to. Maybe she didn't realize? Maybe she didn't know about 'The Breathing Room'? Didn't understand?

What if she just hated Super? What if his whole life's work was just an annoying aside to her? Maybe she was one of those people who heard his songs on the radio and thought 'not these jokers again' before changing the station? Would it matter?

He was disgusted with himself, but he had to admit – it would.

CHAPTER SIX

LUCY

Lucy stepped out of her heels in the entryway, tiptoeing through the dappled wash of a nightlight until she spotted Chloe's bedroom door open, and the lights off. She was still out with her bridesmaids. At least that was one less thing Lucy had to think about.

She didn't know how she would explain her relationship with Nicky Broome to Chloe if it came to that. Truthfully, she had a difficult time explaining it to herself. Even after all the years that had passed.

It had been decades, plenty of time to come to terms with the hows and the whys. They'd only had one night. Less than twenty-four hours. It was no time at all, really, in the grand scheme of things. If Lucy added it all up, she'd probably spent more time picking out nail polish, or untangling charger cords in the span of her life. Their time together had been a flash, a blink of an eye.

But it was also forever.

CHAPTER SEVEN

LUCY

1990-Something

'What are you doing over there? Planning out your *Sassy* photoshoot?' Kim said as she waddled into the living room on her heels. Her toes were freshly painted, but Kim being Kim, she couldn't just sit down and wait for them to dry.

Lucy looked up from the display of outfits and accessories draped over the living room chairs and rolled her eyes at her best friend. 'Don't pretend like you don't have an outfit ready. Because I know you do.'

'As a matter of fact, I have two,' Kim said. 'I'm trying to decide between so tight it's almost dangerous, and so short it's almost pornographic.'

'Oh good, a classic.'

'Well, it is our first weekend at the beach. I feel an impression should be made,' Kim retorted with a dignified lilt.

'An impression of Mike Pellegrini's hand on your ass, you mean?'

'Exactly.'

Kim Rusike and Lucy Rollins were almost exactly the same age. Separated by only two days in March. Thanks to the alphabet, they'd been seated next to each other in school for nearly their entire lives. They were a perfect match in personality, but somehow, Kim had managed to become infinitely more self-possessed and sophisticated in the same eighteen years it had taken Lucy to become, uh, not hideous.

Lucy accepted that she gave off fairly sharp tough-cookie vibes while, even at eighteen, Kim managed elegant and refined without really trying. Kim's eyes were a shade of golden amber so arresting it could stop a man's heart. Her skin was buttery smooth and absolutely blemish-free at all times (even during her period, which Lucy thought was completely unfair of the universe).

Thanks to Kim's dad, a black former Eagles defensive end, and her mother, a white, extremely blond professional spender of football money, Kim had a combination of features that was utterly unique, especially in Delaware. She was complete supermodel material, from the top of her smooth black hair to the tip of her neon pink toenails. If Kim had any inclination whatsoever, she would already be walking a runway somewhere. Pity for fashion photographers the world over, she desperately wanted to be a lawyer instead.

Lucy looked over her choices one more time. The black-and-white-striped cropped tee and button-fly jeans was the winner. Especially if she wore her leather motorcycle jacket and the Mary Jane Docs she'd gotten for graduation. She gathered up her stuff.

'I vote tight, Kim. It'll probably be windy. And it's never really hot after dark down here.'

'Good point. Okay, skintight, long Calvin Klein tube dress and cropped Benneton jacket.'

'The one with the patches?'

'Yeah. Heels?'

'We're going to the football house, not a club.'

Kim tilted her head in thought. 'Platform flip-flops?'

'Perfect.'

'You sure? I'm going more for *Vogue* than Delia's.'

'Kim, if you wore a grocery bag it would look like it came from *Vogue*.'

Kim clutched her chest with mock sincerity. 'This is why I love you.'

Lucy rolled her eyes. 'I love you, too. Now go get dressed. It's almost nine.'

*

The fifteen miles of Atlantic coastline from Rehoboth Beach to South Bethany was a veritable hive of eighteen- to twenty-five-year-olds. From June through August, they worked menial jobs in food service to support the perfect summer balance of binge drinking, sleeping with all the wrong people, and not using enough sunscreen. This was carved-in-stone Delaware tradition. As such, Lucy and Kim had dutifully signed on for minimum-wage gigs at the new Grotto Pizza location on the boardwalk and moved into Kim's dad's house in Rehoboth.

Lucy and Kim sat on the wooden benches of the Jolly Trolley for the short ride from Rehoboth to Dewey, headed for a party. The party was with all the same high school dipshits they'd been hanging out with forever, but it was at the beach. Therefore, it was infinitely better. Close proximity to the ocean gave almost everything a glimmer of possibility and magic. And, if there wasn't any magic, at least there would be beer.

Rumbling along in the open-air carriage with the salty sea air ruffling her bangs, Lucy finally felt like summer had arrived. Senior year had been a long slog, each day slower than the one before. And God, every little thing had been so fucking *important*. Graduation requirements, GPA, ACT, SAT, college applications, the final ever *this*, the first ever *that*. With graduation over, and college months away, Lucy finally felt free.

The girls hopped off the trolley in the heart of Dewey Beach and made their way to a wide dead-end street on the bayside. All the houses on the block were the same shade of dingy white and all of them had wraparound porches cluttered with mismatched furniture, damp towels, and drunk people.

Lucy and Kim headed for the house with the most raucous party – the Football House. So named because of the twenty or so former high school football players that passed out there each night. (A couple were probably even on the lease.)

Snoop Dogg's 'Gin & Juice' thumped from somewhere

deep inside the building and people spilled out onto the lawn, sipping from red Solo cups between drags of their cigarettes and joints.

'You think it comes pre-treated with the piss-and-vomit smell, or did they manage it all on their own in the week since graduation?' Lucy quipped.

'Oh, I bet it's all them,' Kim replied. Then added, 'Football boys.' As if that explained everything.

Lucy and Kim walked through the front door and were immediately greeted by a guy named Chris K (as opposed to Chris G and Chris S) from their graduating class. His massive chest strained the bounds of his Jane's Addiction T-shirt to the point that the three naked ladies on it were cracked and cleaved into about fifty pieces.

''Sup ladies,' he said to Kim's cleavage.

'Hey, Chris,' Lucy replied to his oversized neck.

Chris brandished a Sharpie and jotted their names on two red plastic cups, then handed them over. Kim's said 'Kimmy.' Lucy's was 'Rollins.'

Lucy never could get a cute nickname. She'd just have to console herself with the knowledge that her genitalia had earned her free beer. Woohoo! The patriarchy pays its dividends!

'Keg is in the kitchen,' Chris called to their backs.

The friends walked through the house, past a group of guys who clearly appreciated Calvin Klein's work on the tube dress, waved at a couple of classmates, and hung a left at the quarters game.

Standing around the keg in the kitchen were Mike

Pellegrini and two other classmates, best friends that always wore ponytails and whom everyone simply called 'the Melissas.' Not ironically, mind you. They were both named Melissa. Talking with them was like trying to converse with a *YM* article. It was all, like, 'How to Decode Your Boyfriend's Feelings by the Color of His Boxers' or '101 Unforgettable Curling Iron Tips & Tricks.'

Mike handed one of the girls a cup marked 'Melissa 2,' then took Lucy's cup in his large quarterback's hand. Mike was tall with a deep suntan and freckles on the bridge of his nose. Everything about him was chiseled – his jaw, his abs, his damn calves. He wore a red sweatshirt that said 'Rehoboth Beach Patrol' and Lucy was positive he hadn't bought it at a souvenir shop.

Kim reached around Mike to hand him her cup, pressing her chest against his back and placing her hand firmly on his shoulder. That got him.

Mike handed Lucy her full cup, then looked to Kim. First her chest, then her lips, finally landing on her eyes.

'Hi, Mike,' Kim smoldered.

'Hi, Kim.' Those were the words that came out of Mike's mouth, but buried in the tone were subtitles reading: *Fuck, yes. Let's go.*

Kim led Lucy out of the kitchen.

'You gonna finish that with Mike?' Lucy asked.

'Oh, we'll *finish*,' Kim replied. 'He'll come to me.'

'I think you mean come *on* you.' Lucy chuckled.

'With any luck,' Kim said with a wink. 'Let's go out and have a smoke with the Melissas.'

'I'll be there in a minute. I'm going to find the stereo and see if I can fix this . . . situation,' Lucy said, waving her hand around in the air above her. 'This is the third time I've heard "Gin & Juice" and we've been here for twenty minutes.'

'Doing the Lord's work,' Kim joked.

'You know it,' Lucy replied.

Kim sauntered away, while Lucy followed the crackling sounds of an overtaxed subwoofer to a small nook off the living room. There she found a haphazard collection of CDs and a newish stereo with a tangle of speaker wires erupting from the back like a limp ponytail.

She flipped through the CD selection with dismay.

'Anything good?' said a deep voice behind her.

'I hate to admit it,' Lucy replied, 'but whoever picked these two songs did us all a favor.'

Lucy turned, ready to add something about her concern for the cultural fate of her generation, but the words got caught in her throat.

It was Nicky Broome.

Gorgeous, amazing, singular Nicky Broome.

They had technically known each other for six years, since he'd materialized from who knew where – probably the ancient spawning ground of unfairly beautiful boys – and joined sixth grade. They'd had classes together once or twice. She'd seen him in the halls. He was the sole occupant of a small but exclusive corner of her brain right between John Hughes plot devices and all her hopes and dreams.

In Lucy's hormone-addled imagination, Nicky Broome was the *Weird Science* lovechild of Brad Pitt, Jake Ryan, and the sexy guy who worked at the Sam Goody in the mall on Fridays. To be fair, this was probably true for most of the girls in their high school. Actually, it was probably true of *everyone* in their high school.

Nicky Broome could charm anyone. Students, teachers, that weird guy who cleaned the floors in the gym. He had confidence and attitude. He also had a smile that was ever-present, completely sexy, and utterly irreverent.

Nicky Broome did things people talked about. He wore a Clash T-shirt to graduation. He hopped up on stage during Junior prom and played a couple of songs with the band. He drove a beat-up old Jeep that was impossibly cool. Most of the time it had no doors and it always had the keys dangling from the mirror – and no one ever stole it from the student parking lot. Not once. Nicky Broome was a goddamn high school legend and the ink on his diploma wasn't even dry.

As Nicky stepped forward into the little nook, he tucked his long glossy, sun-kissed brown hair behind his right ear.

'Hey,' he said, not really looking at her.

'Hey,' she answered back.

It was the first time they'd ever spoken other than the rare 'did we have homework?' or 'can I bum a pencil?' because only two teenagers could see each other three thousand times a day for years and never actually have a conversation.

Nicky Broome was taller than Lucy; her head reached

only about as high as those shoulders of his that she wanted to climb. He smelled like clean ocean, peppermint, cigarette smoke, and some dark, mysterious *something* that was either an off-brand deodorant or pure, unfiltered hot guy pheromones. Combined, they made one word throb in Lucy's brain: *tasty*.

As they each set about digging through the piles of CDs, the soft hem of Nicky's Beastie Boys tee brushed against Lucy's hand. She felt it like an earthquake. It made her list in his direction and question the stability of the ground beneath her feet.

Lucy willed herself to breathe. And not sweat. And calm her thudding heartbeat, which she was sure the whole house could hear over Snoop Dogg.

'Wow,' Nicky said, holding up an Ace of Base CD for Lucy to examine.

'Yes,' Lucy replied, coming back to her senses. 'And then there's this,' she said, holding up an Enigma album.

'I'm getting a European theme,' Nicky said with a smile, holding up a cardboard-wrapped Culture Beat single.

'You might be right, because what else could explain this?' asked Lucy, proffering an Erasure CD.

'I'm afraid, there is no explanation for that,' he deadpanned.

Lucy laughed.

Nicky cracked a little smile. His eyes slid to Lucy's mouth, and back up to her eyes.

Then he started laughing.

And, because Nicky Broome's laugh was like some kind

of irresistible spell designed to unhinge teenage girls, Lucy laughed harder. Until her stomach ached and a tear slipped from the corner of her eye.

It really hadn't been that funny.

When Lucy caught her breath, she noticed that Nicky was staring at her. His mouth twitched with the faintest hint of a smile. His eyes communicated something unfamiliar. Curiosity? Interest? Maybe he thought she was a lunatic?

Lucy couldn't figure it out, so she grabbed her beer from the table and took a slow sip to cover her face and work out exactly how Nicky Broome looking at her hit in such a way that she could physically feel it. In her stomach. And maybe somewhere a bit lower.

'Here,' Nicky said. He pushed the stop button on the stereo, then the eject button. 'Better switch to the radio for a minute,' he instructed her.

Lucy fiddled with the radio dial until it read 102.7 and The Cranberries floated from the speakers.

'Ah-ha!' Nicky exclaimed. He showed Lucy the back of the Snoop Dogg CD. A streak of something (hopefully mustard?) was stuck to the surface.

He rubbed the back of the disc unceremoniously on the leg of his jeans. Then scraped at a stubborn spot with his thumbnail. He held it up to the light to check it, before carefully polishing the CD with the inside of his shirt.

As he worked on the disc, his shirt slipped up. And up. Lucy stopped breathing for a moment as she glimpsed the honeyed skin of his abdomen and the barest suggestion of a happy trail that disappeared beneath his waistband.

Tasty.

While Lucy tried to restart her heart, Nicky plopped the CD in the tray and it closed with a whoosh. He cued up track eight and hit play.

The first notes of 'Who Am I? (What's My Name?)' filled the house and Nicky grinned at his own success.

Cheers erupted from all over the house. Leave it to Nicky Broome to get a standing-o for hitting play.

'You get that reaction to everything you do, don't you?' Lucy teased.

'You don't?' he asked, feigning confusion.

Nicky Broome flashed Lucy that devastating smile of his and focused his green eyes right on hers. And, because Lucy was a heterosexual female with a pulse, she had little choice but to smile right back. There may even have been some egregious eyelash fluttering, to her eternal shame.

Lucy said, 'I'm going out on the deck.' She produced a pack of cigarettes from her pocket and held it up. 'You wanna?'

'Yeah,' he replied. 'Sure.'

Lucy led the way, scooting sideways through the crowd in the living room, which was now on its feet drunkenly grinding to Snoop. She raised the arm with her beer to avoid spilling.

Nicky took the beer from her hand in mid-air. 'I got it,' he said.

They stepped through the sliding door into the cool night air. He handed her beer back.

'Thank you.'

'You're welcome.'

Lucy made brief but eventful eye contact with Kim, who was across the deck chatting with Mike Pellegrini and the Melissas. Kim's eyes widened to saucers and then blinked in a way that Lucy easily interpreted as 'what the fuck? Oh my God! Nicky-fucking-Broome!' Lucy gave her best friend one long blink in reply, then focused her attention back on Nicky.

Lucy offered him her pack of smokes. He declined, producing his own from his back pocket.

They each lit their cigarettes. Lucy blew a puff of smoke up in the air toward the thin sliver of a moon that hung over Rehoboth Bay.

'So, not a fan of European bands?' Nicky asked.

'I wouldn't say that,' Lucy said, leaning back against the porch railing. 'I mean, that would have to include Led Zeppelin and The Beatles, right? So—'

'But it would also include Milli Vanilli and Wham!,' Nicky responded with a wry grin.

'Any category that could include both The Beatles and Milli Vanilli is obviously so broad it's useless.'

'You may have a point there,' Nicky conceded.

'I mean, U2?' Lucy added.

'UB40?'

'The Smiths,' Lucy said emphatically.

'Golden Earring,' Nicky threw back.

'Queen.'

'Europe.'

'Oh, man,' she gasped as though the very mention of the band Europe hurt her physically. Then she tossed him, 'The Cure.'

'Falco,' Nicky said triumphantly.

'Bzzzzz,' Lucy said, smacking an imaginary buzzer on the deck railing. 'Falco does not fit the category.'

'What? Falco is Austrian!' He looked up at the stars for a second, then back to her. 'Wait, *Australian*?' he chuffed.

'Austrian,' Lucy confirmed. 'But a solo act, not a band.' Lucy couldn't help the smug grin that had spread across her face.

'Shit,' Nicky grumbled, pretending to look dejected.

'If it makes you feel any better, the mere mention of Falco will now have "Der Kommissar" running through my head for days.'

'That does make me feel better.'

'That's a little bit evil, Nicky Broome.'

'Maybe,' he said, tossing his cigarette into a bucket full of sand and cigarette butts.

Then, he stepped into her space. Close. Close enough for Lucy to notice his chest rising and falling. Close enough to feel the heat of him shifting the cool ocean air around her.

'I wonder what else I could have running through your mind for days,' he said, almost to himself.

The line should have been cheesy, but not from Nicky Broome. From him it was an irresistible invitation. It was a question she was meant to answer.

And it was the moment. One that Lucy would look back on throughout her life. In times when she faced a choice that required a blind jump, an act of daring that was terrifying but rife with the potential for something new and amazing. It was the moment that taught her every single thing she would ever know about risks and rewards.

Lucy jumped.

'Do you want to get out of here?' she asked.

'Where?'

'My place in Rehoboth.'

'Yeah.' He grinned. 'I do.'

'Cab?'

'I have my car.'

'You good to drive?' Lucy asked.

'Stone-cold sober,' he replied.

'Just let me tell Kim.'

Nicky nodded. 'I'll meet you out front,' he said, before heading down the porch stairs into the yard.

Lucy crossed the deck and pulled Kim aside. 'I'm going home.'

'Why?'

'Because Nicky Broome will be there.'

'Holy. Shit,' Kim exclaimed.

'Quiet. Listen, are you okay here or—'

'I was going to stay over with Mike anyway.'

'Okay. You sure?'

'Totally,' Kim replied. 'I'm good. I'll be back tomorrow by ten. I have a shift at noon. So, be decent and not fucking on the coffee table when I get there.'

'I'll try.' Lucy laughed.

'Is he okay to drive?' Kim asked, concerned.

'Yeah. Sober.'

Lucy turned to go, but Kim stopped her with a hand. 'Wait.'

Kim reached into the pocket of her jean jacket and pulled out a book of blotting paper. She ripped off a sheet and tapped it on Lucy's nose.

'Do you have condoms?' Kim inquired with a motherly tone.

'Of course,' Lucy replied.

'Did you remember to take your birth control this morning?'

Lucy joked, 'Yes, Mom.'

Kim reached into her pocket again and came up with a tube of Lip Smacker, dabbed it on Lucy's lips.

Kim capped the lip gloss dramatically, then swept Lucy's bangs out of her eyes with her long French-tipped pinky nail. 'Remember,' Kim said earnestly, locking those shocking amber eyes on Lucy. 'He's just a boy.'

'I know,' Lucy lied.

CHAPTER EIGHT

NICKY

1990-Whatever

Nicky pulled the Jeep up over the curb and right into the front yard of the Football House so that the passenger door was even with the stairs from the deck. He knew for a fact that Chris and Mike did it all the time, and he liked the idea of surprising Lucy Rollins. Truth was, he liked *all* the ideas of Lucy Rollins. Had for a while. In middle school when she knew all the answers in science class. In sophomore year when she got three studs put in her left earlobe. And, God, those fucking hair buns. He'd had full-fledged fantasies about tugging down those hair buns.

He couldn't believe his luck, running into her. He'd never had the guts to approach her before. Mostly, women came onto him. It sounded like a stupid-ass problem. Not a problem at all, except it made him extra nervous when he had to do the picking up. He'd thought Lucy wasn't interested. She'd never even looked at him except when he faked needing a pencil in class or something, just to make her. But school was over. There'd be no more accidental run-ins with Lucy Rollins. She'd be off to college in a few months, and he'd be off to . . . wherever the fuck he ended up going off to.

Lucy walked out from around the side of the house and shook her head with a laugh when she spotted him in the Jeep. Perfect reaction. Perfect smile.

'Need a ride?' he teased.

'Yeah,' she said, opening the passenger door.

Thank fuck he'd remembered to put the doors and the lid back on the Jeep before he left Dover. Sometimes girls got weird about maybe plunging to their deaths on the pavement.

Once Lucy was buckled in tight, Nicky punched the tape deck to start it up and took off toward Rehoboth.

'Where we headed?' Nicky asked.

'Stockley Street. Two blocks off the boardwalk. At the Funland end.'

'Got it.'

He turned left at the light onto Coastal Highway and spotted Lucy tapping her fingers on her jeans to the beat. Singing quietly along to the song.

'You know this song?' Nicky asked.

'Sure,' she said in a tone that was halfway between *duh* and *how dare you*. 'It's Brad.'

'No one knows this band,' Nicky retorted.

'Obviously, that's not true, because I just proved that I do. Plus, I'm a bit of a Pearl Jam superfan so . . .'

'Okay,' he said, bringing his finger to the car stereo with perfect accuracy – practice made perfect. He hit fast-forward for a beat, then play. 'How about this one?'

The tape started up right in the middle of the chorus of the next song.

She huffed, like it was the easiest ask ever. 'The Verve,' she replied, *correctly*.

At the next red light, he hit the buttons again and a new song came through the speakers.

'Oh, getting tricky on me, are you? This is a live album, Jeff Buckley.'

'Damn,' he said, impressed. 'All right, how about . . .'

He hit fast-forward for a little longer this time. Pushed play with a flourish and cranked up the volume, one-hundred-percent sure he'd stump her.

Sweet, fluid guitar riffs filled the Jeep. The steady thump of a slow drum echoed in the background like a heartbeat, just the framework for the groove and improvisation of the guitarist.

They traveled a mile or more, without a word from Lucy. Nicky glanced over at her. Her eyes were closed, and a smile played over her lips, just as sweet as the guitar.

'Having trouble, sweetness?' he asked wryly.

'No,' she said, grinning at him. 'Just wanted to listen.'

His heart kicked up double time.

Her face lit up in triumph as she said, 'It's Stevie Ray Vaughan's "Little Wing." And I love it. I do miss Hendrix's lyrics, though.'

Nicky felt like someone had hit him with a bat. Right to the skull. Or, maybe the chest, because his heart was hammering against his ribs.

'You're the real deal, aren't you, Lucy Rollins?'

'I suppose that depends on your definition,' she said as she leaned her head back against the headrest and closed her eyes once more, like she was soaking in Stevie Ray Vaughan through her skin.

Mine, he thought. *My definition.*

Nicky pulled the car over abruptly. Blocking the driveway of some ritzy, oversized house in Silver Lake.

Lucy looked up in shock. 'What's wrong?'

Nothing was wrong. Things were so incredibly right Nicky couldn't take it anymore.

'Couldn't wait,' he said, throwing the Jeep in park.

'Wait for what?'

Nicky leaned toward her and slid his hand over her jaw. She looked up at him, her eyes nothing but thin bands of blue in the darkness.

He put his mouth on hers, and she opened hers immediately. Her hand reached around and grabbed the sleeve of his shirt, twisting and pulling it as though trying to drag him into her lap.

He smiled into the kiss, and he could feel her smiling back. Felt her chuckle on his tongue.

Who knew laughing and kissing at the same time could be so hot?

They went at it like that for a while, kissing like it was a job they were both determined to do well. They kissed until his cock against his fly was painfully hard. Until Lucy's cheeks were pink and her lips raw. Cars passed, headlights streaming over them like strobes. Nicky's knee jangled the keys in the ignition. The music around them drifted in and out from one song to the next.

Finally, Nicky came up for air. Made the long, slow trip back to reality. 'Shit, where am I?' he breathed against her lips.

'Here,' she said, laying cool fingers on his cheek. 'Couple more blocks to the house.'

Nicky threw the Jeep in gear and peeled out.

CHAPTER NINE

LUCY

Present

Lucy woke up in a Nicky Broome–induced haze. She had somehow managed to keep functioning, but had to battle past Nicky-shaped thoughts and memories at every turn. She found herself starting a task, and then slipping into deep contemplation over the possible subtext embedded in 'I want to take my time with you,' only to snap out of it and find that twenty minutes had passed.

Her plan had been to get some work done before the day's wedding madness began, so she'd grabbed her laptop and a mug of steaming coffee and built a nest of pillows on her king-sized island of a bed. She then spent at least thirty minutes staring at the weirdly compelling hotel room art across the room, and exactly zero minutes working on the requests for external review she'd intended to finish.

The upcoming twelve-to-fifteen-month marathon of

tenure review required slow, steady progress. Deadlines loomed just all over the damn place. Personal deadlines, committee deadlines, tentative deadlines that depended on other deadlines.

While Lucy had been allowed a lighter teaching courseload for the fall semester so that she could focus on tenure, it was hardly a break. She was to be inspected, reviewed, assessed, and judged by no less than three different committees and four different administrative bosses. There were external reviews, internal reviews, and probably a cavity search at some point – the notification of which was likely buried in the fine print of one of the thousands of forms she'd filled out both online and on ancient onionskin in triplicate.

Tenure review was the culmination of six years of work at the small liberal-arts college where Lucy was an associate professor. It was also the final leg of a journey that had begun at eighteen when she'd fallen head-over-heels in love with life on a college campus.

There'd been some detours that delayed her trajectory. When she married Brandon and then when Chloe was born, she'd taken years away. But then she'd gotten back on track. She'd earned her PhD and begun work as an assistant professor. Turned that post into an associate professorship on a tenure track. She'd stuck through the hard times, like the time she thought another university somewhere, maybe out west, might offer her more freedom. But Lucy had made the best of it so that Chloe could get all four years of high school in the same place.

Later, she'd muddled through other professional bullshit

when Chloe decided to stay in town to go to college. Something about the allure of free tuition, with Brandon waiting in the wings to drop a hundred grand a year, had almost made Lucy feel like the balances with her ex were even. Now, the finish line was finally in sight. She'd done her time. Put in all the effort humanly possible. She would finally become a fully tenured professor.

Tenure would mean a raise and job security. She might be able to buy a hybrid or something, or finally travel somewhere other than conferences. She could study what she wanted, come up with inventive new classes, write when she felt compelled to and not because she needed to pad her review package to impress her colleagues. It was all she'd worked toward for decades.

The only thing that worried Lucy just a little was that she wasn't the least bit excited about it. But surely that was normal? The excitement would come after, when the goal had been achieved. She was sure of it.

Lucy's phone buzzed from somewhere, the sound muffled by the thick bedding all around her.

She dug the thing out of its fluffy tomb.

KimmyR: Landed. Should be at hotel in 15.

Great, she'd gotten nothing done, and she was late.

*

Lucy rode the special dedicated elevator to get to the special dedicated lobby, because naturally the Lusso Resort had *two* lobbies. The entrance for regular folks was spitting distance from the gaming tables and slot machines, and glitzy in an obvious 'as seen on TV' way. The other lobby, exclusively for penthouse guests, was hard to find and out of the way. In Las Vegas, hard to find and out of the way were privileges one paid handsomely for, apparently.

The Penthouse Tower lobby was bathed in rich, comforting earth tones, from the plentiful soft seating to the lush carpets. It had high ceilings, wood paneling, and in keeping with the Las Vegas custom of never letting humans see daylight ever, it perpetually felt like ten p.m. in a very exclusive gentleman's club. It was impressive, but Lucy couldn't escape the uneasy feeling that she'd somehow been transported inside her ex-husband's brain.

Lucy spotted Kim the moment she glided through the revolving doors.

'Oh my God! It's so good to see you!' Lucy cheered as they swept each other into a big bear hug.

'It has been too damn long,' Kim said sincerely in Lucy's ear. 'Holy shit, where are we right now?' Kim added, looking around the space.

'I fear that we're inside Brandon's id,' Lucy replied.

'God, I hope not,' Kim grumbled, with her eyes on a massive chandelier.

'Wait, is this cashmere?' Lucy exclaimed, holding out her friend's arms to take in the finely knitted cream halter top and lounge pants set her friend was wearing.

'When traveling first class to Las Vegas,' Kim preened.

Only Kim Rusike could wear cream-colored cashmere

on an airplane and come out the other side looking like she stepped from the pages of a magazine.

'You're damn gorgeous. I would have ketchup down my front and a suspicious brown stain on my ass, for sure.' Lucy laughed.

'You're right,' Kim teased. 'You would.'

'Thank God you're here.' Lucy beamed.

'Uh-oh, that sounds ominous.' Kim tugged on her rolling suitcase. 'Let me get checked in, then tell me everything.'

*

By the time the two friends were marching down the fortieth-floor hallway, Lucy had spilled all the dirt on her encounter with Nicky Broome.

'Which one is his?' Kim whispered.

'That one,' Lucy whispered back as they passed room 4023.

Kim only hummed, and pressed on toward the end of the hall, right across from Lucy and Chloe's.

As they crossed the threshold, Kim's shoulders visibly relaxed.

'Enough about me,' Lucy said, suddenly feeling bad about the info dump she'd just laid on Kim. 'What's going on with you?'

Kim was a partner in a law firm that worked with lobbyists, politicians, and other unsavory types.

'Just the usual,' Kim griped, slumping into the sofa in the suite's living room, mostly supine on its goose-downy depths. 'Hate DC. Hate politics. Hate the hours. Hate the job. Just like you.'

'Like me?' Lucy asked, genuinely confused.

'Lucy, you've whined to me about the department chief . . .'

'Chair,' Lucy corrected.

'The Dean of the Candidates . . .'

'College.'

'The President Pro Tem . . .'

'You mean the provost?'

'Whatever. My point is, you're worn out. Same as me.'

Was she? Sure, things had been a bit tougher lately. Her patience for the bureaucracy and office politics had become extremely thin. And okay, lately the balance between frustrations and achievements often tipped toward the negative. But worn out?

Lucy deflected, 'Have a solution yet?'

'Eh,' Kim grunted. 'I don't want to get into all that. Right now, what I need is a week in Vegas.'

'What a coincidence, you're in Vegas.'

'Am I? Because this feels like the Mandarin Oriental in Tokyo. Where's all the Elvis tat?'

Lucy looked around at the one-bedroom suite, which was at least as tastefully over the top as hers and Chloe's.

'I think you have to request that in advance,' Lucy deadpanned. 'But if you call the concierge, I bet you could have a rhinestone jumpsuit up here in ten minutes flat. You could probably have a hot, willing man *inside* the rhinestone jumpsuit if you gave them fifteen.'

'I'll keep that plan on standby,' Kim said, sitting up and donning her full Lady Boss persona – spine stiff, those amber eyes piercing.

Lucy tamped down a feeling of dread. The Lady Boss pulled no punches, and she wasn't sure she was sturdy enough to handle the blows.

'Nicky Broome,' Kim said sharply. 'He was not great to you all those years ago. And, this may be a stereotype at work here, but surely decades in the rock-and-roll business haven't *improved* his character.'

Lucy couldn't say really, one way or another. Nicky seemed funny and thoughtful. He had been interested in her, listened and teased. It had felt . . . *easy* between them, at least once they'd gotten over the initial awkwardness. Plus, Kim didn't have the full picture. She didn't know about the song, and what came after. The pain and regret. It was probably the one and only secret Lucy had ever kept from her best friend of some forty years. And it was a big one. Huge, really. But it was a lie by omission that was as fixed as bedrock. The maelstrom of Nicky Broome was something Lucy had kept for herself. If she was the only one who knew, no one could minimize it. Nobody else could own even a little piece of it for themselves. *No one* knew.

'This isn't some big thing,' said Lucy. 'I just ran into an old friend.'

'Flame,' Kim corrected.

Lucy pushed back, 'Friend.' She took a deep breath, knowing just where Kim was headed with this topic. 'Look, I know I'm absolute garbage when it comes to men. I make bad choices. I made at least three pretty big ones. I've come to terms with that. No more ex-husbands for me, thanks. My collection's complete.'

'I know this is a novel idea, but you *can* feel things for someone without marrying them. I have felt plenty of things and have exactly zero ex-husbands.'

'I know what you've felt, Kim. And it's mostly anatomy,' Lucy said.

Kim shrugged, not the least bit bothered.

Lucy went on, 'I have no intention of getting all wrapped up in anyone. I'm not doing that anymore. Not even for Nicky-rock-star-Broome. Even though he actually makes panties melt all the way off whenever he so much as walks by.'

'That is a very niche superpower,' Kim retorted. 'And, by the way, I think you can do it. I believe in you. I know you can get all up in his anatomy and not come out with an ex-husband. Let him melt those panties repeatedly.'

'That sounds really . . . *unsanitary*,' Lucy chided. 'But yes. I think I will.'

'Good, you need a break as much as I do. More. You've got the bride, the family bullshit, the goddamn dads convention.' *God, the dads*. She hadn't allowed herself to dwell too much on that particular wedding gift. Ex-husbands were truly the gift that kept on giving. 'Take time this week to decompress. Enjoy a distraction.'

'I'll try,' Lucy replied, mostly meaning it.

'Decompress *under* Nicky Broome, *over* Nicky Broome—'

'Yeah, I think I understand what you're getting at.'

'Good,' Kim said, clapping her hands to her knees as though she'd really just done some damn business. 'Now, if I'm not mistaken, we have some bridesmaids to endure.'

'*Kim*,' Lucy warned gently.

'Sorry, I mean *enjoy*. Enjoy! Of course, I meant enjoy.'

CHAPTER TEN

LUCY

There was a lot of giggling. Given the amount of complimentary champagne in the room, this was not entirely surprising. Still, the giggling was different. It bordered on manic at times, and seemed to be contagious. Occasionally, tears accompanied the giggles; other times, they came interspersed with exclamations of joy. There had been a brief but unsettling Taylor Swift sing-along. There were a lot of selfies. A lot of talk about angles.

Lucy and Kim reclined side by side in matching pink velvet chairs in the center of the circular room. Around them, each on a separate pedestal, were Chloe's four bridesmaids. They were all lovely, none of them were above the age of twenty-three, and there was So. Much. Giggling.

A battalion of seamstresses in smart black tailor's coats bustled around pinning, stitching, and consulting with one another.

'I feel like a sociologist plopped down in the middle of a

strange, isolated tribe. I don't know what this ritual is, but it's fascinating,' Kim said in a low rumble, her eyes fixed on Chloe's friend Alexis. Alexis was stupidly gorgeous and could easily be a long-lost Kardashian (of the Jenner variety). Kim added, 'I don't think we ever giggled this much.'

Lucy replied, 'That's because we're Gen X miscreants raised feral.' Lucy couldn't drag her eyes away from Chloe's cousin Hannah, who was attempting a viral social media dance in floor-length lavender silk. 'We were fully formed jaded malcontents by age twenty. We were too world-weary for giggles.'

'I find that oddly comforting,' Kim said, before taking a healthy sip of her champagne. 'In related news, it turns out I enjoy drinking before noon. Will all these events involve day drinking?'

'Yes,' Lucy replied matter-of-factly.

'Excellent.'

'Well,' came Chloe's sing-songy voice, dripping in triumph. 'Here they are!'

The four bridesmaids turned away from their mirrors to face Lucy and Kim.

Lucy couldn't help but smile. Even with pins and tailor's basting dotting their garments, the ladies were magnificent. So happy and fresh and pretty in their different gowns all in the same shade of rich, dusty lavender.

'You are all drop-dead gorgeous,' Lucy announced.

'Amazing,' Kim added, holding her champagne flute up as if toasting.

Chloe clapped her hands together in glee, her bright blue

eyes – just exactly like Lucy's own – glistened with happy tears. Her fair skin was tinged with a splash of pink that made her look so much like little middle-school Chloe that it took Lucy's breath away. She got up and hugged her daughter fiercely.

'It's going to be a beautiful wedding, Clo,' Lucy mumbled into her daughter's hair.

'I can't wait,' Chloe replied.

With a deep, cleansing sigh, Chloe pulled back and fixed her gaze on Lucy.

'Okay, Mom. Your turn.'

Lucy groaned. Well, it had to be done, whether she was ready or not. 'All right, let's do it.'

*

There were pins in very inconvenient places along the back seams and underarms of the mother-of-the-bride dress that Chloe had helped Lucy pick out. It was a simple silhouette, a sleeveless column dress with surplice detail at the bodice that dipped into a deep V. Lots of cleavage. *Probably too much cleavage.* The slit on the left thigh was maybe, possibly, too high to be appropriate for a wedding – even one in Vegas.

The real stunning bit, though, was the beading. Every inch of the thing was covered in tiny sequins and baubles. Shades of rose gold and pale pink glimmered over every curve. The gown was beyond beautiful, heavy and, thanks to her ex-husband's explicit directions to 'put everything on the AmEx, Chloe,' completely free. For Lucy, that is. Chloe refused to tell Lucy how much of a dent it was putting in Brandon's millions, rightfully guessing that Lucy's brain would explode at the number.

Lucy stepped into the gallery room flanked by two of the seamstresses with their measuring tapes and jangling pins. She took her place on one of the pedestals and faced the assembled crowd – Kim, the bridesmaids now back in street clothes, and of course, Chloe.

The first words were from Kim – a sharp: 'Holy. Shit.'

Lucy freaked. 'Oh, God! It's too much, right? There's too much boob? The slit is too high. Is it too sparkly?'

A multi-part chorus of 'no' rang out.

'It's fucking gorgeous,' Kim declared. 'You are stunning in that.'

'Thank you, but that's not the point. Is it?' Lucy tried. 'I mean, it's Chloe's day. I don't want to look like I'm trying to outshine her. I should be a Rose or a Dorothy, not a Blanche.'

The young women in the room looked at her like she was speaking a foreign language.

Lucy tried again. 'I need to be a Charlotte or a Miranda, not a Samantha.'

Only Chloe seemed to understand.

Good Lord. Lucy searched her mind.

'Oh!' she chirped. 'I need to be more of a Vanessa or Blair than a Serena or Jenny.'

The bridesmaid crew all nodded in understanding. Kim only looked confused.

'You should not!' called Chloe. 'You should be a Carrie.'

'You're the Carrie in this situation, Clo,' Lucy tried.

'There will be no missing me in the big white dress. There's no reason you shouldn't shine, Mom. You're amazing.' Chloe turned to her squad. 'Ladies, am I right?'

Alexis chimed in, 'It's perfect, Lucy.'

'Beautiful,' said Gabby.

'You should definitely introduce her to Chandler's uncle Shane,' said Hannah.

Chloe glared at Hannah with such force, Lucy was surprised not to see two smoking hollows where Hannah's eyes used to be.

'Uncle Shane?' Lucy asked Chloe.

When Chloe refused to respond, Lucy looked to Hannah.

The poor thing could only grimace and shrug.

'It was just an idea,' confessed Chloe.

'I don't—'

Chloe raised her hands to cut Lucy off. 'I know you don't. But he's smart. He's a journalist. And he's nice.'

'And hot,' added Alexis.

'*Alexis!*' Chloe admonished.

'Well, he is!' Alexis fought back. 'Uncle Shane is a complete silver fox.'

Oh, holy Mary, Rhoda and Phyllis, am I in my silver fox era? When the fuck did that happen? How do I make it stop?

Lucy took a gulp of air – because she couldn't reach the booze.

Chloe turned to Lucy and leaned in conspiratorially.

'Look, I know it's going to be a lot with the dads and, well, *all* of that. I thought Uncle Shane might be a nice distraction.'

What was it with everyone and their decompressing and distracting? Lucy wasn't fragile. She had never been fragile. She handled stress and chaos and every other damn thing like a champ. Why did everyone suddenly think she needed coddling? And *fondling*?

Lucy had no choice but to put on her stern motherly hat. She said gently, 'That is very kind of you, Chloe.' She turned to the bridesmaids, 'You too, girls. But I don't need a silver fox.'

Kim silently mouthed the words, 'Yes, you do.'

Lucy cleared her throat and continued, 'I'm great as is. Now, are you sure this dress isn't too over the top?'

Even the seamstresses chimed in with their noes this time.

Well, guess that's settled.

CHAPTER ELEVEN

NICKY

Time was a stubborn bastard. It sped up and slowed down, flexed and contracted with no discernable predictability as far as Nicky could tell. And that was just while he was in the drive-thru line at Starbucks or sitting on the tarmac waiting to take off.

The way time lived in Nicky's mind was even more confusing. He could remember some things with such clarity that they felt like they'd just happened. Other things, even things that had once seemed important, faded away. Leaving behind only the memory of a memory, like a file with a name but no contents in his internal hard drive.

So it was that Nicky Broome, lounging in his boxer briefs in a chair overlooking the Las Vegas Strip, concluded that time was meaningless.

How else could anyone explain being in the same room with Lucy Rollins almost thirty years after the first time and feeling both like no time and *all the fucking time* had passed simultaneously? Time was obviously nothing but an illusion, a trick of the mind.

If he could still summon the old magic, he would write all these thoughts down in one of the crisp new Moleskine notebooks he still kept in his carry-on. They were there, waiting. He couldn't say if it was out of habit or hope, but they were there. Even though he hadn't been able to hear the music for a goddamn age.

That thing inside him, the one that had guided him through so much trouble and given him so much joy, was silent. It had been for a while. A year, maybe more. No songs. Who was he kidding? Not so much as a single note or word – for more than a year.

That, too, was a subject for contemplation. But for some other day. The silence was too frustrating and painful. It made him feel lonesome, maudlin, and restless.

Anyway, what he really wanted to do wasn't write. What he really wanted was to be in the same room with Lucy again. Any way he could have her. And there was one stretch of time in particular that his mind could play at will, as clearly as an IMAX film in 3D.

CHAPTER TWELVE

NICKY

1990-Whatever

Lucy pointed at the house, a small, gray-shingled thing with a screened-in front porch so big that it seemed to swallow the rest of the place.

Nicky parked the Jeep all the way down the driveway, near the detached garage that had a long string of lightbulbs coming off it, zigzagging back and forth from the house and the fence so that the whole backyard was lit up.

'Nice place,' Nicky said as he held the car door open for Lucy and watched her hop down to the drive.

'Yeah,' she replied. 'It's Kim's dad's. His bachelor beach shack after her parents got divorced.'

'You've got it for the summer?'

'It was his graduation present to us. Free rent in Rehoboth.'

'Sweet.'

'Yeah,' she said, gazing up past the lights to the sky. 'It really is.'

Lucy dug inside the pocket of her jacket and pulled out a key as she stepped up a couple of stairs to the back door.

Nicky followed her, close but careful not to get too close. He didn't want to pressure her, or for her to feel like he was only there to get in her pants. Of course, he did want to get her right out of those jeans and peel off the leather jacket that was making it impossible to see her tits. But he thought it was important not to be completely obvious about it.

The back door opened right into the kitchen. Lucy shucked her jacket and hung it over the back of a chair.

'Want a beer?' she asked, opening up the fridge.

'Sure.'

'I've got Rolling Rock or Yuengling,' she offered.

'Yuengling's good.'

She popped the tops off two bottles with one of those old-fashioned opener thingies that was bolted to the heavy white cabinets.

Nicky took a long guzzle. To settle his nerves. To keep him from saying something stupid like 'where's your bedroom?'

Instead, he blurted, 'Where's your stereo?'

Lucy just chuckled and nodded her head toward the front of the house. 'My CDs are on the porch.'

She led the way through a little living room crammed with oversized furniture that looked like it came from a much fancier house. A lot of leather and dark wood.

Lucy flipped on a lamp behind the sofa as she passed it, then went straight for the front door.

They walked out onto the deep front porch that stretched across the width of the whole house. The porch seemed much more lived in than the rest of the place, with ashtrays and empty soda cans. Bottles of nail polish and a stack of fashion magazines.

Lucy stopped at the coffee table and lit a couple of candles with a nearby lighter. Then she went over to the corner and grabbed a massive binder with a zipper all the way around it. She hit play on a boom box and handed the heavy binder to Nicky. He plopped onto the sofa, the fabric slightly damp from the humid beach air.

'Speedy Marie' kicked up in the background, and it made him smile.

'Frank Black?' he asked, busying himself with the CD case so he didn't come off like a damn grinning goob.

'Yeah, it's a mix,' she said as she sat next to him and looked down at the CDs on his lap.

Thank God for the binder, because the heat of her next to him against the cold ocean air blowing through the porch screens gave him a raging fucking boner. The light from the candles and the glow coming in from a streetlamp down the block made her look like a damn dream. A good one that he'd had before.

He cleared the lust from his throat and managed to croak out, 'What else is on the mix?'

'Um, on this one I've got some Liz Phair, some Zeppelin. New York Dolls. Runaways. Sugarcubes. The Cure.'

'Cool. What do you call it?'

Lucy angled her body toward him slightly. Her breast skimmed the skin of his forearm as she slung an elbow on the back of the sofa. He could feel her eyes on him, so looked up.

Her eyes locked on his, and without a single fucking blink she said, 'Lucy's Make-out Mix.'

It was hard to say who moved first, but somehow within seconds Nicky's hand was splayed on Lucy's back and her fingers were in his hair. Her tongue slipped past his teeth and the relief of it made him actually shiver.

The CD case slid to the floor with a bang. Lucy must have taken it as an opening, because she pulled her knees up on the sofa and slung one around his hips, straddling him.

Nicky's hands slid up her thighs and wrapped around her ass, pulling her closer. So close. Not close enough.

Lucy broke the kiss, rested her forehead on his as she tried to catch her breath.

'I love this song,' he mumbled as the first chords of 'Summer Babe' by Pavement started up.

Lucy laughed. The sound made his heart thrum like an Eddie Van Halen guitar solo. Half admiration, half longing.

'Should I go back over to my side of the couch?' she teased. 'Let you listen?'

'No,' he said into the hot, salty hollow of her neck. 'I can do two things at once.'

He pulled her hips in hard to his, the fly of his jeans pressing into hers. She groaned, a frustrated kind of bellow.

'More,' she demanded.

'Bedroom?'

Her lips said, 'Yes,' but her tone said, *Finally*.

She scrambled out of his hold and headed for the door. She flipped a light switch as she went past, and the music around him went dead.

Her voice drifted out from somewhere inside the house. 'Nicky! Are you coming?'

He blew out the candles and took off after her.

Nicky found her down a little hallway, an open door with a soft haze of light drifting out. As he crossed the threshold, 'Summer Babe' started up again, this time from a small pink boom box on the nightstand.

'The same mix?' He laughed.

She nodded. 'Copies.'

'I always knew you were a smart girl,' he said.

She crossed the room to him, and immediately grabbed the bottom of his shirt, pulling it up over his head in one swift tug.

'What's yours called?' she asked as she went to work on her own shirt, whipping it off without a hint of self-consciousness.

Nicky's brain shorted out. Her bra was black and lacy, and he could just make out her nipples. 'My, uh, what?'

She tugged off an elastic band from one hair bun, and then the other. They came loose with a pop and unfurled like a magic trick. Long, smooth brown hair cascaded down over her shoulders.

'The mix. In the car,' she said, unbuttoning the fly of her jeans.

Oh, Jesus. Matching black lace panties.

Nicky watched her legs slide out of the jeans. Slowly. One, and then the other. He spotted her tan line. Bikini. God he'd love to see her in a bikini.

'Earth to Nicky,' she said with a smile.

Right, the mixtape. 'It's called, uh . . . Kitty.'

One eyebrow lifted up into her bangs as she asked, 'As in . . . *pussy?*' She pulled at the scrap of black lace at her hip and it snapped back with an audible *smack*.

'Yes,' he said. Both an answer and a plea.

Lucy took one step closer to him, and unbuttoned the top of his jeans. Slid the zipper down so slowly against his dick that he thought he might lose it right then and there.

She peeled the jeans wide and he watched as a grin spread across her perfect lips. He knew what the grin was about. The Joe Boxers with the yellow smiley faces all over them. Goofy as hell, but comfortable.

Lucy looked up at Nicky, through her lashes, focusing her eyes right on his.

'Mind if I take these off?' she asked, just above a whisper.

'Please.' All plea.

She slipped her hands inside his boxers, cupping his ass. Then, dragged her fingernails down his thighs as she pulled his jeans and boxers all the way down. The sensation sent shockwaves blasting in his chest.

When he looked down, she was on her knees. Like she had no intention of coming up.

With gentle hands, she helped him pull his feet free. Then she stayed down there, looking up at him.

Lucy licked her lips.

Licked her fucking lips. And leaned in, dragging her tongue from his balls straight up to the tip of his cock.

Nicky felt the room spin. He grabbed at the nearby dresser, just in time to keep himself upright. He'd been with plenty of girls over the years. All kinda girls, all kinda ways. Nothing – not anything – had ever felt like *that*.

As she gripped the base of him with firm fingers and he felt the soft, wet heat of her mouth close over his dick, Nicky was lost. His thoughts were nothing but miles of tan skin. Black lace. Soft brown hair. Blue eyes. The curve of her back. Her lips. Her hands. *Jesus Christ, her tongue.*

Nicky's skin was electric. The Zeppelin starting up on the stereo was the sound of his blood pumping.

'Bed,' he scraped out like sand in gravel. 'Lucy, baby,' he said, stroking her hair, then the smooth curve of her back. 'Get on the bed.'

He helped Lucy to her feet, then wrapped his arms around her. Kissed her. All teeth and tongue and growls. He was hungry for her. Felt it in his bones. In the hairs on the back of his neck. Starving for her.

She sat on the bed and reached her arms back to unhook her bra.

'No,' Nicky said, sitting next to her. 'Let me.'

She turned her back to him to give him access. Nicky brushed her hair forward over her shoulder, revealing those tan lines again, a narrow stripe across her back. He traced it with the tip of his finger before opening the bra clasp.

Nicky slid the bands slowly off her shoulders, and watched as goose bumps erupted down her arms. He couldn't say why, but he felt sort of proud that he could do that to her.

He guided her to her back, gently resting her head on the soft white pillows. He resisted the urge to dive right on her and lick those sweet pink nipples, standing hard and ready for him. Instead, he grasped the panties at her hips and slid the lace over her long firm thighs. He dropped them to the floor and stood up, to get a better look.

'Fuck, you're beautiful,' he said.

Her eyes lit up with delight, and maybe a tiny bit of mischief. 'You're not bad yourself, Broome.'

Then Nicky did move over her, taking one of her nipples in his mouth and smiling at the gratified moan she made as he slipped between her thighs. He ground his dick shamelessly into the mattress to relieve the ache her noises were stirring up.

He felt Lucy's leg slide up, her knee gliding against his arm. Her fingernails found his scalp as he licked and nipped at her breast. Her hips rose and fell beneath him, seeking him out.

'Are you ready for me, Lucy?' he rasped.

'Yes!'

The intensity of her answer sent a chuckle bursting out of him. He laughed into the smooth skin of her stomach, which set her off, too. He felt her laughter in his lips, felt it move the hair falling over his eyes.

Still laughing he pushed up and said, 'Let me get a condom.'

'Bedside table,' she instructed, before pulling him back down to her and kissing his shoulder.

He slid his body higher, reaching for the drawer and she licked at his neck, dug her thumbs into his hip bones.

As Nicky's hand fumbled around the drawer feeling for condoms, The Cure started up on the stereo and he couldn't help but smile. It was perfect. Sweet and bubbly and right, like grape soda on a hot day. It was everything he felt in his gut in that moment. *Happy*, he realized. He was happy.

It had been so long since he'd felt that way, it rushed over him like cool water, like diving into a swimming pool. He felt like he could float on it.

Nicky finally set his fingers on something vaguely condom-like and pulled it from the drawer, whooping in victory as he spotted the Trojan label on the wrapper and sat back to rip it open.

Suited up, and pretty sure he was going to blow his load any second, he looked down at Lucy to settle himself.

That was a fucking mistake, because with her knees up and open for him he could see everything he was in for, all the hot, wet glory of it. His cock twitched like it was screaming 'what's the holdup?'

Still on his knees, he touched the tip of one finger to the glistening pink core of her. Inside of her. Soaking. So ready. Amazing.

'Nicky,' she begged, as his finger trailed lazily over her clit.

'I'm coming, baby,' he whispered.

He crawled up over her again and nestled himself between her legs. Used his hand to line up and drag his cock through her wetness.

She moaned and he smiled. Again. Had he ever smiled so much during sex before?

Nicky pushed his hips forward and slid inside her. Slow and easy so he didn't lose his goddamn mind.

He watched her then, watched her mouth make a perfect rosy circle as she whimpered.

He pushed in further and marveled as she inhaled, sharp and infused with something like disbelief or amazement.

'So good, Lucy. So fucking good.'

She nodded in agreement, eyes locked on his, as though she couldn't even form the words.

He began moving then, pushing and pulling in and out, Lucy matching his rhythm with her hips. He could feel the place on his bones where he'd have a bruise from hers. He wanted it, relished it. The pleasure and the pain of it. The black and blue mark that he might have as a souvenir.

He leaned in closer to her, dragging his teeth over her bottom lip, her neck, anything he could reach.

Their breathing synched up somehow so that he could feel her exhale in time with him.

It was different. New. Wasn't just two bodies doing a thing biology made them want. It wasn't just two people in their own heads, in their own worlds, using each other to get off. Looking at Lucy, with sweat beading around her temples and her lips raw from his kisses, it struck him how fucking stupidly lucky he was that this smart, beautiful woman let his dumb ass see her bare and raw. That she let him into her body. He was grateful and awed by her. How she looked him right in the eye as he thrust inside her. Her unbelievable blue eyes right there with him.

Nicky adjusted his position, and pulled her knee up high to her shoulder. He slid up and down, in and out so that each stroke grazed her clit.

'Oh, fuck,' she screamed.

Jackpot.

'That's it, baby.'

Her hands slapped against his ass, pushing him forward, and holding him hard against her for a beat each time he was balls deep inside her.

God, she was sexy. Every damn thing.

Nicky's pace increased, his body shifting to a higher gear without any input from his mind.

He felt the tiny flutter of the muscles inside her, right before she wrapped her legs completely around his hips, holding him hard and fast inside her. With small, purposeful movements he ground into her, increasing the pressure on her clit.

And then Lucy goddamn detonated.

She panted his name, over and over as her back arched and her legs quaked. Her body squeezed his cock so hard it was just short of painful. So unbelievably good as he rocked inside her.

He alternately cursed and prayed into her hair as spasms of release racked his body. His whole fucking body. His earlobes. His kneecaps. Every-fucking-where.

'Holy shit,' he rasped as the flashes of light began to clear from his vision. 'Holy shit.'

'Yeah,' Lucy breathed. She laughed, pure and unrestrained as her hands worked a clumsy path over his back.

'What was that?' he asked, like a complete moron.

He felt a little less like a doofus when she answered, 'No fucking clue. I really don't even know.' And then began laughing again.

They lay like that, laughing like weirdos as he slowly went soft inside her.

Then Nicky kissed her, tender sweeps of his lips. Her mouth. Her cheekbones. Her eyelids.

Suddenly, he realized he was probably suffocating her with the full weight of his body and rolled off to her side. He quickly dealt with the condom, tossing it in a garbage can that was so close he didn't even have to get up.

He breathed out a sigh and maneuvered himself and Lucy, bendy as a rag doll, so that his arm was wrapped around her and her head was on his shoulder.

The bed was a disaster. The comforter was in nine different kinds of lumps under them, with pillows hanging half-off the bed, but it didn't matter. Her head on his shoulder was everything he needed.

The song on the little stereo turned again, another Cure song, and Lucy's eyes closed. She smiled, like she had in the car when 'Little Wing' was playing. Her foot, with its neon-blue-painted toenails, began moving in time with the music.

'Which one is this?' Nicky asked.

'"Just Like Heaven."'

'I need to listen to The Cure more.'

'Good idea,' she muttered dreamily.

Then she rolled over, folding her arms on his chest and gazing up at him, little wisps of her bangs stuck in her long eyelashes.

'You know a lot about music,' she said.

'So do you.'

'But I'm just a fan,' she said, curling her leg over his. 'You actually play. Do you write?'

The sappy-ass grin that took over his face couldn't be helped. Couldn't be resisted. He was that fucking gone for this girl.

He smacked a kiss to her nose and said, 'Wait right here!' before hopping off the bed.

Nicky ran out of the room and through the house.

He heard her laughter and a garbled 'Where are you going?' from behind him.

Nicky barreled out the back door and hissed at the cold night, cursed June in Delaware because it was a ball-shriveling sixty degrees at night. Like it was geography and not the fact that he was buck-ass-naked that was the issue.

He raced to the Jeep and yanked his battered old guitar case from the back. A gift from his mother. A parting gift, as it turned out, before she ran off to Florida or wherever the fuck she went first.

Nicky's bare feet slapped on concrete and grass. On wood planking and then the cold linoleum of the kitchen. He made sure to lock the door behind him and then charged back into Lucy's bedroom holding his guitar case up like a prize.

'Wanna hear a song?' he asked.

'Yes!' she screamed.

'Good,' he replied, pulling a little chair out from against the wall. It had a slightly damp bath towel draped over it, which seemed as good a cushion as anything. He sat down and pulled the guitar out of its case.

Lucy sat up on the bed, still gloriously naked. She hadn't even bothered to get under the covers or put a shirt on or anything. And he was beyond fucking thankful. And amazed. And humbled. Though, he had to focus on tuning the guitar and not looking at her tits because he was already chubbing up again.

She reached over and shut off the stereo, then waggled her ass deeper into the comforter. She crossed her legs and rested her elbows on her knees, excitement on her pretty face.

With the guitar on his bare knee, and probably too much enthusiasm, he played Lucy Rollins a song he'd been working on. He'd been calling it 'Rain Delay' but didn't know if that would stick. Truthfully, he didn't know if any of it would stick. But he played it anyway, managed to sing without dropping the tempo or any notes. Remembered all the lyrics he'd just finished two nights before.

When the last chord drifted off, he finally found the courage to look up at her.

'Holy shit, Nicky. That was fucking *great*,' she said. With awe. With amazement. The truth?

'Yeah? You don't have to say that just because you want my dick again.'

'Ha!' she tutted. 'Trust me, if I didn't like it . . . well, I might not tell you because your dick *is* pretty great. But I would've said something like. "Oh, that was nice" or, I don't know . . .' She stopped to think. 'Maybe something like "your fingering was very accomplished."'

'My fingering *is* very accomplished,' he said with a wink.

'I meant the guitar, you horndog.'

'Sure, you did.'

'Come to think of it, I might have just said, "Touch my tits," to distract you from my non-answer.'

He laughed, but she continued on. 'Nicky.' Her voice more serious. 'I really mean it. That song is *good*. Like, put it on the radio good. Do you play for people? Like bars and whatnot?'

'The whatnot thing, for sure.' According to his dad the guitar wasn't practical. Wouldn't get him into college. Wouldn't ever pay the bills. So instead of trying to make a few bucks playing for people somewhere, he spent all his free time working in a damn diner.

Her eyebrows scrunched up in confusion. Her head tilted to one side as she asked, 'Got any more?'

'Maybe.'

'Play 'em,' she demanded.

She smiled at him, and that was all it took. He strummed out another song, and then another.

And somewhere in the middle there, with Lucy Rollins listening to him – really listening – and moving her toes in perfect time, he was finally able to breathe.

It was like he could suddenly see that maybe the weight that he'd been feeling in his chest all year wasn't actually drowning. Maybe it was just the pressure of expectations and intentions and fucking *potential* that his dad had been piling on since senior year started. The weight wasn't *inside* him. It wasn't doubt from within him. It had been on the outside all along. He could peel it off and finally fucking breathe.

It wasn't like Lucy gave him permission to let go of all the bullshit. It was more like she gave him confirmation. Dreams are fragile things, easily destroyed by doubt and conflict. Sometimes it's easier to convince yourself you're crazy than it is to convince yourself to take a chance.

Nicky sang out the last note of a song, and Lucy leaned back on her elbows, stretched her legs out, crossing them at the ankles.

She said, 'Look, I'm not an expert by any means. I don't know the first thing about the music business. Not really. But to my ear, those are *real* songs. Like, you could have strummed out some bullshit to me and I think I would know the difference. A terrible song is a terrible song, right? There are plenty of those on the radio, too. I think I could tell. But what you played me was not terrible. Not even close.'

Nicky tossed his guitar in the case, then kicked it aside. He jumped on the bed, making Lucy's whole body pop up and land back on the mattress.

He pulled her into his lap.

'You're going to be here all summer?' Nicky asked her, with that stupid grin plastered all over his face again.

'Yeah.'

'Then so am I.'

'Right in this room?' she teased.

'I mean, I hope every once in a while, you'll let me in. But I'll crash with Mike and those guys. Or I have a buddy, Travis, who has a place in Bethany.'

'Really?' Lucy asked, like she was shocked or something.

'Really,' he replied, with the kind of certainty that can only be delivered by the very young.

Lucy shifted in his arms and wrapped her long, bare legs around him. She rested her arms on his shoulders and pressed their chests together.

'Okay,' she breathed, before canting her hips to press her heat against his growing erection.

'Good,' Nicky said against her lips. 'Now, about this accomplished fingering . . .'

CHAPTER THIRTEEN

LUCY

Present

The glow of Las Vegas was a very different experience from the rooftop deck of the Lusso Resort. Even Lucy's suite on the penthouse floor didn't have quite the same perspective. Up where she and Nicky were, out in the desert air some five hundred feet up, Lucy could see the neatly marked squares of the streets branching off the Strip, exponentially dimmer than the casinos. Beyond that, the impenetrable dark of the desert lay on the horizon. Pitch-black and empty. It was a reminder that this freaky town was a kind of island, set apart from the rest of the world and its rules. Set apart from reality. It was a place founded on trickery and illusion. Nothing about it was real. Knowing this only compounded the dreamlike quality of the whole evening, drinking champagne while nestled in an oasis of potted palm trees and squishy sofas with Nicky Broome.

They had eaten dinner as the sun set over Las Vegas. It was a show to rival any in the casinos. The scant clouds all around them had turned shades of purple, orange, and yellow against the azure backdrop of the sky. They'd talked about the weather, and some movies they'd both seen. They'd brushed over politics, but decided it was too depressing. Then tried the music business before Nicky had declared it more depressing than politics.

Now, they were lit only by the ambient glow of the millions of bulbs below them in the city and enjoying each other in silence. There was no awkwardness at all, though. Just peace as the traffic and frenzy of the Las Vegas Strip became a barely audible hum under the music from a portable speaker Nicky had brought along.

'Chloe's dad, what's his name?' Nicky asked, reclining against one side of the enormous sofa they shared. He looked every bit like the figment of a dream, in his jeans and white T-shirt, his feet propped up on the rattan coffee table.

'Brandon,' Lucy replied flatly, wiggling herself deeper into her corner of the long sofa.

'Tell me about him.'

Lucy groaned. Childishly joked, 'Do I have to?'

'No,' Nicky answered. 'But I'd like to know.'

Right. Okay. Big-girl pants. 'We met our senior year of college. Dated for a long time. Got married late 2001. We were in New York. And after 9/11 things felt so—' Lucy didn't know exactly how to say it. 'I mean, it's all hindsight now, you know?'

Nicky nodded.

'I see now that things were *unsettled*. The world was unsettled. Everything felt so precarious. So unstable. In New York, especially. I think we were clinging on to each other for safety almost?'

'I get it,' Nicky said.

He couldn't. Not really. So, she added, 'Brandon was supposed to start a job at Cantor Fitzgerald in October of 2001. Do you remember—?'

'Shit. Yeah, I remember.'

'His entire department. The one he was supposed to start with was just . . . *gone*. Hundreds of people. People we knew. Guys he went to Columbia with. It was . . . hard.' Hard really wasn't the word. It was an understatement of massive proportions, but Lucy still didn't really have the proper words to describe it, even all these years later.

Nicky sat quietly, listening. Waiting.

Lucy went on, 'It was the trauma really, I think. That pushed us forward. I had misgivings about him before we were engaged.' Lucy stopped, corrected herself. 'No, not misgivings about him. About *us*. About how we worked, but we just kept moving forward, but at an accelerated pace because of everything that happened.'

'It's understandable.'

'Twenty-plus years later and all grown up, yeah. It is.' Lucy took a sip of her champagne. 'I was the one who saw it first, though. The one who realized. So, he was the one who got to be angry. It was . . . *bitter*.'

Nicky nodded his understanding.

The sweet sounds of Dave Grohl's rhythmic guitar spilled from the speaker, just as Lucy became desperate for a change in conversation.

'Oh, God,' she said. 'I love this song.'

Nicky's eyes brightened. He swung his legs off the table and ticked the volume up on 'Everlong.'

'Some people say it's the greatest rock love song of all time,' Nicky said, feigning nonchalance like a champ.

Shit. Shitshitshitshit. Alarm bells went off in Lucy's head. *Retreat! Abort!* She'd just opened the door on a whole line of conversation she'd been trying to avoid. Namely another, very specific, rock love song that people sometimes called the greatest of all time.

'I agree,' said Lucy. It was honest. But it was also a deflection. The best she could hope for in the moment.

'*Really?*' Nicky drawled devilishly.

'Yep,' Lucy said, practically licking the last drops from her champagne flute.

'What are some others?'

Fuck. She knew what he was getting at. She could sense it in the expectation in his tone, in the sudden avid lean of his body toward her.

'Mmmm, okay. Are we talking rock only, no ballads?' she stalled.

'No ballads.'

'"Maps,"' Lucy said.

'Yeah, Yeah, Yeahs?'

Lucy nodded.

'I can get behind that, and . . .'

Lucy went on, '"Lovesong," "Friday, I'm In Love."'

'I think we can safely just add the entire catalog of pop-era Cure,' Nicky said, pointedly.

Aaaand she'd just accidentally waded into deeper water. Memories of their night a million years ago came swelling to the surface. They were memories he clearly also had judging by the pointed flash of triumph in his eyes.

'More?' he asked.

'Okay, but I'm going to need my phone for this,' Lucy tried.

'Be my guest.'

Lucy picked up her phone, willing her hands not to shake. She flicked open Spotify and scrolled through her playlists.

'"Such Great Heights,"' Lucy said, her eyes still on the phone.

'Yeah, okay,' Nicky replied.

'"Supernova,"' Lucy added.

'Hold up,' Nicky exclaimed. 'You mean Liz Phair's "Supernova"?'

'Yeah,' Lucy said, now more defensive than anxious.

'"Supernova" is a sex song not a love song, Lucy,' he said firmly.

'It is not. There's sex. But clearly, she loves him.'

'Uh, she says his dick's like a volcano.'

Lucy laughed. 'Excuse me, I think he fucks like a volcano,' she teased.

'Oh, yeah, that makes it *less* of a sex song.' Nicky chuckled.

Lucy defended, 'But he's also everything to her. See, says so right here,' she said, pointing to her phone.

'Scroll down a bit more,' Nicky instructed. He smiled. 'There's also a lot of friction. And blasting.'

'Okay, agree to disagree on that one.' Lucy laughed. She looked back at her phone. 'Oh, well here's a couple, but—'

'But what?'

'I don't think you'll accept them,' she said, holding the phone away playfully as he scooted closer and tried to have a look.

'Why not?'

'Sammy Hagar,' she said slowly.

Nicky looked to the sky, pretending to be exasperated. He looked back down at her. 'Okay, let me guess.'

He was close now. So much closer than he'd been just a minute before. She could smell the faintest hint of his cologne or bodywash. It smelled expensive and fucking delicious.

He locked those wild green eyes of his on hers. There was a twinkle there, roguish and hungry at once. It made Lucy's heart beat faster. The man was flat-out mouthwatering.

'"Why Can't This Be Love?"' he asked. For a second, as Lucy's heart climbed into her throat, it struck her as a question. For her. A few terrifying seconds passed before she realized that it was the title of a Van Halen song.

'Uh-huh, that's one of 'em,' she breathed, breaking contact with his voodoo rock-star eyes. 'One more.'

'"Love Comes Walking In,"' he said.

'The title is actually "Love Walks In,"' she said. 'But

yes.' It came out breathless, an answer to the questions she felt pulsing off him. Questions she was unable to resist answering in the affirmative.

Nicky edged ever closer to her, a microscopic increment in the practical, but the sensation was something altogether different.

'Any more?' he asked, the words skimming across her skin in a tempting gust. 'Maybe by someone else?'

Lucy felt her skin come alive, like a wave of sparks had shot down her arm and into her chest. Or maybe it was just a heart attack. Either way, she knew her life was about to take a turn.

'Nope,' she said defiantly.

'*Lucy*.'

'What?' she scoffed.

'*Really?*'

'Really.'

She resisted connecting with his damn eyes again, but in the end it was futile. Lucy had to accept the sad truth that if Nicky Broome wanted to look at her, she would be there, looking right back.

'Hey, Lucy?' Nicky whispered.

'Yeah?' she whispered back.

'I want to kiss you.'

She breathed, 'I thought you wanted to take things slow.'

'I realized something last night,' he said into the fine hairs at her temple. He inhaled as though with an objective, taking a long, deep draft of her.

She stuttered, 'What?'

'Twenty-eight years between kisses is really fucking slow. Mission accomplished.'

Nicky leaned forward, so close that the heat of his breath skated across Lucy's lips and lit up every forgotten nerve between her head and her heart.

'No,' Lucy blurted.

She didn't know where the instinct came from, but as soon as she uttered a refusal, Lucy felt the tension in her chest begin to unwind.

'No?' he repeated.

'You were right,' Lucy added.

'No, I wasn't,' he droned.

'You were.'

'No, I was *wrong*.'

Nicky suddenly had a look of desperation about him. His brow crinkled. He shook his head. His cheeks went pink. And something about it made Lucy absolutely effervescent with delight. It tingled in her limbs, lively and potent, like a shot of tequila.

'Slow is good,' Lucy said. *Fast is rash. Dumb. Dangerous. Always has been.*

'No, it's not,' he mewed.

'But it is,' she said firmly.

Nicky Broome's slack-jawed despair – his dopey look of confusion and disappointment – hit Lucy like the drop in a stadium anthem. She was lighter than air. She wanted to stand up and cheer. Scream into the star-studded desert sky and float up there after it.

The grin that spread across her face couldn't be helped because the feeling of Nicky Broome wanting her – even just a tiny fraction as much as she'd wanted him over the years – was like pure, distilled female power. She let it cascade over her. Sat in the euphoric buzz of it.

Lucy carefully placed her glass on the table. She leaned into Nicky's heat and bussed him on the cheek with world's most chaste peck.

Allowing herself one last glorious glance at Nicky Broome, she drank in his shock and frustration like gulps from a red Solo cup dipped in the fountain of youth.

As Lucy stood up and stepped away from Nicky Broome, she couldn't escape the feeling that she'd begun the night as Lucy McManis, ho-hum college professor, and had somehow transformed into Lucy Rollins – nearly forgotten Badass Bitch.

'Goodnight, Nicky,' the Badass Bitch cooed.

Then, with zero fanfare and a whole lot of attitude, Lucy Rollins walked away.

CHAPTER FOURTEEN

LUCY

'I thought you were just gonna hit that and move on?' Kim griped.

'You're such a poet,' Lucy deadpanned.

Lucy and Kim sat jawing under the hairdryer chairs in the Lusso's salon like a couple of old grannies in a sitcom. Lucy's head was cocooned in a hive of plastic wrap. Kim was foiled like she was trying to pick up ham radio with her hair follicles.

Meanwhile, Chloe and the bridesmaid crew were fussed over by a gaggle of aestheticians. Being gleefully trimmed, glossed, highlighted, and generally gilded like the gorgeous young lilies they were.

Kim nudged, 'Well?'

'I was. I am. Probably,' Lucy dithered. There had been a moment there, after she'd said no, that had felt a lot like *relief*. 'No' was easy. Comfortable. Safe. Like a cozy sweater. 'But the look on his face, Kim. I'm telling you; it was priceless.' Lucy tried to recreate it in her mind. Tried to channel the sensation of seeing Nicky-fucking-Broome want her like a drowning man wants oxygen. 'I know it's twisted, and probably the sign of a serious mental issue. A God complex or clinical narcissism or something, maybe? But rejecting him felt like . . . like *winning*. The Super Bowl. Or an Oscar. If I could bottle that shit, I'd be a billionaire. And women would rule the earth.'

'Consider me your first guinea pig when you figure it out,' Kim quipped.

'Done,' Lucy replied. She closed her eyes and tried again to capture those Badass Bitch feelings that had sizzled in her veins and made her feel young again, and in control.

'But you're not feeling, like, *feelings*? Right?' Kim's words sliced through Lucy's revelry. Her tone was light, but after decades of friendship, Lucy could sense the undercurrent of worry just beneath the surface.

'No,' Lucy replied reflexively. 'It's more like the echo of feelings. From far off and a long time ago. Not the real thing. Don't worry.'

'I'm not worried,' Kim lied. 'Why would I worry?' Then a moment later: 'Should I worry?'

Lucy patted Kim on the hand. 'I'm fine. It's fine. He's just a boy,' Lucy said, offering the phrase that had practically been the mantra of their youth. 'Just. A. Boy.'

CHAPTER FIFTEEN

NICKY

Nicky shoved his hands in his pockets and absentmindedly glanced around at the collection of family sedans and high-end SUVs parked in the garage beneath the Lusso Resort.

He was nervous.

Nicky couldn't remember the last time he'd wanted to impress a woman. Or, to be completely honest, the last time he'd had to. After a certain number of platinum records, impressing women wasn't so much a desire as a nasty side effect of fame that he did his best to ignore. But suddenly, he really wanted to impress Lucy. Since the moment she walked away from him on the rooftop, he'd been sort of obsessed by the possibility of it, actually.

'Okay, here I am,' came her voice from behind him.

Nicky turned, and felt his boxer briefs get a little tighter at the mere sight of her. Dark jeans, white T-shirt with fine black stripes. A pair of red Chuck Taylor's. Her hair was kind of curly and wild. Beautiful.

'You look amazing,' he said.

'It's jeans and a T-shirt, Nicky,' she said, looking down at her outfit.

'I know.'

He smiled, and she smiled right back. The silent communication was so ordinary, commonplace. Still, it made his heart bang.

'Mr. Broome? Ms. McManis?' A large bald man in a black button-up and gray jeans approached them. 'My name is Sonny. I'll be your guide and driver for the evening.'

Nicky shook the man's hand. 'Good to meet you, Sonny.'

'Where are we going?' Lucy whispered, coming up to Nicky's side.

He took her hand. 'You'll see.'

*

The Las Vegas Strip spilled out around them, a kaleidoscope of flashing light and color, just beyond the cool comfort of their black SUV. Flashes of red and orange flickered across Lucy's face as she peered out the window.

'It really is the most American kind of crazy,' she mused beside him. 'This insane circus of greed and excess in the middle of the desert.'

'We absolutely do crazy better than anybody else,' said Nicky.

'We're so good at it,' Lucy added with a grin that he felt in his stomach.

'We've reached our first stop,' came Sonny's deep voice from the driver's seat. He pulled the car into a parking spot and turned to face them. 'You may recognize the California Casino and Hotel from the explosive opening sequence of *Casino* starring Robert De Niro. The California is one of the oldest surviving casinos in Las Vegas. Many of the film *Casino*'s other exterior locations have since fallen to the wrecking ball, as Las Vegas is a city in a constant state of renewal and reinvention.'

Lucy turned to Nicky, her eyes sparkling with excitement. 'Are we on a movie tour of Las Vegas?'

'We are,' he replied.

Lucy trilled, 'Nicky Broome!' in a sing-song tone. Nicky went ahead and translated the giddiness and the giggle that followed: *Nicky Broome, you goddamn fucking dreamboat. You're a bona fide genius.*

Over the course of the next hour, Sonny took them to locations from *Natural Born Killers*, *Leaving Las Vegas*, *Fear and Loathing in Las Vegas*, *Showgirls*, *Vegas Vacation*, and *The Hangover* movies.

'Our next stop,' Sonny said, 'is the world-famous Neon Museum, a sign boneyard where the history of Las Vegas continues to inspire awe and wonder. If you'd like, we can go in and have a walk around.'

'Sonny,' Lucy chided, 'I thought you knew me by now. Of course we want to go in.' Then, she threw the door open and raced out.

'I would have opened the door for her,' Sonny said with a chuckle. 'Guess I was too slow.'

'Welcome to the club, my man,' Nicky replied. 'Welcome to the club.'

The Neon Museum was like an electrified fever dream. The signs were enormous, rising fifteen or twenty feet up into the night sky. Nicky could pick out the more important ones by how well they were propped up, how much space they had around them. Others remained unlit, lying on their sides, stacked on top of one another. Sharp, space-age fonts from the Sixties. Big block letters from the Seventies. A cowboy. A showgirl. A neon duck.

Lucy wandered aisle after aisle taking pictures with her phone. Happy. *Impressed.*

'You may find it interesting to know that in addition to films like *Mars Attacks!* and *Fools Rush In*, the boneyard has been the setting for a number of music videos,' Sonny said, mostly to Nicky.

Lucy turned around from where she'd been staring at a sign that said 'Sassy Sally's' and said, 'Come on, Nicky. Give us a taste.'

'A taste of what?'

'The rock-star vibes,' Lucy teased.

Nicky scoffed. 'Excuse me, I always have the rock-star vibes.'

Lucy tilted her head, examined him, pretended to be skeptical. 'Nope.'

'Nope?'

'You're going to really need to turn it on. You know, smolder a little.'

'Oh, sorry. I can't turn on the smolder without a wind machine. It's not safe.'

Lucy laughed and stepped closer, threaded her arm around his. 'Do you guys even make music videos anymore?' she asked.

'Sometimes. But they basically go straight to YouTube.'

'Weird.'

'I know,' he said, guiding her through the aisles of broken old things. 'Remember MTV?'

'I would turn it on as soon as I walked in the door after school, and didn't change the channel until my parents had to watch something dumb like *Murder, She Wrote*.'

'Or *The Rockford Files*,' he added.

'The Nightly News with Dan Rather,' Lucy offered.

'Such a buzzkill.'

'Totally.'

On the way out of the museum, Nicky shoved a wad of hundreds into the donation box in the souvenir shop and bought Lucy a T-shirt that said 'I got lit at The Neon Museum' just so she had to put it on and he could take her picture.

CHAPTER SIXTEEN

LUCY

Sonny stopped in front of The Bellagio. Its gently curving, cream-colored façade rose up behind the massive blue fountain, the perfect marriage of elegance and ostentation. The Bellagio was now a landmark of Las Vegas, as easily identifiable as the columns of Caesar's Palace or MGM Grand's enormous pyramid.

On a night when the temperatures still hovered around the eighties, the volume of water outside The Bellagio struck Lucy as breathtakingly bold and irresponsible. But also, magnificent in that way that bold and irresponsible things often are.

'Even I know this one,' said Nicky beside her in the back seat. '*Ocean's Eleven*.'

Up front, Sonny nodded. 'Got it in one. I'll let you two off here and swing around in a bit. The fountain show begins every fifteen minutes.'

'Thank you, Sonny,' Lucy said as she hopped out of the car.

As Sonny rolled away, Lucy said, 'He deserves a big tip.'

'He does,' Nicky agreed. 'I'll take care of it.'

Lucy and Nicky made their way, side by side, to the intricate concrete railing at the edge of the fountain. Its elegant curves and balustrades gave the impression of classical permanence, like a monument in Rome. Of course, as they had learned on their tour, nothing in Las Vegas was forever.

The water beyond them was still and dark. But the proximity of it made the air feel cool and misty. The perfume of light chlorination surrounded them; a smell that always gave Lucy a little thrill. The relic of a thousand happy summer days, their freedom and ease.

'So, should we do it?' Nicky asked.

There was a long list of things Lucy had thought about doing with Nicky Broome, so she wasn't sure exactly which one he was referring to.

'Here,' he said, 'like this.' He leaned his elbows on the railing.

Ah, right. The movie.

Lucy followed his lead, rested her arms on the concrete and looked out over the water. Waited for the magic to happen.

The fountain began to hum and the first jets of water erupted, swaying and dancing.

Then, she heard it. Music. Not from the fountain show, but from beside her.

'Clair de Lune.' Debussy. Just like the movie.

'God, this song,' she moaned.

'Pretty incredible,' Nicky said quietly, stowing his phone

in the front pocket of his T-shirt so that it seemed like the music was coming straight from Nicky. From inside him.

Nicky stared out over the water. But it wasn't the fountain that had Lucy spellbound. She watched the dancing lights glimmer on Nicky's eyes. Saw his mouth turn up – the whisper of a smile. So achingly beautiful that it took her breath away.

'How do you do that?' she sighed.

He turned to her. 'Do what?'

Make me want to cry and laugh and jump headfirst into the water to escape and also let you crawl under my skin.

But she didn't say any of that.

'How did he put notes together that make a person *feel*?' she asked, then cringed internally remembering that she was asking a guy who had actual Grammys for songwriting tucked away somewhere. 'I mean, these are the same notes used to make the "Happy Birthday" song, and a toothpaste jingle.'

Nicky hummed. A warm, fuzzy, philosophical sound. 'It's about focusing on a moment. A single, small moment,' he said softly as he angled his body toward her. 'If you feel it, the notes that come out are texture, touch, air. They *are* the emotions.' He leaned closer and whispered, 'The secret isn't in the notes, Lucy. It's that despite all the evidence that makes us doubt it, the human experience is universal. Emotions are our common language. A songwriter is just someone who knows how to translate it into sound.'

Why does he have to be so damn amazing all the time?

Nicky turned back toward the water.

'Hey, Nicky?'

'Yeah?' he asked, facing her again.

'I want to kiss you.'

There was no hesitation as Nicky's hand came to her face, cupping her jaw with the barest of pressure. He brought his lips to hers and Lucy dissolved into his kiss – his desire, his longing. It was a memory. A song.

Somewhere, far off in the real world, there were cheers and clapping. The Debussy swelled from Nicky's pocket and floated off into the ether along with all of Lucy's willpower and a chunk of her good sense.

CHAPTER SEVENTEEN

LUCY

In the elevator, there was no subtlety in Nicky's lips as they crashed on Lucy's. There was only determination and pure, overwhelming lust. It came over her like a fever, hot and immutable. She was powerless to it. To him.

Lucy grabbed at his T-shirt. At his tattooed arms. Her hand found its way to his scalp and he groaned.

The elevator doors opened to the penthouse floor and they tripped out into the hall, a tangle of limbs and lips.

'Yours? Mine?' Nicky mumbled into Lucy's neck. Then pulled away, with a cringe. 'Neither?'

'Mine,' she purred.

Nicky threaded his fingers through hers and guided her down the corridor with determined steps. When they reached Lucy's door, Nicky reached into her back pocket. He only lingered for an extra second or two on the swell of her ass, before pulling her keycard out and slapping it to the lock.

Thank goodness Chloe was out with her friends. Lucy had answered 'mine' before giving the logistics of the thing a second thought. She'd been bamboozled by the sudden ache for Nicky.

Lucy guided Nicky past the kitchen and through the living room of the suite. To the left. To her bedroom. To the extra-large bed that looked in that moment like it could easily host the entire cast of Cirque du Soleil on its acres of fluffy white blankets.

Lucy stepped out of her Chucks as Nicky fell back on the bed, flicking his own sneakers off from the heels and sending them flying across the room.

She laughed at the sheer glee written all over his face and the way he called her over by waving his arms, like she wasn't moving fast enough for his liking.

She plopped down next to him, and he immediately threaded his hand through her hair, gripping the back of her neck. He sidled up closer. Kissed her slowly. As though he truly were taking his time. And Lucy kissed him back with an equally languid ease, but only because his mouth was a thing of enthralling and consuming beauty and she could linger there indefinitely.

His hand slid under the hem of her T-shirt. Strong, callused fingers made a path across Lucy's stomach, then gripped the curve at her waist before splaying across her back.

It felt like he was holding on, keeping her close.

Something about it made Lucy bristle, want to push away. It was irrational; she knew this. Still, she nudged him gently to his back and straddled him, saying a little prayer of thanks to a couple of years of yoga and Pilates.

She pushed his shirt up and helped him wrestle it over his head. There, she found more ink. Everywhere. A riot of color and image that was too much to take in at once. An amazingly detailed scene of evergreen trees with mountains in the background gave way to the bear from California's state flag. She spotted a fine line tribute to the angel on the cover of Nirvana's *In Utero*, but the angel's upturned hands weren't empty. One held a human heart, the other a flame. She felt over his tattoos with her fingertips as though she might be able to divine their meaning by touch.

'Jesus!' she exclaimed suddenly.

'What? The ink?' he asked, frantically looking down at his own stomach.

'No, the abs,' Lucy huffed. 'You have an actual six-pack.'

He smiled. 'Nah, more like four. At best.'

'Excuse me,' she said. 'I am a college professor. I can count to . . .' She touched each ripple with her finger. 'One, two, three, four, *five*, *six*.'

'America's youth is in good hands, professor,' he teased. Then added, 'I do crunches when I can't sleep.'

'Well, insomnia is really working for you.'

'Thanks, I think.'

Nicky tugged at the hem of Lucy's shirt. She stopped him with a hand on his.

'Fair warning,' she said. 'I eat Cheetos when I can't sleep, so there's only one ab under here.'

Nicky chuckled. 'I don't care what you have under there. Whatever it is, I want it.'

She hoped that was true, because she wasn't eighteen anymore and didn't have the money required to try to be. Lucy had never been particularly self-conscious about her body and she wasn't exactly out of shape for a forty-something woman who spent all day in a desk chair. But also . . . time. And . . . gravity.

Lucy pulled her shirt over her head in one smooth movement, then unclipped her bra, tossing both over her head.

Nicky moaned low and soft, like Lucy did when there was pasta in the room. His hands went straight for her breasts, kneading them slightly and dragging his thumbs slowly over their stiff peaks. The sensation went straight to her core.

'I like your ab,' said Nicky in a faraway voice while pinching her nipple.

'That's not my ab,' Lucy managed to croak as her hips pushed down on him of their own accord.

Nicky raised himself up using all those abs and sucked her nipple into his mouth. She grabbed hold of his shoulders to keep herself from collapsing.

'Nicky?' she asked.

His mouth slipped off her breast with a pop. 'Yeah?' he replied before kissing his way toward her other breast.

'Can we go ahead and get naked now?'

His eyes tracked up to meet hers. She brushed a stray hair from his lust-drunk eyes.

'Yes, please,' he replied.

Lucy rolled off him and stripped herself of jeans and underwear with zero grace and ridiculous speed.

Nicky tried to do the same, but one of his socks was locked in a wrestling match with his jeans, trapping him.

Lucy laughed at Nicky's frustrated groans as he lay on his back struggling with his foot in the air, jeans whipping around.

'Here, let me,' she said.

She unknotted the tangle at his ankles and slid his pants to the floor. His wallet and phone clunked noisily to the carpet.

Then she looked up and saw Nicky-fucking-Broome sprawled on the bed – naked, inked, amazing. Everything about him was bigger than she remembered. But then, her memories, cherished and well-loved as they were, featured a boy of eighteen. There was nothing boyish about Nicky anymore, and she was grateful for it.

'You're a work of art,' Lucy breathed. 'Literally.'

'I've been told I have a tattoo problem.'

'I wouldn't call it a *problem*,' she said, feeling the tingle between her legs intensify.

Lucy crawled her way over him again, seating herself on his legs and watched as his cock tapped impatiently against the skin below his navel.

She canted her hips, gliding her wet heat along the base of his shaft.

'I have condoms,' he said breathlessly. 'Wallet.'

'IUD,' she said. She didn't add that her (now former)

gynecologist had referred to her internal lady bits as geriatric and the possibility of conception as statistically insignificant. (*Thanks for that, Dr. Jackass.*) Lucy added, 'I was tested recently and I'm all good.'

'Me too,' he said. 'Haven't been with anyone since.'

'I'm game if you are.'

'Oh, yeah,' he agreed with a fervent nod.

Lucy leaned over, and dragged her lips slowly over his. She nipped at his bottom lip, then made a slow trail over the slight stubble on his jaw, and around to the smooth stretch of skin behind his ear.

His hands worked at the soft flesh of her hips before sliding to her ass.

Lucy reached her hand between their bodies, wrapping her fingers around his shaft. She lifted her hips and guided him to her entrance.

In one swift jolt, she drove her hips down and took him deep.

Lucy's forehead dropped to his as they both groaned at the pleasure of it.

She moved her hips up again, but was met by his hands on her ass, pressing her back down.

'Lucy, baby. Hold up. I need a second. Pretty sure I'm having an out-of-body experience.'

'You sure it's not a stroke?' she asked, maybe only half-teasing.

'No,' he replied with a smile.

They both laughed – deep, silly, champagne-fueled belly laughs.

Nicky's wide pupils snapped to hers. 'Oh my God. I can feel you laughing. From *inside*.'

That made her laugh more.

He grunted, 'That is seriously the sexiest thing in the history of the universe.'

She smiled down at him, rocked her hips forward and back again, catching her clit as she did, and sending a wave of hot sparks down her spine.

'You okay now?' Lucy asked.

'More than okay,' he replied. The sincerity in his tone, and the unspoken words that seemed to linger in the silence that followed, was too much for Lucy. It was too difficult to reflect on, laced with too many emotions. She had to close her eyes against the force of it.

She pushed up onto her hands and put all her focus on her body.

'Dreamed about this,' he panted. 'You over me. Dreamed about it.'

Lucy closed her eyes more tightly. Concentrated on her breathing, on the sounds their bodies made when she slapped her hips against his. Anything but what might lie behind his words.

She sunk into the pure bliss of Nicky's body against hers. Of his big hands gripping her waist. The sensation of sweat trickling down her back.

Then came the sensation of her hamstring begging for relief because she was definitely not eighteen and was a CrossFit dropout.

Lucy pulled at Nicky's body and he followed her with

no resistance. Rolling, still connected, to their sides. Lucy wrapped her aching thigh over his hip as he thrust more forcefully inside her.

'Lucy. Open your eyes, baby,' he begged. His hand gripped her hip with purpose. 'Look at me.'

To keep them closed would reveal more than simply complying. So, she did.

And it was devastating.

He wasn't looking *at* her. Those loden eyes were peering *inside* her. She felt like he could see the truth that she'd been trying to hide. The hurt he'd caused. All the years that he'd been there, but not there. She knew 'The Breathing Room' and its thorny legacy was written all over her stupid, uncooperative face.

She blinked hard.

'Don't go,' he panted. 'Stay with me.'

Lucy opened her eyes again, and he was right there. His eyes almost glowing in the neon streaming in from the window. His focus was so intense, so unguarded, that she felt it in her chest. A weight. A burden.

Then his hips shifted, and he hit a place inside her, deep and undiscovered. The pleasure there was so raw and vivid that it took her by surprise.

She gasped his name as her orgasm hit like an explosion, everywhere at once.

Lucy clawed at his back, trying to hold on. Trying to keep herself tethered to reality even as her thoughts scrambled and fractured into nothingness.

She felt his pace increase, but only tangentially – as

something happening somewhere else. His eyes remained locked with hers, and Lucy couldn't look away. In that moment, she truly felt that they were the only thing holding her together.

Nicky called her name like a chant, over and over, as she felt him pulse and release inside her.

He buried his head in the crook of her neck. 'Oh my God,' he said, struggling to catch his breath. 'Oh my God.'

'I know,' Lucy whispered.

'Lucy,' he tried, with a kind of amazement that made her heart trip. He clung to her tightly.

'I know,' she replied. 'I know.'

That was the last thing Lucy remembered before falling into a dreamless sleep, still clinging to Nicky Broome like a lifeline.

CHAPTER EIGHTEEN

LUCY

'Mom?'

Lucy's eyes struggled to open. The blazing desert sunlight was firing like laser beams through the window and her eyelashes were glued together.

Must have forgotten to wash my face last night, she thought lazily.

It was then that Lucy realized other parts of her were equally sticky, and the whole situation struck her as both odd and disconcerting. She rolled to her side sleepily contemplating all the variously gluey and aching aspects of her person.

Chloe's voice filtered through the bedroom door again. 'Mom! Where are you? You're not answering your phone. Mom!'

Lucy managed to pry one eye open and spotted a swath of brightly decorated skin beside her. Nicky Broome, face down, with his back roasting in the sun.

The previous night whooshed back into her consciousness so quickly that it made her stomach lurch.

Shit. Shitshitshitshitshit.

'Nicky!' Lucy whisper-yelled while shoving his shoulder. He only groaned and rolled away.

Shitshitshitshitshit.

'Mom!'

'Nicky!' Lucy tried again, with a shake.

'Huh?' he asked blearily, shielding his eyes with an arm.

'My daughter! She's here!' Lucy hissed.

Lucy scrambled off the bed and almost face-planted when her right hamstring refused to cooperate.

She grabbed the closest item of clothing and dove into it, realizing only after that she'd slipped into Nicky's tee from the night before. It smelled like him. She resisted the urge to sniff it and went about grabbing clothes from the floor.

When she looked back, Nicky was up watching her with pure amusement on his face.

She slipped into her terribly unclean panties from the floor.

'Come on!' Lucy urged. 'Get . . .' She looked around. 'Get in the closet.'

Nicky laughed.

'Quiet!'

'Why—?'

Lucy cut him off by thrusting a pile of his things into his arms.

'The closet!' Lucy implored.

'Okay, okay,' he said through a chuckle.

Nicky hauled himself off the mattress with a groan – completely naked except for about a million tattoos.

Lucy opened the door to the closet and flipped on the light switch. It was a walk-in so she didn't feel too guilty about it when she hurried him in with a single poke to his perfect ass.

He laughed as he stumbled in and Lucy closed the door behind him.

'Mom?' Chloe said, as the door to the bedroom opened.

'Hi,' Lucy replied.

Act. Casual.

She tugged at the shirt to try to cover more front . . . and back bits.

'Uh, hi?' Chloe said, looking her mother over with blatant curiosity.

Chloe was dressed and ready for the day in a pale pink romper. Her silky brown hair was curled; makeup perfect.

'You look nice,' Lucy said. 'Going somewhere special? Did you, um, stay here last night?'

'Not going anywhere,' Chloe answered. 'It's just eleven-thirty so . . . *dressed*. I stayed with Chandler last night.' She was talking to Lucy, but she was not looking at her.

Lucy tried to scuttle into her field of view.

Nope. No dice.

Chloe's eyes were focused on the things scattered around on the bedroom floor.

'Mom?' Chloe asked, a grin slowly spreading across her face like the damn Joker. 'Is there a *man* in here?'

'*Whaaaat?*' Lucy spluttered. 'No!'

Chloe stepped further into the room and picked up a

single black Vans sneaker by the laces. It dangled from her fingers as a single eyebrow arched. 'When did you start wearing size twelve Vans?'

'*Busted*,' came a deep voice from the closet.

Chloe's jaw dropped, her eyes glistening with a ridiculous combination of smugness and delight. The shoe clunked to the floor and Chloe crossed to the closet, yanking the door open.

'Ho-ly shit!' Chloe laughed, in that impish everyday-is-Christmas-morning way that was her signature.

Chloe stepped back and *bam*. There was Nicky Broome wearing a single white sock and a pair of tight black boxer briefs that left absolutely nothing to the imagination.

Nicky smiled that irritating smile of his, oozing charm and sex appeal (and just plain sex) all over the place.

'Hi,' he said and gave a sheepish wave.

Chloe looked from Nicky to Lucy and back again, her mouth absolutely agape. Obviously stunned and amused in equal measure.

'It's not what it looks like,' Lucy blurted.

'Mom? Did you get it on with a rock star in your Las Vegas hotel room?'

So, maybe it's exactly what it looks like.

'Oh, I like her,' Nicky said cheerily to Lucy. He turned to Chloe, extending a hand. 'I'm Nick Broome. Good to finally meet you.'

Chloe absentmindedly slipped her hand in Nicky's and shook it. All the while she stared at Lucy with something like admiration.

'Chloe,' her daughter said to Nicky. 'Nice to meet you.'

Nicky leaned against the closet doorframe, and had the temerity to cross his socked foot over his un-socked foot like this was just a casual social gathering. In the closet. In his underwear.

'Is she always so uptight in situations like this?' he asked.

Chloe leaned a shoulder casually against the wall like she was settling in for a good long chin-wag. 'Yeah, pretty much. Though there was this one time with my high school boyfriend—'

'Oh my God,' Lucy grumbled. 'Nicky, can you put some . . . pants on or something?'

Without another word, Nicky winked at Chloe and closed himself back in the closet.

'I'm sorry, Clo.' Lucy grimaced and buried her gritty eyes in the heels of her hands.

'Are you kidding me? This is epic, Mom. Completely badass. Good for you. Are you bringing him to the wedding?'

Lucy shook her head vigorously. 'It's not . . . it's not like that. Nicky and I knew each other a long time ago. You remember I told you he was in my graduating class? Ages ago?'

Lucy did. She remembered it perfectly because Chloe had dug out Lucy's old yearbook and upon finding Nicky's picture had said, 'I'd hit that.' Oh, those cherished mother-daughter memories.

Lucy blabbered on, 'We just ran into each other randomly . . . by accident actually, and—'

Chloe chuckled. 'You accidentally ran into his dick?'

Deep masculine laughter drifted out from behind the closet door.

'Chloe!'

'Mom, chill. I'm glad you're having fun. You didn't, like, traumatize me or anything. I've seen you in your undies before. And seeing Nick Broome in *his* didn't exactly scar me for life.' She mumbled quietly, 'Yikes, he's a smokeshow.'

'Thank you,' came Nicky's voice again.

'You're welcome,' Chloe replied to the door. Turning back to Lucy she said, 'You should bring him to the wedding. Bring him to *all* the wedding stuff.'

Lucy's pulse ticked up. 'Nope. No. Nonononono.'

'I'd love to,' said Nicky through the door.

'Good!' Chloe exclaimed.

Chloe made for the bedroom door just as the closet opened again. Nicky stepped out in his jeans and that one stupid sock.

'Don't forget, tonight is the bachelorette.' She turned to Nicky. 'Sorry, that's ladies only.'

'Understood,' Nicky replied.

Chloe went on, 'But tomorrow is brunch with the dads.' She turned to Nicky and asked, 'You'll be her plus-one?'

'I'd be honored,' Nicky replied.

Lucy protested, 'But Kim—'

'Kim will come, too,' Chloe declared. Her smile brightened. 'Don't you worry, I'll make all the arrangements. See you later, Nick.'

'Can't wait, Chloe,' Nicky replied.

Chloe, who never could resist a parting shot, called out over her shoulder as she closed the door, 'Make good choices, you two!'

Lucy could hear her daughter's triumphant cackle as it drifted deeper into the suite.

'What the fuck was that?' Lucy mumbled.

'I finally got to meet your daughter,' Nicky replied. 'She's great. She looks like you. In the eyes.'

Lucy stared at Nicky, all those tattoos and abs just fucking everywhere. She found it hard to clear her head and focus with all of his *everything* in her face.

'You really don't have to go anywhere or do anything. Chloe is . . .'

'She's pretty amazing, from what I can tell.'

'Definitely amazing,' Lucy said, 'But also enthusiastic about her social life. About *everyone*'s social life. You probably have things to do and it will be . . . a lot. Too much.'

'I promise I'll tell you if it's too much,' Nicky said stepping toward her.

It's insane. 'It's insane,' she told Nicky's California bear tattoo as it closed in on her.

'It's not insane,' he said, threading his fingers through hers. 'Also, if there's one thing I've learned after getting married a billion and a half times it's that the bride always gets what she wants.'

Nicky slipped his free hand under the T-shirt Lucy was wearing. His fingers drifted up, grazing against the skin of her stomach. Along the curve under her breast.

'What are you doing?' Lucy grunted, holding back a mewl.

'Getting my shirt back,' he huffed into her neck.

'I really need a shower.'

'Me too,' he said before pressing his lips against hers. 'Let's go do that.'

He pulled her by the hand into the adjoining bathroom.

'What are we doing? Are we just going to—?'

Nicky turned to her and squeezed her hip with his hand. 'Right now, we're going to take a shower.'

'The wedding is on Saturday,' Lucy tried. 'I'm flying out on Sunday night.'

'Perfect, I'm leaving for the tour on Monday.'

'Tour?'

'Europe.'

Of course. Of course, he is. He's a big-time fucking rock star, Lucy. You dolt.

'So, until then?' she asked, as he twisted the hot water on in the cavernous shower.

'Until then,' he said with finality. He pulled the T-shirt over her head and trailed kisses across her collarbone.

Lucy took a deep breath. She should be grateful. She *was* grateful. At least she could see the end coming this time. She could brace herself and prepare for it. She wouldn't get all twisted up. It would be casual. Easy. No big deal.

Nicky turned around and put his hand under the water. It was then that Lucy caught a glimpse of a tattoo she hadn't noticed before. Under his right shoulder blade was a cassette tape, slightly smaller than life-sized. It was done in fine black lines that had drifted a little, smudged as though from age. The fact that he had a cassette tape tattoo wasn't odd, it made sense, really. What *was* odd, though, was the strip on the tape where the album title should be. There were only four letters there – L-U-C-Y.

She wanted to ask about it. Figure it out. Understand. But before Lucy could form a sentence, Nicky dropped his jeans and boxers.

The words never came.

(Oh, but she did.)

CHAPTER NINETEEN

NICKY

Nicky ran a towel over his hair after his second shower of the day. The first one hadn't really been about getting clean, though, so he didn't feel guilty about it. Even if he was in the middle of the damn desert during a drought.

He found his phone on the coffee table of his suite's overlarge living area and hit the button for Damon.

As always, his assistant answered the call on the second ring.

''Sup, Bossman?' Damon chirped.

'How's everything in LA?'

'Right as rain. Without the rain.'

'Good. Look, I'm going to need to change the travel plans this weekend,' Nicky said.

'Let me get a pen.' After a moment of rustling and clanging Damon came back with: 'Okay, hit me.'

'I was supposed to go out on Sunday morning, right?'

'Yeah, with Vinny and the tour managers.'

'Can I hop on Gill's flight Monday instead?'

'Yeah. Not a problem. I'll get the manifests squared today,' Damon replied. 'I'll synch the updates to the schedule in the app. Should pop up in a bit.'

'Awesome. Perfect, thanks.'

'Easiest thing I've done all day.'

Nicky laughed. 'Man, please. You've done nothing but smoke up all day. I know you.'

Damon just laughed his deep, goofy stoner's laugh.

'Just remember to water the plants in the kitchen. And not with bong water this time.'

'They *loved* it.'

'They *died*.' Something else occurred to Nicky and he knew damn well that Damon would not be this coherent later. 'Oh, Damon?'

'Yeah?'

'If I needed to add another person to the flight, how much notice would you need?'

'Like two hours, maybe. Sooner the better, though. The FAA loves their fucking paperwork.'

'Got it. Thanks.'

Nicky said his goodbyes, then collapsed into the sofa.

He had hope. Maybe it was hope of the idiotic Pollyanna variety, but it was still there. And it made Nicky feel lighter than he had in forever. Over the years optimism had become his drug of choice. He loved it as much as Damon loved his OG Kush. Nicky had been missing it for a while, the enthusiasm and hopefulness. They had slowly dimmed behind the shadows of hollow, broken relationships with women who'd ticked the 'hookup with a rich, famous guy' box on their career day survey, and under the weight of professional obligations and the hamster wheel of recording, promoting, and touring.

The band had been enough for a while; there had been mountains to scale, songs to write, records to make and break. But now? Now all Nicky really wanted was a little slice of normal. Some calm and contentment. So, he leaned into his Pollyanna hope.

Maybe Lucy was the spark, or maybe she was just the breath of fresh air that reignited his own. Either way, he could feel the glow and warmth of *possibility* catching alight within him. It was both familiar and new, comforting and thrilling.

Nicky sat with that feeling, focused on it and willed it to expand.

Then, in the peace and quiet of his hotel room, with the desert sun warming his face, Nicky heard something. Inside him. Ringing out bright and bold in the empty, silent caverns of his mind.

He bolted up and raced into the bedroom. He got on his hands and knees and dug through a closet just like the one he'd been shoved into earlier that morning. His hands closed on his battered carry-on duffel. He unzipped everything he could, searching until he found a crisp, clean Moleskine notebook and a pack of pre-sharpened pencils.

And began to write.

CHAPTER TWENTY

LUCY

Except for the purple penises bobbing over her head and the burning sensation in her thigh, Lucy was feeling pretty good. The bass in the place had made her mostly deaf, but the ringing sound in her ears muffling the house music was actually sort of soothing. The three margaritas she'd had didn't hurt either.

Lucy tried to look cool and relaxed from her spot on the absurdly long corner booth they'd reserved for the bachelorette party. She stared across the room at the people drunkenly gyrating on the dance floor, keeping her eye out for the one set of bobbing penises that were lit up with flashing LEDs – Chloe.

'Hey,' panted Kim as she slid into the booth. Naturally, Kim managed to make her hot pink bouncing penis headband look like some kind of avant-garde Barbie-core fashion statement. Unfair. 'Brought you another green one,' she said, handing Lucy a lollipop penis.

'Score!' Lucy yelled over the music. 'The green is surprisingly delightful.'

'It is,' replied Kim, licking her own green candy appendage.

'What are you doing over here?'

'Can't dance anymore,' Lucy grumbled. 'You'll be happy to know, I have a sex injury.'

'Awesome,' Kim said, clearly impressed. 'Whatcha got?'

'Pulled a hammy,' Lucy replied.

'Aw, that's not too bad.'

'It's not a concussion,' Lucy said, waggling her eyebrows. 'That was not my finest moment.'

'Ah, but watching you explain it to your dad in the hospital was *mine*.' Lucy opened her lollipop and took a good lick. 'What was that dude's name?'

'Oh, man,' Kim said, squeezing her eyes together as though forcing her sloshed brain to remember. 'Derek? Dominik? Something with a D.'

'Oh, there was a D all right,' Lucy said before bursting into margarita-induced laughter.

Kim followed her right over, the both of them laughing like teenagers before clinking their green penis-pops together in a toast to good old D-whoever.

'Is there THC in these dicks?' Kim gasped through tears of laughter.

This sent them into a whole new round of guffaws that made Lucy's stomach hurt and wish she hadn't eaten the *whole* burrito at the restaurant beforehand.

As Lucy gulped for air and clutched at her stomach, the

entire club went nuts. The song had changed. She could actually feel the vibration of the dancers through the floor, even from across the massive room.

The song was fast, new. But somewhere there in the background was a sample. Something she recognized.

'Oh, shit,' Lucy said, dropping her chin in her penis-free hand. She stared at the bright pink bouquet of flowers lying forgotten on the table. The same one that had bounced down the hallway past Nicky's feet that first day. Lucy mumbled, 'Is this—?'

'Your man?' Kim asked. 'Yep.'

The sample behind the dance beat was 'The Breathing Room' sped up slightly and laid over some other guy's hip-hop/dance/rap combo. It was different, but it was there. All of it. As familiar as her own name, and just as ever-fucking-present.

Kim scooted closer, leaned in so that her shoulder rested against Lucy's. A comforting hand came to Lucy's back.

'It's all right, Luce. It's okay.'

Lucy's head turned to Kim. Shocked. Panicked.

'Oh, God. Y-you know?' Lucy stuttered.

'I'm like the smartest person you know, so . . .' Kim said, shrugging.

Oh, God. She *knew* knew. About the song. About Nicky Broome.

'I should have told you,' Lucy burbled.

'No. You didn't have to. I love you like a sister. You are the most important person in my life. My *whole* life. But that doesn't mean you have to tell me everything. I don't tell you everything.'

'You don't?'

Kim's slightly glassy eyes scanned the table, squinting in thought. 'Well, okay. I actually do. But I don't *have* to.'

Lucy sucked on the unreasonably delicious green penis, then said, 'The first time I heard it, I was on the street. Listening to the radio on my way to class. On my Walkman. Remember the Walkman?'

'Yep,' Kim replied dryly.

Lucy exhaled a sigh. 'I knew from the first note that it was him. I knew from the first chorus it was about me. I started sobbing. Like uncontrollable sobbing. On the sidewalk. I mean, it was New York so people mostly tried to ignore me and give me a wide berth but . . .' Lucy could remember that day perfectly. It was firmly imprinted in her psyche. 'Never made it to class.'

'The Breathing Room' ended up becoming the undisputed heavyweight song of the year. A breakout hit by a little band no one had heard of called Super, featuring a dynamic and beautiful lead singer named Nick Broome.

The song was everywhere. *He* was everywhere. TV, the radio, posters in the Virgin Records down the block from her dorm. In the background at every party.

From the very start, people theorized who the song was about. It was a luscious secret, like the subject of 'You're So Vain,' only fueled by a burgeoning internet and fans whose every drunken two-a.m. musing could be shared with the whole fucking world in an instant. Over the years,

'The Breathing Room Girl' had stamped itself on American culture, become a shorthand phrase for an enticing and unknowable mystery.

Nicky never told anyone. If he'd only said publicly that the song was just fantasy, or that it was about some girl he knew once, the whole mess might have blown over. But he didn't, and the mystery of the thing made it tantalizing. Compelling. Made it last. Well, the song did that too, Lucy supposed. Because it was amazing. Beautiful and powerful. A love song you could dance to, rock out in the car and scream at the top of your lungs.

When Super's first album was rereleased for the ten-year anniversary, the fervor really ticked up. The lyrics, reprinted in the CD liner notes (because that was still a thing) included new punctuation. A question mark, of all things. Websites popped up, dedicated to pondering the addition of a fucking question mark. (*Was it always supposed to be there? Was it added now for a reason? What did it mean?*) A few tiny pixels of difference between the original lyrics printed in the late 1990s and the ones from the 2000s made the subject relevant again.

At the twenty-year anniversary, there was a call from a music magazine willing to pay a million dollars – one million actual American dollars – for the answer to the mystery.

'Who Is the Breathing Room Girl?' was a funny human-interest blurb on *The Today Show*, the local news, in the damn *Wall Street Journal*. *You too could be a millionaire if you just speak up, people!*

Lucy didn't. Even though a million dollars would have vastly improved her net worth.

'Jesus,' Lucy exclaimed to Kim. 'You could have made a million bucks off that info.'

Kim shook her head, pink penises swaying dramatically from side to side. 'I don't need a million dollars as much as I need you.'

Lucy's eyes went all misty. She felt a lump of emotion forming in her throat. *Damn, margaritas and memories are a terrible combo.* 'I love you,' she told Kim.

'I love you, too,' replied Kim, slinging her arm across Lucy's shoulders. 'There is one thing, though.' The statement came with a grimace, and a look of contrition Lucy could never remember seeing on her best friend's ever-confident face.

'What?' Lucy prodded.

'The question mark.'

'Not you, too!'

'Well, come on! It's a fucking national mystery. It changes the whole meaning of the song, dammit! Have you asked him about it? Do you understand it?'

Lucy's body curled in on itself. A teensy bit of shame washed over her. 'I've been avoiding the subject.'

'You haven't mentioned the song?' Kim asked, clearly floored.

'No.'

'At all?'

'No.'

'God,' Kim said under her breath.

'I don't . . . *want* to,' Lucy sputtered, feeling childish and weak.

Kim pulled her phone from her back pocket and typed furiously with her thumbs. She propped the thing up against the flower bouquet and scrolled.

The lyrics to 'The Breathing Room' glared up at them in glowing black and white. Lucy didn't really need to read them; she knew all the words by heart though she avoided the song at every possible opportunity.

Kim placed her hand over Lucy's, a tangible reminder of the unwavering strength of the nearly forty years of friendship and support between them.

For the first time, Lucy read the lyrics – really read them.

'The Breathing Room'
Music and Lyrics by Nick Broome

Gazes like smoke and whispers
Strokes of sparks like wishes
Sharp breaths, panted names
Beginnings and endings
Sometimes feel the same

Doubt like ocean wind within
Burdens and hassles without
Weight lifted under the weight of you
Wanted to spend all summer
In that breathing room

There with you, that was it.
It was the calming.
It was the fit.
In the Breathing Room,
You gave me breathing room.

Praises like balm, a zephyr
A draft to ease the pressure
Soothed and strong over the heart of you
Should have spent all year
In that Breathing Room.

There with you, that was it.
It was the calming.
It was the fit.
In the Breathing Room,
You gave me breathing room.

Gasps, fiery and resounding
Sated and restless, I cling
Come undone, life changed
Endings and beginnings . . .
Sometimes, they're the same

There with you, that was it.
It was the calming.
It was the fit.
In the Breathing Room,
You gave me breathing room.

Everything from you.
Anything for you?

'Ugh,' Lucy groaned, throwing her head in her hands.

Kim exhaled dramatically. 'I mean . . . whoa.'

'I know, okay?' Lucy griped. 'But in the end, it's just a song. One of about a million he's written over the years.'

'Sure, but it's a question, Luce. The song is a question. For you. You get that, right?'

'You think he's been waiting twenty-some-odd years for me to answer?' Lucy asked, disbelieving.

'You don't?'

Lucy knew that Nicky had been trying to get her to bring up the song since the moment they ran into each other; she *knew* that. She could feel it lingering in his avaricious dive into her Spotify app. In the way he jumped on the swing to rock love songs in their conversations.

She should bring it up; they should both get it all out on the table. Lucy was a grown-ass woman; she knew how to talk about difficult things. However, she was also really fucking adept at denial and deflection. And she'd been avoiding all talk about 'The Breathing Room' for decades. It was a form of self-protection that was second nature to her now.

'It doesn't matter, Kim. It's old news.'

'You had sex with him *last night*,' Kim objected, punctuating each word with a finger stab at the table.

'And I'll be going back to Ohio and tenure review on Sunday. He's headed off on a European tour on Monday. *A European tour*. Because he's a certified rock god. He doesn't even live in the real world, Kim. This is just another weird fling. We'll probably meet up again when we're in our seventies.' The thought of that sent a sick feeling washing over her. *It was probably the burrito.*

Kim tapped at her phone again. Lucy caught a glimpse of the Google doodle before Kim tipped her phone away.

After a moment, Kim huffed, 'Oh, boy.'

'What?'

'Spain, France, England . . . fucking *Monaco*.' Kim scrolled up on her phone. 'A show every two or three days. Sometimes four days between countries. It goes from the end of July to . . .' She groaned, '*Next year*. In July. It's a full year. In Europe. Damn, a lot of these shows are already sold out.'

Lucy's heart sank. She felt it settle on the overlarge burrito in her belly and tap out a sad tune. *Dumb. This is a short-term thing with Nicky. Till Sunday. Nothing more.*

'See?' Lucy said, gathering the futile little scraps of hope that had somehow formed without her noticing. She shoved those pesky things right into a familiar old mental box marked 'Nicky Broome' and locked them up tight.

'Shit,' Kim said before exhaling heavily and putting her phone down. 'Okay, it's like I said before. A nice distraction.'

'Yep,' Lucy agreed, wishing she'd gone for the fourth margarita instead of water.

The beat from the speakers slid into a rhythm that had a Pavlovian effect on Lucy. It felt like bouncing in a tub of joy bubbles. She couldn't help but smile.

'Oh, hello!' yelled Kim. 'I believe they're playing our song! Sex injury or no sex injury we're going out there.'

Kim took Lucy's hand and dragged her out of the booth, their dick headbands springing to the beat of the Notorious B.I.G.'s 'Hypnotize' as they sauntered to the dance floor.

There, Lucy lost herself in the music, screaming the lyrics with Kim until she was hoarse and dancing until the pain in her hamstring was nothing but an afterthought.

CHAPTER TWENTY-ONE

NICKY

The door to Lucy's suite swung open before he even had a chance to knock.

'Who knew rock stars were so punctual?' Lucy joked. Then she stopped as though stunned, and looked him over. Breathed, '*God*.'

'What?' Nicky asked, rattled. He looked down at what he'd thought was a perfectly respectable Tom Ford button-down and black pants. He really only had seventeen different kinds of sneakers, so he'd gone with the limited edition Jordans. Maybe he should have ordered some real grown-up shoes from the Prada in the casino shops?

'Do you always look like you were spit out by *GQ* or is this just a Las Vegas thing?' Lucy teased.

Phew.

'All of this is too much for just one city,' he teased back.

'Sounds about right,' she quipped, ushering him into the room.

Lucy walked to one of the bedroom doors and knocked on it. 'Chloe, get a move on!' Then, to Nicky she said, 'I told the wedding planner that brunch the morning after the bachelorette was ambitious, at best. But she insisted that it would all work out. She must be accustomed to dealing with *responsible* adults.'

'Well, you look beautiful,' Nicky said. Meaning it.

Lucy was wearing another ballet-pink sleeveless thing on top. Tight this time, with her strong arms looking good enough to lick. Snug black pants led down, down, down, to some seriously hot black heels. Gold hoops peeked out from her bob. Sexy as hell.

Lucy caught him checking her out. Her shoulders shook with a chuckle as she flitted around the suite grabbing things and shoving them in a handbag.

'Well, all of this,' she said, waving her hand in front of her face. 'Is thanks to about twelve pounds of concealer, and the fact that I'm standing is only the result of near toxic levels of caffeine. So, don't get your hopes up. Eventually, I'm going to crash and melt like the Wicked Witch of the West. Maybe not in that order.'

'Fine by me,' he said.

She stopped, looked at him with concern. 'You really don't have to do this, you know.'

'Do you not *want* me to go?' he asked.

'It's not—' Lucy heaved a sigh as though rethinking what she was about to say. 'You are top-notch eye candy, Broome.' She smiled, and God he wanted to kiss the pink lipstick right off her mouth. 'But it's a lot. It will for sure be uncomfortable. And this—' she waved her hand between them '—is just supposed to be fun and casual, right?'

He nodded, even if the word *casual* was entirely inaccurate from where he was standing.

'All of this completely bonkers family and wedding stuff isn't . . . exactly . . . uh, *that*.'

Now she was getting it.

'I *want* to go with you,' he stated simply.

'Oh,' she chirped, tilting her head as though trying to figure him out. 'Okay, then.' Lucy turned back to Chloe's door. 'Chloe! We've got to go, kiddo.'

A feminine voice called back, 'Almost ready!'

A few seconds later, Chloe emerged from her room looking every bit a young bride. She swept out in a cloud of flowery perfume, white cotton, and buoyant expectation that made her look exactly like her mother.

'Okay,' Lucy said, shoulders drooping, her voice laden with apprehension. 'I guess this is it.'

'Relax, Mom, you're not headed for the firing squad. It's just a simple little brunch with at least four guys you've slept with. No big deal.'

'At *least*?' Lucy asked.

Chloe didn't miss a beat. 'There'll probably be waiters there, maybe a maître d'? I don't know what you've been getting up to in this hotel. I mean, you let a strange rock star spend the night. How am I to know how far you might go?'

Chloe winked at Nicky conspiratorially, and it struck him right in the chest. The woman was smart, quick, and wickedly funny. She was confident and special. He admired Lucy all the more for having raised such a person.

Lucy grumbled, 'And again, improv comedy summer camp rears up to bite me in the ass.'

'I *loved* that camp,' Chloe whispered to Nicky.

Nicky laughed and threaded his fingers through Lucy's as they trooped out of the suite.

*

They were escorted to a small, private dining room with tall windows showing off a third-floor view of the Strip below. It was bright and cheerful, all white linen and gold-trimmed dishes. There was an enormous round table in the center and a whole lot of empty chairs.

Nicky took a deep breath to center himself, like he did before he went onstage. *Nothing could be as terrifying as singing in front of thousands of people, right?*

As though he had summoned the terror, it walked in – Kim. She shot Nicky a look that would shrivel a normal man's balls to raisins. Luckily, Nicky had never been normal.

The tall, slender blast from the past sauntered in wearing jeans and one of those fuzzy Chanel jackets favored by his New York booking agent.

'Oh, good. You're already here!' Lucy exclaimed with relief. 'I thought you might get smart and sleep through it.'

'Never!' Kim said, hugging Chloe. 'Just went out for some hair of the dog.' She waggled a large Bloody Mary at them.

Lucy turned to him. 'Kim has recently discovered the delights of day drinking.'

Kim took Nicky's proffered hand and shook. She purred, 'It's most likely not becoming a problem.' Her grip was firm, pointedly so, as she said, 'Long time no see, Broome. I think the last time was at the . . . *beach*?' The words were friendly, but the tone was damn near venomous.

'Yeah. Good to see you, Kim.'

Nicky barely had time to get the feeling back in his hand before a group of people filed in. He sucked in a deep breath, and Chloe noticed.

With a twinkle in her eye, she said, 'Yeah. Better buckle up.'

'I guess this must be the place,' said a jocular man of about Nicky's age and height. He was sewn into a gray linen suit, expensive and new. He had the look of a frat boy made good, lots of gym-hewn muscles and overpriced cologne. 'There she is,' he exclaimed, opening his arms to Chloe.

Must be Brandon.

'Hi, Daddy,' Chloe cooed. 'I'm glad you could make it.'

'Wouldn't miss it, Cricket,' he said softly into Chloe's hair.

Behind Brandon was a young, pregnant woman. Instinctively, Nicky wondered if she was a half-sister or something until Chloe said, 'Jenna, this is Mom's friend, Nick Broome. Nick, this is my dad's wife, Jenna.' She pointed to Jenna's silk-clad belly and added, 'And in there is my little half-sister.'

Oh boy.

The room went silent, and Nicky knew that all assembled

were beginning to piece together who he was and what exactly the word 'friend' implied. This particular reaction wasn't uncommon, especially if he was showing up at a place unannounced. These people were expecting to have a family gathering and had come face to face with someone they'd only ever seen on TV. He imagined it would be a bit like waking up and finding a space alien in your living room. Amusing maybe, but also jarring.

The whispers he'd been expecting started up soon after. As did the awkward gaping looks as he shook hands with a rugged, bearded guy named Sam, Lucy's second husband, and his new spouse James. And then again when Devin, Lucy's apparently much younger and third ex-husband, tried to smash Nicky's heavily insured fingers in a bone-crushing handshake.

'Chandler's not joining us?' Brandon asked as all assembled found seats.

'No, he and his parents are on a thrilling tour of the Hoover Dam today,' Chloe said, unfolding her napkin. 'Just my side of the family for brunch.'

Nicky, who had spent the majority of his youth with his father as his only family, had a hard time wrapping his head around the whole scene. It was amazing that Chloe had so many people willing to truck to Las Vegas and show up for her. It was even more astonishing that all of Lucy's ex-husbands could sit in the same room. Nicky tried to imagine his ex-wives doing the same, and could envision only a heap of smashed china and broken fingernails, with Andy Cohen doing the color commentary.

'I tried to warn you,' Lucy whispered to him from behind her water glass.

Nicky slid his hand under the tablecloth, and onto Lucy's thigh. Gave it a good squeeze. 'It's all good, Lou.'

He watched her struggle to swallow. Then, stared at her stunning profile – probably a bit too long – when she turned back toward the table.

After a waiter had been in to take their orders and drinks had arrived, Chloe said, 'So, Nick, let me give you the SparkNotes version of the family.'

It sounded great if only he knew what the fuck a SparkNote was.

Lucy leaned in before he could even exhale and whispered, 'Like CliffsNotes, if you were born after the cell phone.'

Ah, got it.

Chloe continued, 'Brandon is my bio dad. He lives in New York with Jenna where his business is making money reproduce like bunnies by exploiting the stock market in ways that are mostly legal.'

'Excuse me,' Brandon objected. 'Don't forget the bond market.'

'Sorry,' Chloe said to her dad, then added, 'and the bond market. He and Jenna have been married for three years. She's growing an online knitting business. And a baby.'

'Got it,' said Nicky, returning Jenna's warm smile.

'We won't be offended if you need your Notes app to keep track of all this, by the way,' joked Chloe. 'There *will* be a test after.'

A rumble of laughter circled the table, from all but

Devin. He seemed to be trying to grind his perfect white teeth to dust.

'Next,' Chloe said dramatically, 'is Sam. He was with us when I was in elementary school. Sam is the reason I can ride a bike and throw a punch.'

'Because I taught her those things,' Sam said to Nicky, running a hand over his beard. 'Not because she had to ride away or punch me back.'

'Yes,' chimed Chloe. 'He married James when I was fifteen. I remember because I was the only flower girl in history with braces.'

'You were perfect,' offered James, tipping his glasses further up his nose.

Chloe smiled. 'I was very awkward and distributed the flowers poorly, but thank you, James. Oh, Sam is a professor, too, like Mom, and James does something in city government.'

James rolled his eyes as though this was an old family joke. 'I'm the mayor,' he told Nicky.

Chloe waved a hand to her left at the fit young guy who seemed uncomfortable in his khakis and polo shirt. 'And last, but certainly not least, is Devin. He was with us when I was in high school and gave great advice on the twisted minds of teenage boys and never ever told Mom about that time he had to pick me up because I was sloshed.'

'Two times,' Devin corrected, with a smile. 'There was that time at Grant's when—'

Chloe waved her hands dramatically. 'Oh, wow. Yeah. Okay, let's not go into those details.'

'What details?' Lucy asked.

'It was fine!' Chloe said cheerily to Lucy. 'See, I'm here and I'm fine.' Chloe turned to Nicky. 'Devin is the women's soccer coach at the university where Mom and Sam work. Phew, so there. That's everyone, yeah?'

Nicky said, 'Thank you.' Desperately trying to infuse it with the sincerity he felt. 'I do hope you were joking about that quiz, though.'

Conversation turned to the wedding, with Chloe answering questions about flowers and cocktails and all sorts of things Nicky didn't have a clue about. He simply nodded, and tried not to stare at Lucy as she smiled and laughed along with Chloe.

It was only after the food arrived, and Nicky was three bites into his eggs Benedict, that he noticed the room had gone completely silent. He looked up and found three pairs of eyes on him.

'Oh, God. Sorry,' said Sam.

James offered, 'I told him not to stare.'

James had been staring, too, but it didn't seem the time to mention it.

'Can we talk about it now?' Sam asked as he eyed various people around the table.

'Talk about what?' Lucy asked dryly, fooling no one.

'Ugh, okay,' Sam said, laying down his fork with a chunk of breakfast ham still attached. 'I know I'm supposed to be cool about it and not freak out. But, *dude*,' he said, looking at Nicky, 'you're *Nick Broome*.'

Nicky couldn't help but laugh. 'Uh, yeah. I am.'

'Holy shit,' Sam said.

'Funny, that's what my mom calls me,' Nick joked.

'I'm just . . .' tried Sam. 'My mind is blown.'

A bunch of heads nodded. Kim's sort of shook back and forth as she stared at her fruit salad.

'I saw you in Philly. In 2016,' Devin grumbled, as though suddenly pissed about it.

'Oh, yeah?' Nicky did some quick math and scanned his mind over the roughly seventy-million shows he'd performed in his life. 'Was it the one where Dave Grohl came on for a few?'

'Yeah,' said Devin.

Lucy's hand stopped midway to her water. Nicky eyed her curiously, wondering if she was all right.

Nicky added, 'That was a good show. At least from up front. I hope you had a good time.'

'Yeah,' he grumbled, even more pissed about it. 'I did.'

Lucy turned slowly toward him. 'You *know* Dave Grohl?'

'Sure,' Nicky replied. 'Why?'

Lucy replied, 'Um, this may be out of line but . . . can you tell him that I love him with all my heart and that *The Colour and the Shape* changed my life. And that I love him. Oh, and that his eyelashes are mesmerizing. And he's the best drummer ever.' She paused. 'And also, that I love him.'

'Yeah, you said that already.' Nicky laughed.

'Said what?'

'That you love him.'

'It bears repeating. You can say it as many times as you feel comfortable with,' Lucy instructed. Then added, 'As long as it's no fewer than three.'

Nicky cracked up at both the earnestness and complete insanity of that statement. 'You really want me to say that to him? Word for word?'

'Yes, dammit!' Lucy slapped his arm playfully. 'I've been wanting to say that to him for about thirty years, give or take a month.'

'She had a Dave Grohl poster on her wall in high school, Nick,' chimed Kim. 'Not Kurt Cobain. Dave Grohl.'

'Got a thing for drummers?' Nicky asked.

'Just one. *That* one,' Lucy replied.

Note to self, lose Dave Grohl's number.

'Okay,' Nicky said matter-of-factly.

Lucy sputtered, 'Really?'

'Sure. I'm going to call him.' Nicky pulled his phone from his pocket. 'Right now, as a matter of fact,' he said, calling Lucy's bluff.

'That's okay,' Lucy said, smiling. 'I don't mind. He needs to know.' Her grin widened. 'That I love him.'

Nicky scrolled through his contacts. Actually clicked on Grohl's contact page. 'Was that two times that you love him?'

'Three,' Chloe piped up cheekily. 'Minimum.'

'Thank you, Chloe,' Nicky replied.

Moving with ridiculous speed, Lucy snatched the phone from Nicky's hand and shoved it between her ass and the chair.

'You are probably committing an actual butt-dial right now.' Nicky laughed.

'Since it's your phone, I don't feel bad about it,' Lucy teased.

'It's cute how you think I won't just dive in there and get it,' Nicky said, raising an eyebrow for effect.

'Try me, Broome.' Lucy chuckled.

The sound of someone loudly clearing their throat pulled Nicky's focus back to the table. It was Kim, covering her mouth with a napkin, but obviously trying to get their attention.

Then Nicky realized that the entire table was ogling them, their eyes bouncing between Nicky and Lucy like they were a couple of zoo animals copulating in front of an observation window. Devin, especially, gave him the feeling of being examined and considered like a specimen behind glass.

Nicky and Lucy both silently went back to work on their food, Lucy's ass still warming his phone.

Sam tried to cover the awkwardness by blurting, '"The Breathing Room" was the first dance at our wedding.'

Nicky's heart traveled directly to his throat, making it next to impossible to swallow the bite of eggs he was chewing. He coughed. Tried to breathe.

His head whipped toward Lucy, whose blue eyes had shuttered, even as her fork moved around her plate.

'It was,' James said dreamily, looking at his husband.

Nicky let go of the breath he hadn't realized he'd been holding. It was *Sam and James*'s first dance. Not Sam and Lucy's.

Fuck.

Nicky didn't have time to ponder why the idea of Lucy dancing to 'The Breathing Room' at her wedding to some other guy had made his chest feel too tight.

'That's great,' Nicky said, struggling to get the food down past the lump in his throat. 'I've heard it's a popular song for that. Weddings.'

'What's your first dance going to be, Chloe?' Kim asked.

'"Grow Old With Me,"' Chloe replied. 'No offense, Nick.'

'None taken,' he said. 'John Lennon?'

'Tom Odell,' she said.

'Solid choice.'

The rest of the meal passed with Nicky feeling increasingly sick to his stomach, a condition he did not attribute to the excellent food.

He was asked about his Grammys and where he kept his platinum records. Chloe offered further details on the honeymoon. Brandon spoke about the Hamptons. Devin said something about a marathon. Nicky couldn't seem to hold on to any of the threads of conversation.

He knew he and Lucy had to get the song stuff out in the open. Intellectually, he recognized it as a barrier. A fixed stopping point to anything more that he might hope to have with her. He just really didn't know how to bring it up. Or, to be honest, what to say.

Nicky was beginning to suspect that the song meant something to Lucy. He had felt her stiffen next to him when Sam brought it up, couldn't help but note how her eyes had closed as though pushing it away. And it scared the shit out of him.

CHAPTER TWENTY-TWO

LUCY

The whole bizarre circus that was Lucy's family said their many, many goodbyes in a little atrium outside the restaurant. Beyond their strange bubble was a shopping area chock-full of luxury brands and the tourists ready to indulge in them.

Lucy had hugged all of her exes, save one. As Brandon finally approached her, she heard Jenna tell him that she was going to pop into Bulgari and for him to meet her there.

'Have a minute for a quick chat?' Brandon asked, more to Nicky, who was standing behind her.

'I'll just . . .' Nicky said, pointing a thumb over his shoulder toward the riot of color and checkerboard in a MacKenzie-Childs shop window. He walked away, looking back at her twice.

Brandon eyed Nicky, then gazed back to Lucy. Her ex-husband looked different, younger. His brown hair had lost all traces of gray since meeting Jenna. His face was smoother, more relaxed. Either he had a very talented plastic surgeon, or Jenna and the new baby on the way were a calming influence. Her money was on the surgeon.

Brandon took a deep breath, inhaling like he was preparing to say something, while smoothing the lapel of his perfectly tailored linen jacket.

The words Lucy was expecting didn't come, though. Instead, Brandon just exhaled loudly and shoved a hand in the pocket of his sportscoat.

'Maybe we should, uh, sit down,' he said, tipping his head toward a bench nestled into a planter filled with tropical plants.

Usually, Brandon didn't talk so much as confidently instruct. His gentle tone and stuttering speech had piqued Lucy's curiosity. 'Sure, okay,' Lucy replied.

When they were seated on the bench – and Nicky had moved to keep her in his line of sight – Brandon said, 'I'm sorry.'

'For what?' Lucy asked, shocked. Brandon didn't apologize much. Or, *at all* that Lucy could recall.

'I think when we met, I was looking for Jenna.'

Wow, didn't see that one coming. Lucy feared the sudden shift to the distant past had given her whiplash.

She said, 'Well, Brandon, I hate to tell you this, but if you had found Jenna instead of me back in the old days you'd be in jail, because you'd have found her in a kindergarten classroom.'

'No, I don't mean Jenna specifically. I mean—' Brandon

looked down at his perfectly polished bespoke loafers. 'Look, when we split up, I was angry.'

'I noticed,' Lucy tutted.

'But I'm realizing now, after *many* long, expensive hours with a therapist, that I wasn't really angry with you. I was angry that you couldn't be what I wanted. I see now, it was on me. My expectations were unrealistic. You were you, and I was me, and neither of us was going to change.'

Lucy was stunned. She didn't know what to say to that. Brandon was in therapy. He had a *feeling*.

He continued, 'I'm sorry that I was an asshole. While we were married and after. You didn't deserve it.'

Lucy sighed. As much as she'd love to bask in her ex-husband's contrition, it wouldn't be honest. Lucy said, 'It wasn't just you, Brandon. I probably should have known that I wasn't that girl. The one who wanted to stay home with the kids and summer in the Hamptons and do the whole Wall Street wife thing. I tried. But I think deep down I knew, even before we got married, that I wasn't going to love it.'

'We were so young and naïve,' he said with a half-smile.

'We were.'

A long moment of silence passed between them, maybe a nanosecond for every year they'd been angry with one another.

'For what it's worth, I like him,' Brandon said, nodding toward Nicky who seemed to be studiously inspecting a black-and-white checkered espresso machine.

Lucy muttered, 'Oh, it's not—' but then couldn't decide how to finish the sentence.

Brandon smiled softly. 'It could be, Luce.'

Lucy suddenly had the uncomfortable feeling that therapy had made Brandon psychic as well as introspective.

'Thanks,' she said, hoping to end the whole weird conversation.

'Forgiven?' Brandon asked.

For Lucy, the pain between her and Brandon had been just the memory of an old ache for years. Still, she'd gotten into the habit of pushing on that healed bruise in preparation to meet Brandon and his ever-simmering anger. It would be nice to just exist around him, instead of posturing on a constant state of alert, waiting to react to whatever rancor he might throw her way.

'Nothing to forgive,' Lucy lied.

'Someday we might have to be together in the same room as grandparents.' He laughed.

'Oh, shit!' Lucy exclaimed. 'We could be grandparents!'

'Fucked up, right?'

'Jesus, I barely have this parenting thing figured out.'

'Tell me about it,' Brandon said, his eyes following the path Jenna had taken.

'I bet it'll be easier this time,' Lucy said.

'You think?'

'Sure,' Lucy lied again – a kind, gentle lie – for old times' sake.

CHAPTER TWENTY-THREE

NICKY

As they slowly meandered down the hotel hall toward their suites, Nicky heard Lucy sigh heavily. A weary-to-the-bone sort of sigh that he felt himself, but probably not for the same reasons.

He wanted to be near her, to keep her with him. They had agreed on four more days. Till Sunday evening when her plane took off. If that was all he was going to have, he didn't want to miss a minute of it. He should probably take her to her suite. Tuck her into bed and leave her to it. But Nicky was selfish, and his door was the first they came to. He headed for it, pulled her gently forward by their intertwined fingers.

'Am I coming over?' she asked.

'Yes.' He opened the door.

'I just really want to get into some sweatpants and take a nap,' she groaned.

'Okay,' he said, closing the front door and pulling her toward his bedroom.

'My sweatpants are about fifty yards that way,' she trilled, pointing.

'You can borrow some of mine.'

She smiled. 'But mine are right there.'

Nicky went to his dresser and pulled out a black T-shirt and gray joggers, handed them to her in a bundle.

'Just sweats. No funny business,' he said with a wink. 'Change in the bathroom to keep me honest.'

She rolled her eyes, but did as he instructed and headed for the en suite.

When Lucy emerged, he was lounging on the couch in the living room in another pair of sweatpants. He'd considered the bed, but was pretty sure that he wouldn't be able to get *funny business* off his mind if they were anywhere near it.

Only a sliver of desert sunlight peeked through the closed living room curtains. It was cool, dark, and cozy. Nicky reached for the TV remote and patted the seat next to him.

'It smells like you,' Lucy said absentmindedly, as she pulled the shirt up to sniff it.

'What do I smell like?'

'Soap. Salt. Man.'

Lucy snuggled in next to him, curling her feet up beneath her.

'Just generic *man*?' He laughed.

'Never generic,' she said, taking another whiff. 'Not you.'

'Not generic,' he said, while pulling the throw blanket from the back of the sofa and tucking them both under it.

'I'll stow that in my back pocket in case I decide to start a Tinder profile.'

She smiled weakly – tired, wrung out.

'Hangover any better?' he asked, flicking the TV on.

'Just a dull throbbing behind my eyes now,' she quipped.

Nicky got up and went straight to the kitchen where he found his stash of Tylenol and a bottle of water.

He handed two pills and the water to Lucy. She swallowed them down and said, 'Thanks.'

He tucked himself back under the blanket with her, and said, 'Chloe's dads all seem nice.'

Lucy's head fell back against the sofa. 'You were very tolerant of their questions and gawking. It was kind of you.'

'It sort of goes with the territory. I've had worse.'

'What are your exes like?' Lucy asked, eyes on the ceiling.

Nicky tutted. 'Not like yours.'

'Meaning?'

'Meaning, my first wife is basically a normal person who only wants me to be slowly eaten by sharks once in a while. My second wife believes I am the worst human to ever walk the Earth, but only because she's pissed at herself for signing a prenup. And my third wife doesn't exist because we weren't really married. Remember?'

'*Right*,' Lucy said with a grin.

'But it's safe to say, I can't imagine them sitting in a room together getting along. And I certainly can't imagine any of them apologizing to me.'

She cringed to the ceiling. 'You heard that, huh?'

'I don't think it qualifies as eavesdropping since it was all because of the extraordinary acoustics in that atrium.'

'The acoustics.'

'Yeah.'

Lucy sighed again, even more heavily than before. She snuggled deeper into the cushions, more closely into his side. 'Brandon's time was always more valuable than mine. His minutes could be calculated in dollars – thousands of them at a time. We agreed that I would continue with school, finish my master's, and go for a doctorate. But what value did my intellectual curiosity about the cultural significance of boy bands have? Monetarily? None. Less than none. Or maybe some paltry sum, years in the future. It didn't stand a chance. My dreams were insignificant. Hard to justify with logic. So, I took time away. It made me resentful. Whereas it made him happy. Hence the conflict.'

Nicky breathed out. 'Makes sense.' And it did, but he truly wished that it didn't. Mostly because he could feel an echo of that very same argument somewhere off in the distance. Wrapped up in his tour and his Pollyanna hopes for the two of them.

'And you had Chloe full-time?'

'Brandon had a month every summer. Every other Christmas.'

'That must have been hard,' Nicky said.

'Sometimes,' she said, closing her eyes as if remembering. When she opened them again, she added, 'But I had it easier than a lot of people. Brandon is filthy rich, so a lot of those concerns weren't an issue. You just keep going, right? As a parent. You just keep working and doing and going. Plus, I had a month every summer to work. Write my book, articles, whatever.'

'You wrote a book?' he exclaimed, unable to subdue the excitement.

She chuckled darkly. 'All part of the job. Publish or perish.' It came out like a groan, and Nicky wondered about it, but didn't want to push. Not when she was just freely offering up all this good stuff.

'Can I buy it?'

'Not on Amazon or anything but—'

Nicky grabbed his phone. 'Website. Now.'

Lucy laughed and took the phone from him, clicked the browser. 'It's boring. Not exactly what I'd hoped. My department chair—' She stopped herself. 'Anyway, doesn't matter, just expect to use it to cure insomnia or as a doorstop.'

She handed the phone back and he saw the book, *Pop: American Culture in the 20th Century* by Lucy McManis. He noticed that the site took Apple Pay and in seconds had it ordered. He made a mental note to get Damon to ship it out to wherever he happened to be when it finally arrived in LA.

Nicky asked, 'What happened with Sam?'

'He fell in love with James.'

'Really?'

'Yeah. Sam and I were really good friends. He's bi. I knew it all along. That part wasn't a surprise or anything.

But I thought we were sort of . . . comfortable. I guess I should have noticed that it wasn't everything he wanted. Then he fell in *big* love with James. All the trimmings. Honestly, it didn't hurt that much when it was over. I was happy for him. To get the full package deal.'

'Very mature of you,' Nicky said.

'Or maybe we shouldn't have gotten married in the first place.'

'Devin seems like—' Nicky couldn't decide how to word it.

Lucy finished, 'He wants me to be slowly eaten by sharks?'

Nicky laughed. 'A little?'

'Yeah.'

'I caught that. He's younger, right? Like, thirty-five?'

'On the nose,' Lucy replied. 'We were uh, hot and fast. He's a jock through and through and it just . . . fizzled. We had nothing in common. The physical part was there, but everything else was . . . missing, I guess? It was fun and great and then it wasn't. It was a terrible idea to get married. His, but still. I knew better. I *knew* it. It was dumb of me. A recurring theme, in case you hadn't picked that up.'

Nicky had never seen a broken marriage – his or anyone else's – that didn't have some culpability on both sides. He wondered why she kept putting so much of the blame on herself.

'Think you'll ever get married again?' Nicky asked, grateful that she had her eyes closed and her head tipped toward the ceiling. It was a crazy thing to ask, and he regretted it the second it was hovering there in the air between them.

Lucy laughed. 'The only way I'll get married again is accidentally.'

'How does a person accidentally get married?' he teased.

Lucy smiled. 'I don't know, someone asks "do you want chicken for dinner?" and you say, "I do" and there happens to be a priest there?'

Nicky followed her wild thinking. 'You're sightseeing in a church and you stumble through a door and find yourself on the altar just as the guy is saying "do you take this man to be your lawfully wedded husband?"—'

'And I hear, "did you take a wrong turn, dumbass?"'

'And answer, "yes."'

'Exactly!' Lucy chuckled. 'Like that.'

In her laughter, Lucy's head had migrated from the sofa to his shoulder, and it felt like a gift.

'You know what I miss?' Lucy said softly.

'What?'

'Smoking.'

'Oh, God. Me too.'

'It was so fucking relaxing.'

'And fun.'

'Yeah,' she sighed dreamily.

Nicky reached over to the coffee table and picked up his phone. Tapped a few buttons.

'What are you doing?' she asked, her eyes cracking open just a sliver.

'Nothing,' he said, not at all subtle with the lie.

Still, she just hummed again and closed her eyes.

Then, he clicked a few buttons on the TV to cue the

internet up to a site he'd been damn near obsessed with since he'd found it a few years back.

As soon as the voice started up introducing the show, Lucy's eyes opened up.

'*120 Minutes*?' she asked.

'Yeah, discovered the Internet Archive on a long flight from Prague to Brisbane and I can't seem to stop.'

'I've dug into the Archive for research, but not *120 Minutes*, and never just for fun. It's brilliant,' she said, rolling her head to smile right at him.

Really, watching the MTV of his youth was self-indulgent and a little bit pathetic if Nicky thought too hard about it. So, he just *didn't*.

'Nineties commercials!' she exclaimed, her face scrunching up with delight.

'Sometimes,' he replied. 'You never know. It's like pulling the prize right from the top of the Cracker Jack box when you get 'em.'

'Amazing,' she breathed, fully entranced by a thirty-year-old Frosted Flakes commercial.

A quiet knock came at the door.

'Don't move,' he said before popping up.

On his way to the door, he found his wallet on the entry table, and pulled a crisp hundred-dollar bill from the fold. He opened the door and made a quick exchange before heading right back to Lucy.

Her eyes lit up as they landed on the pack of cigarettes and lighter in his hand, then at the shit-eating grin on his face.

'How the hell?' she asked.

'Concierge.'

'You have the concierge on speed dial?'

'We call it text here in the twenty-first century, but yeah.' He held his empty hand out to her. 'Come on.'

Without balking for a second, Lucy slipped her hand in his.

They bounced through the suite, hand in hand, like a couple of teenagers. Into the primary bedroom where Nicky slid open the balcony door. The tiny outdoor space wasn't exactly luxurious. Not a stick of furniture, a temperature just a touch cooler than the surface of the sun, and glass safety panels that extended up five feet, but it was something.

Nicky whacked the pack a few times on his wrist, then opened it, handing Lucy a cigarette.

'You're a bad man, Nicky Broome,' she said, completely giddy.

Nicky played it up. 'You know, every one of my albums has a parental advisory sticker.'

'Such a bad influence,' she cooed, holding back a laugh.

'Hardcore,' Nicky corrected.

He lit her cigarette. Then his.

She took a drag and groaned with pleasure in a way that made his boxers a tad too tight.

'So good,' she mumbled, exhaling a cloud of smoke into the sweltering desert air.

The look on her face was that good. Better than the cigarette. Better than almost anything he could imagine in that moment.

'Here we are, smoking on a balcony again,' she mused.
'Couple of hoodlums,' he teased.
'Slackers,' she added. Then: 'It didn't last long enough.'
'What didn't?'
'Youth.'
'Wasted on the young,' he said, leaning back against the cool glass of the sliding door.

'That is bedrock truth, right there,' she said, exhaling again and joining him in his lean. 'Do you know what bothers me the most about living on a college campus?'

'Tell me.'

'I see these girls – these young women – every day. They're everywhere. Fresh and bright, and so full of optimism. And I remember being like that. I remember the feeling of life stretching out like an endless field of stars just waiting to be captured and explored. Out on my own, independent, but also so safe and protected. The amazing and wonderous just *right there*. In striking distance. All of the possibility and promise only waiting to be fulfilled. And none of the failures and the fucking grind weighing you down. I think . . . I think maybe I'm a little jealous of them. I think I might have . . .'

Nicky waited for her to finish. When she took a drag of the cigarette instead, he prodded, 'Might have what?'

Lucy sighed. 'I might have done it differently. If I had to do it again.' She flicked some ash to the concrete, smiled. Almost convincingly, too. 'Never mind me. It's probably just a midlife crisis.'

Nicky didn't have the words to fix those feelings for her.

So, he took his free hand and threaded his fingers through hers.

He squeezed her hand and declared, 'You know, I think the midlife crisis gets a bad rap.' He took a drag, exhaled. 'I mean, sure, there are guys who go out and buy a Porsche and a terrible toupee and abandon their family for Margaritaville or whatever. But I think there are also plenty of people who just look back at the first half of their life and then ahead to the second half and just . . . reassess. Reset. Adjust their lives because their dreams are different and their priorities have shifted. Or the world around them has shifted.'

Lucy released a heavy, thoughtful hum around her cigarette, then squinted up at the radiant Las Vegas day.

They stood in silence for a while. Inhaling and exhaling in tandem while Nicky watched the slow crawl of an LED sign offer Keno and free brunch at the casino across the street.

'Oh no,' Lucy said suddenly, clutching her stomach. Disappointment colored all of her features. 'It's making me queasy!' Or maybe that slight tinge of green was from the cigarettes?

He felt it too, but was ready to push past the discomfort to be there with her. Since she'd folded, he admitted, 'Same here. Shit.'

Nicky dropped what was left of his cigarette and took hers from her fingers, ground them both out on the concrete balcony floor.

He opened the sliding door and guided her inside

by their intertwined hands. He closed the door and the curtains.

'Lie down,' he told her, with a kiss to her forehead.

He dashed to the bathroom and made a cool compress with a washcloth.

He found Lucy on her back on one side of the bed, eyes closed again, one hand to her middle. He resisted the urge to stand there and stare at her like a weirdo, and instead placed the washcloth on her forehead. He slid into the spot on the bed right beside her, before pulling the comforter up over them both.

He folded the fingers of his left hand through the fingers of her right, and squeezed.

'I'm too young for the midday nap,' she grumbled – half-laugh, half-groan.

'Relax, baby,' he whispered. 'I won't let them issue your AARP card while you're out.'

Nicky held tight to Lucy's hand and listened as her breathing evened out into the long, slow murmur of sleep.

CHAPTER TWENTY-FOUR

LUCY

Lucy's eyes shot open with a start. She had no idea what time it was, and only a vague notion of *where* she was. The room was familiar, but the bed was positioned differently to the window than what she was expecting. The weird abstract hotel art was the same, but also *not*. Catching a glimpse of her black T-shirt, worn and faded to buttery softness, she remembered lying on the bed with Nicky, his hand in hers.

She spotted her phone and a bottle of water sitting atop a piece of hotel stationery on the bedside table. A note there read, *Had to go do a thing. If you wake up before 5, come meet me in the Scala Theater. I promise to feed you after. x, Nicky.*

Lucy opened her phone and saw that it was 2:30 in the afternoon. She'd slept for hours. She texted to the group chat with Chloe and Kim to inform them that she wouldn't make their scheduled girls-only pool and cabana time.

They both replied immediately with a string of eggplant and peach emojis.

Then, she folded up Nicky's note, chiding her own sentimentality even as she slipped it into her bra. It was the kind of reminder she didn't have of their first time together all those years ago. Unless you counted 'The Breathing Room.' (She didn't.)

Lucy traipsed to her room in Nicky's sweats. She showered and shaved. Exfoliated every damn thing she could reach. Applied three different lotions and mascara. She threw on her own joggers, which were a sexy/comfy combo, and topped it with an old Foo Fighters concert tee – unable to resist subtly needling Nicky about Dave Grohl just a little more.

Helpful signs led Lucy through the main part of the casino to the theater, which was down a long corridor set away from the blinking slot machines and crowds of people willingly parting with their life savings at the craps tables.

She had to try several of the hulking main theater doors by their giant-sized brass pulls before finding one unlocked, then slipped through as quietly as she could.

The theater was mostly dark, with the house lights completely dimmed. LED strips of a muted amber lined the aisles, and she could just make out several stories of box seats behind lavish Italianate arches. The proscenium and stage were lit up, and one of the best-selling, highest-grossing bands in history was on the stage making discordant, incomplete musical sounds.

The shock of it – the *reality* of it – made Lucy's empty

stomach drop out like she was being launched from the top of a roller coaster.

A man stepped out of the shadows to her right and approached.

'You must be Lucy,' he whispered. 'I'm Jacob, one of the tour managers. Have a seat anywhere and enjoy the show. Shouldn't be more than another hour at most.'

'Thank you,' Lucy whispered back.

Lucy tiptoed down the aisle, willing herself smaller and more mouse-like. She shimmied her way down a row so that she was precisely at center stage and midway into the section. If she was in for a private show, she was going to make the most of it.

She took a moment to look around her and spotted maybe five or six other people in the theater. Each of them had an iPad or a clipboard. Some wore headsets. It seemed that Super had a skeleton crew, and an audience of exactly one.

When she glanced back at the stage, Lucy caught Nicky looking up from his guitar with a deep, concerned furrow between his brows. The second he saw her, though, the lines on his face smoothed and he smiled, wide and guileless. Because of her. Lucy was fully fucking slayed by that smile. She was surprised to look down and see her legs still there, not melting to a puddle.

Nicky strummed another chord on his guitar, then silenced it with a slap to the frets. He called out to the cluster of people at stage right, 'Finn, the sound is still weirdly hollow. You get me, man? Like an echo, but not an echo. I think it's the room, not the IEM. But it could be the IEM.'

'Working on it, Nick,' came a grumbly voice from behind one of the iPads.

Behind Nicky, the drummer, a man she knew was named Gill (because she was a woman of a certain age and those guys were just *that* famous) spoke up: 'If we really go hard it's going to sound like a mess.' Then: 'I like Nick's idea of being closer to the audience for this whole thing but, as it stands, they're gonna get nothing but a wall of formless sound.'

'And leave deaf,' added the rhythm guitarist, a guy named Hooper, sporting a man bun and almost as many tattoos as Nicky.

'More sound-deadening or something?' Nicky asked. 'This theater was built for a lounge singer or a string quartet.'

'Maybe we should just do the whole thing acoustic?' asked the bassist, Vinny.

'If you guys stick me back here with some brushes and a single fucking snare, I will murder you in your sleep,' said Gill.

The other three guys onstage just laughed.

'Look,' said Nicky, 'maybe we should just demonstrate.' He shoved a guitar pick between his teeth and ran his fingers through his messy dark brown hair. Then he winked at Lucy.

She felt it in her spine.

Nicky pulled the pick from his mouth and adjusted his guitar strap. 'Sound?'

A disembodied voice from high above called back, 'On it.' Then, a few seconds later, 'Good to go.'

Nicky padded upstage and said something to the rest of the band that Lucy couldn't make out. Then he stepped up to the microphone and began playing a song she recognized. A newer one, 'Mix-up,' that she'd keenly avoided on SiriusXM only a few years before.

She could feel the sound in her chest. In her toes. It was everywhere. *Inside* her.

Jesus.

Lucy felt a gasp leave her chest, but she couldn't hear a thing beyond the band and Nicky's voice. It rattled her, down to the bone.

Nicky was a goddamn vision. The tattoos on his arms rippled as he played, his hair drifted into his eyes. Every square inch of his body was a part of the process. It was otherworldly.

She gaped, her jaw on the floor and her heart racing.

Somehow, she'd forgotten. Forgotten that he could do that. Forgotten that what he did for a living was fucking magic. She had intellectualized 'rock star' as this broad title, shuffling him into a neat stack of other musicians, as one might catalog all postmen or doctors in their own respective categories. But what Nicky Broome did with an oddly shaped piece of wood and metal was unique. Remarkable. His talent – this gift he shared with the world – was superhuman. Rare and precious and powerful.

And the band was so incredibly *good*. Not listening to Super was a form of self-protection that she'd relied on from the first moment she'd heard 'The Breathing Room' in college. That didn't mean they weren't worthy of listening to. They were. Everything Nicky and the rest of Super wrote was next-level amazing. They were skilled songwriters and superior musicians. It wasn't an accident that Nicky had platinum records decorating his bathrooms in LA.

When 'Mix-up' ended, Lucy clapped robotically. Because it seemed the thing to do when her brain and her heart were buzzing in the reflected glare of Nicky's talent.

'How about another?' Nicky asked his bandmates.

'Now taking requests,' Gill said in a goofy tone into his mic, while absentmindedly clicking his sticks against the frame of his snare.

A voice from behind her screamed, '"Stairway to Heaven"!' Which the band simultaneously groaned and laughed at.

From her left another guy yelled, '"Free Bird"!' and they all laughed some more.

Lucy couldn't help herself. She called out, 'Play "Little Wing."'

Gill and Hooper shared glances that said 'why not?'

'Which version?' asked Vinny in her general direction.

Nicky held his hand up to block out the stage lights and locked his eyes right on hers.

'Nicky knows which one,' Lucy replied, trying but failing to keep her tone light.

Nicky turned away from her then, talking to the band.

When he turned back, the first delicate notes of Stevie Ray Vaughan's haunting rendition of 'Little Wing' tripped across the theater. They emerged from Nicky's guitar like flashes of starlight, shooting right to Lucy's core. Obliterating her thoughts.

Gill's drum joined in, grounding the guitars – two now, their notes folding on and entwining with one another. Then, where Vaughan's melody usually drifted further into the instrumental, Nicky's voice cut through with Jimi Hendrix's lyrics.

He sang the words clear and strong. Purred their wistful confession of awe and longing with such emotion that tears filled Lucy's eyes. It was the perfect marriage of Stevie Ray Vaughan's soulful guitar with Hendrix's dreamy acid trip of a story. Just the way she'd always imagined it. When she could bring herself to listen to either version, that is. Most of the time, memories of that summer night with Nicky overwhelmed her and she had to shut it off.

When the notes shifted, Nicky leaned forward to the mic and sang straight at Lucy.

She couldn't breathe. Couldn't keep her heart from hammering against her ribcage. He *remembered*. He remembered *her*. All of it. From their ride in his Jeep that night a million years before and right into the beyond. He had really held on to all of it. That night wasn't just some anecdote he'd made into a song. He'd really felt those things, everything he'd put into 'The Breathing Room.' *All of it*. Her thoughts landed on the image of that tattoo on his back. The one with her name on it.

She could feel Nicky – every tortured emotion – in his guitar solo. Like he was speaking directly to her with each note. The band's serene accompaniment simmered in the background, letting him go. Letting him have his say. Nicky's face twisted; sweat beaded at his temples.

As the music swelled from all four instruments on stage, driving toward the conclusion, Lucy felt herself break.

Every barrier she'd thrown up over the decades began to crumble, piece by piece. They fell away and left her exposed. Raw.

The tears tumbled out of Lucy then, coursing softly down her cheeks and soaking into her T-shirt. It was too much. There was an earthquake rumbling inside her, and the rubble was piling up with no way to stop it.

Lucy stood, willed her feet to get her out of the seats and up the aisle. Behind her, she registered the distant sound of the song ending and of the assembled crew shouting and clapping their approval. But Lucy couldn't stop. She had to go.

As the massive theater door closed behind her, she heard her name break through the din.

Still, she kept going.

CHAPTER TWENTY-FIVE

LUCY

1990-Something

Lucy woke up with an unfamiliar weight on her middle. An arm. Not her own.

Nicky Broome.

He was there. It hadn't been a dream.

Lucy could feel his breath, strong and steady against the nape of her neck. Feel the heat and solidity of him pressed against her back.

She knew she was supposed to be cool about it. No big deal. Whatever. But her stomach didn't get the message. It flipped – a tumble of excitement and glee. She allowed herself a grin and an internal squeal because he was there and they had all summer. All fucking summer.

The smell of the ocean and the morning sun warming the shore drifted into her little bedroom. They mixed with the scent of Nicky's hot, salty, sexy-man smells and Lucy wanted to soak in it forever. It was freedom and joy and adventure and comfort. The summer uncurled like flower petals in her mind's eye – beautiful and infinite. So, she stayed there in Nicky's arms as long as she could, focusing on their touch points in turn. His hand over her belly button. His forearm on her waist. His chest against her shoulder blades. The rough hair on his thighs scratching at the back of hers. The tops of his toes grazing her heel. It was only when her bladder threatened to burst that she finally forced herself to move.

On her way out of the bathroom she slipped into the sexy robe Kim had given her for graduation. She called it a 'dressing gown.' To Lucy it had always felt like a silk costume from *Dynasty* – until she had a naked man waiting for her in her bed.

'Well, good morning after,' said Kim cheerily from the living room, dropping her jacket on the sofa. 'Your stud still here?'

'Bedroom,' Lucy replied.

Kim smiled and gave Lucy the hubba-hubba eyebrows. 'Well, keep all that in there. I've gotta get ready for work.'

'How was your night? You good?' Lucy asked.

'*So* good,' Kim replied. 'You?'

'I don't have the words, Kim.'

'That good, huh?'

Lucy could only nod. She didn't know how to quantify the jumble of things going through her mind. Her body. It was too much to process without caffeine and cigarettes. It was butterflies. Butterflies and rainbows. Fucking unicorns and a bunch of other sappy things that Lucy knew were too much and yet also not enough. So, she vowed to just kept her mouth shut until she could make sentences that didn't sound like a detailed description of Lisa Frank stickers.

'I get off at seven,' Kim said.

'I start at five.'

'Smoke break at six?' Kim asked.

'You got it.'

'I would hug you, but you smell like sex and bad decisions,' said Kim.

'Right back atcha,' Lucy quipped.

Kim blew Lucy an air kiss and disappeared into the bathroom.

Lucy padded to her bedroom and took a deep breath before opening the door as quietly as possible. She planned to lose the *Dynasty* robe and slide back into Nicky's arms. Or maybe wake him up with a blow job. Decisions, decisions.

Instead, though, when she opened the door, he was standing up. His unzipped jeans hung loosely on his hips as he pulled his Beastie Boys T-shirt over his head.

'Good morning,' he said, grinning at her.

'Good morning,' she replied. 'Going already?'

Nicky sat down on the chair, shoved his feet in his sneakers. 'I'm heading to Dover. An hour there. An hour to throw some shit in the Jeep. An hour back. I could be here at, like, three.'

'My shift at Grotto starts at five.'

'Perfect. I'll drive you. That okay?'

'Yeah, okay,' she replied calmly. A real feat considering her insides were bouncing up and down and doing the damn Macarena.

Nicky stood up, zipped his fly. He took a step forward and grabbed Lucy around the waist, lifted her off her feet.

He pressed his forehead to hers and exhaled. 'You make me happy, Lucy Rollins.'

'You make me happy, too, Nicky Broome.'

Nicky brought his lips to hers and kissed her slowly, thoroughly. With purpose. Nicky Broome made her blood fizz like it had been carbonized. He felt important – real and true. Like his kiss was the beginning of something big.

He set her back down on the floor, and reached for his guitar case.

'I'll be back in a few hours,' he said.

And then, he was gone.

CHAPTER TWENTY-SIX

NICKY

Present

Nicky caught a glimpse of Lucy as the doors to the main elevator closed on her and a trio of white-haired ladies with canes. One of them was handing Lucy a package of tissues.

Jesus. She's crying.

His mind stuttered back to work, helped along by the frigid, ozone-dosed casino air crackling against the sweat he'd worked up on stage. He spun around and darted at a run toward the Penthouse Tower lobby, hoping that he could remember how to find it in the maze that was the Lusso Resort.

After a few turns, he got lucky. He stumbled on a hallway he recognized, then blasted through a set of wooden doors. Nicky yanked his keycard from his pocket and sent prayers of thanks to a god he didn't believe in when the doors to the exclusive penthouse elevator opened on the first try.

When Nicky reached the fortieth floor, it was deserted. Not a soul in sight. He eyed the long passage, wondering if Lucy had already made it to her suite, or if the gambling grannies had managed to slow down the regular elevator on its forty-floor trip.

He looked back and forth from the main elevator doors, to the hall, and back again. Unsure of himself. Unsure of damn near everything, if he was being honest.

The light over the elevator lit up, a soft *ding* striking in time with his rapid heart rate. When the doors opened, he took his first breath in what felt like forever. Lucy was there, staring at her hands as they worked over a mangled ball of tissues.

She gasped when she looked up. 'How did you—?'

'Private elevator,' he replied.

She stepped out into the hallway, right past him. 'Nicky, I just can't right now. Okay?'

'Talk to me,' he pleaded to her back.

'Not right now.'

'If not now, when? *When*, Lucy?' he demanded, jogging to catch up.

He scrambled in ahead of her.

She tried dodging him, looking down at her feet.

He tried again. 'What is this about? Why are you crying?'

Nicky *knew*. Really, he did. But he needed her to say it.

'I can't,' she said, walking by.

Nicky raced to the door of his suite and opened it.

When she reached him, he demanded, 'Get in. We're doing this *now*.'

Lucy looked away, down the hall toward her own room. Then – *thank fuck* – huffed loudly, and walked through his door.

When the lock snicked home, he threw the security latch and the deadbolt for good measure.

Nicky followed Lucy into the living room. He watched her pace in front of the picture windows and their vibrant view of the desert sky. She was an avenging angel, up in the clouds, working herself into a frenzy, if the color in her cheeks was any indication.

'This isn't about "Little Wing," is it?' he asked calmly. 'It's about "The Breathing Room."'

'Of course, it is! Of course!' she railed.

Fucking finally.

She continued, 'It's *always* about "The Breathing Room"!' She stepped closer to him, her eyes blazing with fire and red-rimmed from crying. 'You want to know why I don't think "The Breathing Room" is one of the greatest rock love songs of all time? Do you?'

'I really do.'

Lucy's blue eyes locked on his, silently commanding him to him to pay close attention. 'Because to me it's not a love song. It's a fucking tragedy.'

Nicky actually staggered back a step, like he'd been punched. She knocked the wind right out of him.

Lucy went on, her face reddening with anger, 'Of course, I knew it was about me. I was there. How could I *not* know? I was *there*, Nicky. And you made all these promises. Lit up all these fucking fantasies. And then you were gone.

Just – *poof* – vanished. Leaving me with all this stupid useless hope. Like you'd cracked open a treasure chest and then just buried it again with no map.'

Nicky tried, 'I'm—'

'No,' Lucy commanded. 'You want to hear it? Let me get it out.'

Nicky bit his tongue – literally – to keep himself from interrupting.

'When you didn't show up that day. When I had to walk to work on the Boardwalk, I was convinced that you were dead. I was absolutely sure you'd crashed on the highway and were in a morgue somewhere. Then, when your *obituary* didn't appear in the papers I kept buying every morning, I wished you were dead. Because if you were dead, it would mean that it wasn't me. That you didn't just lie to me. Or use me. Or simply not care enough to come back or call me or *something*.' She inhaled and sighed. 'Because I cared so much.'

Nicky pleaded, 'Lucy—'

'Let me finish!' she snapped. 'And then, once I'd finally gotten over it – after waiting and wishing and wondering – there was this fucking song on the radio. And I had to rewrite and question all the things I thought about you. Maybe you didn't lie to me. Maybe I wasn't just some notch on your bedpost. But by then you were this rock star on the cover of magazines, selling out Madison Square Garden.'

'You could have reached out—'

Lucy tutted, frenzied. 'I didn't even have a proper email account until two years after the song came out. It was the damn dark ages. What was I going to do? Write you a fan letter? Mail it to "Nicky Broome, Rock Star, Care of Hollywood, USA"? Stand outside the stage door somewhere and say, "Remember me?"'

'I don't know. I—'

'No, you don't know. You *don't*.' Her voice got quieter, sadder. Nicky wanted to reach out to her, to hold her, but she backed away from him, crossed her arms over her chest and stared out the window. She groaned, '"The Breathing Room" was always there.' Lucy turned to him, arms still covering herself. 'I was on my honeymoon with Brandon, in this backward town in Spain that didn't even have a gas station. We were walking through the town square, bright sunshine, a fountain. It was beautiful. Serene. There was a kid, maybe fifteen years old, playing a beat-up old classical guitar, busking. You know what he played?'

'I can guess,' Nicky whispered.

'Yeah,' she retorted, turning back to him. 'The fucking "Breathing Room." When Chloe hit fourteen, guess what song she became obsessed with when she and her friends would sit around painting their nails and talking about boys?'

'"The Breathing Room,"' Nicky repeated softly.

'Yep. That was a whole new and exciting form of torture, let me tell you. She played it over and over at top volume for weeks. And don't get me started on the grocery store. Or Muzak versions in the goddamn dentist's chair. And every time I hear it, it's like this gaping hole gets reopened. The good sometimes, but mostly just the pain of it. What we could have been.'

Lucy shook her head, resumed pacing in front of the

window. 'If you had just been some guy who promised me things and left, I would have gotten over it. It would have passed. It did pass. Mostly. I was over it. It would have been just this humiliating old memory from when I was eighteen and naïve. Like a bunch of other cringe-inducing mistakes I've made over the years. Big deal. But instead, the song opened up this . . . this old memory of hope. It made everything *unfinished*. Like you'd actually felt all the things I'd felt. Like I wasn't naïve or crazy. But you were also still so fucking far away.'

Lucy ran her hands through her hair, tried to steady herself. When she spoke again it was with more calm. 'There was this epic reminder of it all. With a life of its own. The song colored everything. You were gone, but you weren't.' She stood stock-still before him. 'It's been decades, but it's also only been *days*, because on the way to Vegas the guy next to me in the security line at the airport was humming along to "The Breathing Room" on his AirPods. Do you understand?'

Nicky collapsed into the nearest chair and tried to stop the throbbing in his brain by rubbing a hand over his forehead. Of all the many thousands of ways he'd envisioned Lucy's possible reaction to the song, most involved some form of indifference. He felt stupid now admitting, even to himself, that he'd never considered anything like what she'd just described.

He sighed. 'Yeah, I understand.'

The least he could do now was fill in the rest of the picture. He didn't dare hope that it would lead to forgiveness, but she deserved the truth.

He began, 'The fucked-up irony of the whole thing is that I only had the guts to leave *because* of you.'

Lucy slumped into the chair on the other side of the coffee table. He had her full attention now.

He inhaled a deep breath, gathering the strength to continue. He ran a hand through his hair, stalling for time while he tried to get his thoughts in order. If only he could grab his notebook and write it all down first. No time for that, though.

He began, 'I went back to Dover. When I left you that morning. I was gonna pack up what I could fit in the Jeep and come back down to Rehoboth. But while I was there, I got into it with my dad. He'd been pushing college and the life-or-death importance of getting my shit together.'

Nicky could picture it, as vivid as the sunlight streaming in through the hotel window. God, how many hotel rooms had he been in since that day?

He went on, 'All year long I'd been lying to him. Told him I'd applied to UD and a couple others. But I just couldn't. Every time I thought about it, it just felt . . . *wrong*. Like trying to walk backwards on my hands or something. Like, how was I supposed to go four years like that? Maybe more? Maybe my whole life?'

When he paused, Lucy asked, 'You told him?'

Nicky nodded. 'I can't tell you what that night at the beach meant to me, Lucy. I tried in "The Breathing Room," but there is really no way to describe how important it was to me. It was an actual turning point, a pivot from where I was headed onto a totally different path. It felt like you opened the windows and I could finally breathe. Like I had this weight on my chest, like I was trapped and you lifted it all away. I couldn't hold it in anymore after that. So, I told him.'

Lucy's eyes closed, and he watched a tear fall down her ruddy cheek. 'My dad and I fought, right there at the back of my Jeep. Screaming, yelling . . . eventually punching.' He could still feel the sensation of it. Deep in his chest. Like his heart was breaking and being set free at the exact same time. 'He kept repeating, even as he swung on me, "This is not acceptable! You will not throw your life away! This is not acceptable!"' Nicky let out a gust of air and added, 'I knew – I *knew* – that if I didn't leave that day, that *minute*, my dad would just keep at me. We'd keep having the same argument over and over. He'd find me at the beach and eventually either his bullshit or his fists would wear me down and I'd give in.'

Lucy wiped the tears from her face with the back of her hand. 'Fight or flight,' she whispered.

Nicky pleaded, 'You have to believe me, I was planning to come back. Even after I was driving out West I was going to come back. Somewhere in Illinois. Or Iowa I found a payphone and spent hours trying to get your number at the beach. It was unlisted. I realized later it was because—'

Lucy huffed, hung her head in her hands. 'Kim's dad had played for the Eagles. None of their numbers were listed.'

'Right,' Nicky said. 'So, I called your parents' house in Dover. But I didn't have a number for you to call me back. I just said, "Tell her Nicky called."'

'Jesus,' Lucy breathed.

'You never got the message, I guess?'

'No.'

'I had these teenage fantasies of snatching you up and bringing you back to Seattle with me.'

'That's where you went? Seattle?'

He chuckled. 'I was a dumbass kid musician in the Nineties; where else would I go?'

She shot him a weak, watery smile, and it felt like hitting the damn lottery.

He said, 'I met Gill at a fucking coffee house. In *Seattle*. So damn cliché, right? Ridiculous. Gill knew Vinny, and Vinny knew Hooper. And then it was on. We just clicked. Once we started performing it was like we were hitched to a freight train and I couldn't get off. Not even for a minute. We got a record deal and they scheduled a tour. One album, then another.' Nicky sighed, 'By then, summer had long since passed. And then it was another summer. We were touring in a van, after the first album, before the second – the one that hit big?'

She nodded.

He continued, 'I made them book Rehoboth and Dewey. Drove past the old house on Stockley a bunch of times.'

'I wasn't there,' Lucy said.

'I know.' Nicky gazed at her, wanting her so badly that it was a physical thing, moving through his body along with his blood. Quietly, he asked, 'Do you know how many Lucys were born the same year as you?'

Lucy's eyebrows bunched at the non sequitur. 'No.'

'Three hundred and forty-four.'

'How do you know that?'

'I wanted to know,' he replied.

'Know *what*, exactly?'

'How hard it would be to find you.'

Lucy exhaled, her shoulders sagging.

'Why didn't you? Find me?' she breathed. 'You could have hired a private investigator or something.'

'I could have, but I . . .' He stopped, took a moment to try and understand the impulse himself. 'I sort of wanted you . . . to *want* to be found. For you to find *me*, so I would know—'

Lucy's eyes closed again.

He wanted them open, so he continued, 'So a few years ago, I had this friend. The editor of a music magazine.'

Her eyes snapped open. Gasped, 'No!'

Nicky stood up, crossed the room toward her. 'I went to him with an idea. A crazy fucking stupid idea.'

'Nicky—'

He dropped to his knees on the floor in front of her. Ran a single finger over her thigh. 'I fronted a million dollars. Had a check drawn up and everything. A bunch of lawyers kept it in a safe. Waiting.'

'*Nicky*.' The sound was a murmur, a sigh.

'I just wanted you to answer me,' he said, before pressing his lips to the back of her hand, still damp from tears.

'The question mark,' she rasped.

'Did it mean anything to you, Lucy?' he asked, holding her gaze. His chest tightened by steady increments as he waited for her answer.

She exhaled, 'Everything.'

CHAPTER TWENTY-SEVEN

LUCY

Nicky's thumb swept across her cheek, smoothing away the tears that she'd been unable to stave off.

His eyes were dark, pupils enormous. Their rims of green were more vivid than usual, shades of emerald and pine.

Nicky's lips touched hers gently, a question asked between lovers – a tentative query of the most delicate touch. Lucy answered by opening for him and meeting his tongue with hers. *Now*, she said with her tongue and teeth and lips. *Yes*. And *please*.

Nicky pushed in closer, scooted to fit himself between her thighs. Then groaned – in *pain* – against her lips and clutched his right knee with his hand.

Lucy smiled against his cheek. 'Old stagediving injury?' she teased.

'The mosh pits weren't gentle, Lou.' He laughed.

Something about the nickname, something no one else

had ever called her, made Lucy want to wrap herself around him and never let go. But that was crazy, and impossible. So, instead, she pressed a kiss to his cheek.

'Come on,' she said, taking his hand and standing. 'We're too old for chair sex anyway.'

'Take that back,' he quipped, even as he grumbled himself to his feet.

The bedroom was cool, with shadows painted in sharp relief by the sliver of summer sunlight peeking through a gap in the curtains. The low hum of the air conditioning was the only sound aside from their heavy breathing.

Nicky slithered his fingers under the hem of Lucy's Foo Fighters T-shirt and whipped it over her head. He mumbled, 'Losing Grohl's number.'

Lucy just grinned.

Nicky slipped out of his own shirt, revealing those unbelievable abs and the ink that made Lucy's mouth water. This had her unclipping her bra and shucking the rest of her clothes off double-quick.

She crawled onto the bed, looking over her shoulder when Nicky hissed, 'You're fucking gorgeous.'

Lucy knew that the worst of her cellulite and stretch marks were on full display in that position, but believed every word from Nicky's mouth as he gazed at her with unvarnished awe, stroking his stiff cock slowly – truly enjoying the show.

She lay on her back, torn between wanting to hurry him closer and enjoying the pure carnal decadence of watching him make long, slow pulls on his erection while looking at her.

Lucy didn't get to enjoy the performance for long, though. Nicky climbed up on the bed, impatience in his every movement.

He pressed his lips to the inside of her ankle. Licked a path up her calf. Switched to the other leg and nipped softly at the inside of her thigh, then exhaled a heated sigh against the thin skin at her hip.

Nicky found a sensitive spot at the dip of her waist, and lingered there, making her squirm. He spent ages laving the sharp peaks of her breasts, sucking and swirling his tongue until Lucy's breath was ragged and she could feel the wetness between her thighs dripping to the sheets beneath her.

He worshiped her with his mouth, with the languid trip of his fingers over her flesh. Touching everything. Venerating every inch of her.

It didn't feel casual. Or temporary. Or any of the other words she had repeated to herself. The sensation deep in her chest wasn't some blasé thing she could explain away. It felt as though her heart was breaking apart and remaking itself. As though Nicky Broome was altering her damn DNA.

When his libidinous tour reached her neck, Lucy canted her hips, seeking out the contact that he'd been withholding.

She gasped as he sucked on the tender skin below her ear. She caught a trace of that unique Nicky smell, then pushed her nose into his tumbled brown locks to take in a deep draft of the addictive salty sea-breeze essence of him.

'*Nicky*,' she unabashedly pleaded, clawing at his back and pressing her hips up to meet his. 'Need you.'

He looked down at her, as he finally gave her the friction she'd been seeking. The length of him, the steel and the velvet of it, effortlessly parted her folds and found her molten center. He pushed forward, one tantalizing inch.

Nicky hooked his arms under Lucy's, the full, solid weight of him pressing into her chest and abdomen. She felt surrounded by him, claimed and adored.

His eyes zeroed in on hers, lust-filled and fierce. He panted, 'You were wrong about one thing, Lucy.'

Nicky's hips tilted again, bringing him further inside her, but not far enough. Lucy could only groan in frustration and want.

He continued, 'The song was never *about* you.' He slammed his pelvis to hers. The pleasure and relief of it made her eyes water. Had her spreading her legs as far as they would go. To take more of him. All of him. 'It was *for* you.'

She gasped. At his words, at their earnestness – begging her to understand. And, as he pulled back and slid home once again, she gasped once more, at the mastery he had over her body. She was powerless to it. Lost.

'*For* you,' he grunted. '*For* you. *For* you,' he rasped, punctuating each declaration with a thrust of his hips. 'Every time I've sung it. A hundred, five hundred, a thousand times. Each one. For *you*.'

Lucy's orgasm struck without warning. No gently building preamble. No chasing. It just smashed into her, blasting away the few remaining shards of her rational thought. She was a live wire, exposed and uncontrollable.

Her body quaked and she screamed his name. The muscles deep inside her, electrified and pulsing, clutched at Nicky's cock drawing him even impossibly deeper.

'Fuck. Oh, *fuck*,' he groaned.

The scrape of his skin over her still-hard nipples sent further waves of pleasure coursing through Lucy's body as the movement of Nicky's hips grew erratic and frenzied.

He chanted her name over and over, a beautifully filthy song meant for only her ears. As his body shook, Lucy locked her ankles around his thighs and held on. At the feeling of him pulsing inside her – the hot, wet intimacy of it – Lucy could feel the final vestiges of her fearful barriers fall away. All the cracks in her heart that she'd plastered over and fortified for so many years were exposed, glistening and raw.

It didn't hurt as much as she thought it would.

CHAPTER TWENTY-EIGHT

NICKY

Nicky padded back into the bedroom and quietly made his way to the closet using the flashlight on his phone, but on its lowest setting so he wouldn't disturb Lucy. He stowed his acoustic guitar, the Moleskine notebook, and pencil back in their places, feeling a sense of accomplishment; one he'd been missing for more than a year. Something good was brewing in the chicken-scratched notes he'd been making. He knew it like he knew the crackle under his skin and the restless churning of ideas in the back of his mind. They were familiar old friends, allies in the process. They made it impossible for him to stop, and difficult to sleep.

He shrugged off the hotel bathrobe, leaving it in a perfect white pile on the floor, and slid his naked body back under the covers with Lucy. He slowly moved closer to her until her heat warmed the chill of his calf and he could feel her breathing on his shoulder.

She stirred, rolling on her back and opening her eyes with a flicker of her lashes.

'What time is it?' she asked groggily.

'About three,' Nicky replied.

'In the morning?'

'Yep.'

'Ugh,' Lucy groaned, rolling back over and tucking herself into Nicky's body, resting her head on his shoulder. She threw her leg over his as he curled his arm around her body and settled a hand on her hip. 'My sleep schedule is fucked,' she complained.

'You get used to it after a while,' Nicky said. 'Eventually you find a balance that's a little less vampire-ish.'

Nicky felt her chuckle in his forearm. 'My students will love that. Sorry, you can't go to the bars tonight, guys, class is at midnight.'

Her talk of work was like ice on his skin. It burned, and made him want to jump. To scream. But after their conversation about 'The Breathing Room' he was beginning to understand that his disappearance when they were kids, and the bullshit with the song that came after, were wounds that ran deep. He and the song had both had long, lingering effects on her life. Could be that because it had all happened when she was so young, they'd done something essential – fundamental – to the way she viewed men and relationships. The way she trusted and dealt with things. The guilt was like a weight he couldn't lift. He didn't know how to move it. To change what happened. To fix it. The exhaustion he felt made it worse. And she was in his arms.

He didn't want to waste that time thinking and feeling guilty. That could wait.

'Why don't you go back to sleep and I'll wake you up at some normal hour?'

'Do you even know what a normal hour is?'

He teased, 'Eleven-forty-five?'

She laughed, then he felt her sigh. 'Can I ask you a question?'

'Anything,' he replied.

'It seems like you're alone a lot. Don't hang out with the guys from the band all the time. That just because I'm here or—'

'The band's been together a long time. After all these years we've figured out what works for us, so that we don't end up exploding and taking the whole thing down with us.' Nicky searched for the right words. Sleep deprivation and songwriting had made his thoughts slow and sticky. 'We're basically in each other's pockets for months on end. Soon, we'll be together for a solid year. In the off times we go our separate ways. Like we store up the solitude, time with family, so that when we come back together, we can enjoy it. But we also know we have time away to look forward to when we inevitably start annoying the shit out of each other.'

Nicky's mind drifted, imagining the possibility of storing up time with Lucy. Of holding on to thoughts of her when they were apart. Would it be enough?

'It sounds sort of . . . lonely,' she whispered.

'Sometimes, it is.'

Months in an empty house. Kids grown. A lot *of the time, it is.*

'Everyone always calls you Nick,' she said with a drowsy slur.

Nicky liked her like this. All dozy and unguarded.

She asked, 'Should I call you Nick now?'

'No, Lou,' he said, rubbing a hand over her hair. 'You should always call me Nicky.'

Lucy hummed sleepily, then asked, 'What does it feel like to get on a stage and just expose yourself out there for everyone to see night after night?'

'I never rocked a cock-sock if that's what you're getting at, Rollins. It's a dangerous game to try and out-crazy Kiedis and Flea.'

Lucy playfully pinched his side. 'I'm being serious.'

Nicky cataloged the faint shadows on the ceiling. 'It's both the most terrifying and most amazing thing I've ever done.' Well, it was almost true.

'What's the biggest crowd you've ever played?'

'Wembley. Eighty-nine thousand, one hundred and forty-three.'

'Holy shit,' she gasped. 'Eighty-nine thousand *people*?'

'Yeah,' he replied, practically able to feel the vibration of the stage even as he lay there in the dark.

'What did *that* feel like?'

'Beforehand, for weeks, it felt like this elephant sitting on my chest. Like when you're trying not to cry and your throat is closing up?' He felt her nod her understanding, so continued, 'I kept thinking, "what the fuck is wrong with me? There's no way I'll be able to sing like this." But then, when I was there . . . when they were all there . . .'

Lucy raised up on her elbow, looked down at him. She placed her hand on his chest, right over his heart. He put his free hand on top of hers, to keep it there.

He went on, 'Ninety-thousand people who know your songs. Who just wanted to see you in person. To breathe the same air and hear those words right from your mouth. They wanted to see you so bad that they shelled out the money they worked hard for and got dressed up and got a babysitter. They took cabs and the tube and showed up. For my dumb band, and my goofy-ass songs. I was in awe of it, honestly. Humbled.'

'Was it different than playing a smaller show?'

'I don't know how to describe it, Lou. It was like being plugged into magic. Humanity. And joy. And fucking *love*, as corny as it sounds, just everywhere. All around you. Inside you. Filling you up. It was one of the most amazing moments of my life.'

But not even half as amazing as this. You and me alone. Touching in the dark.

She moaned dreamily, put her head back on his shoulder. 'That's powerful stuff. That feeling.'

'You have no idea,' he replied, all thoughts of London gone. *But maybe someday you will.*

Nicky turned his body toward hers, kissed her forehead, then her cheek.

'Still tired?' he asked to her neck.

'Not really. You?'

Nicky pushed his hips forward so she could feel exactly how awake he was.

She laughed, then squealed, 'I'm not even cleaned up from last time.'

'Doesn't bother me,' Nicky replied, taking one of her gorgeous breasts in his hand and rolling his thumb over the peak. He felt it pebble and stiffen at his touch.

'Who knew you were so dirty?' she teased, pushing her thigh into his rapidly filling cock.

'Me,' he replied matter-of-factly. '*I* knew.'

Nicky dragged his fingers from Lucy's breast, right down her body to the sweet spot between her legs.

He kissed her as he slowly worked her clit with his thumb.

'Mmmm,' he said against her lips. 'Cum, nature's lube.'

Lucy's sputtered laugh erupted like fireworks. 'Wow, took a left at dirty and headed straight for disgusting.'

Nicky laughed along with her, his lips on hers.

Then he dipped a single finger inside her, gathering the wetness there and swirling it over her clit with gentle pressure.

Her head fell back on a moan. 'Nicky,' she whispered.

'I love it when you say my name like that,' Nicky confessed.

'Keep that up and I'll scream it again.'

'Deal.'

CHAPTER TWENTY-NINE

LUCY

Lucy couldn't imagine what it cost to reserve a ballroom in Las Vegas the size of a Space X hangar. 'A lot' was the only number her brain could come up with as she looked around at the reception space. The ceilings were probably thirty feet high, and the width of the room had Lucy questioning her choice of wedding footwear as she could fully envision herself cramping up between the bar and her table.

The wedding planner, a preternaturally chipper person by the name of Tiffy, walked their little group through the early stages of setup. The room was still just miles of ornate carpet and fancy chandeliers with pallets of folding tables and shrink-wrapped linens lined up against one wall.

Tiffy used the word 'fantastic' more than should be legal, and made copious notes anytime Chloe spoke. She had the enviable body and presence of a showgirl, basically all legs and ramrod-straight spine with a hint of cleavage for excitement. She was so striking that Lucy didn't hear anything she said apart from the word 'fantastic' for the entire first hour of their meeting.

Tiffy warbled, 'Each of the dining tables will have a pad beneath the tablecloth to keep the background noise to a minimum. We've actually had all of your RSVPs respond, which is fantastic! Table service should be a breeze even with the special requests for gluten-free, kosher, keto, macro, and vegan!'

'Has the issue with the dessert tables been worked out?' Chloe asked.

Tiffy jotted something in her notebook, then answered, 'Absolutely! Your selection is going to be fantastic! I'm excited to see it all in place!'

Chloe clapped her hands together, and looked to her friends Hannah and Francesca, then to Lucy and Kim. 'Can anyone think of anything I forgot?'

Tiffy responded to the silence with a hearty, 'Fantastic! I'll be in touch via text with any last-minute issues. On the day, Mom will be my point person so Chloe doesn't have a thing to worry about.'

Lucy nodded her understanding.

'Now, I believe it's time to head next door to the Cristallo Salon and rehearse this ceremony!' Tiffy exclaimed, pumping her perfectly manicured fist in the air.

Kim and Lucy brought up the rear of their little group. As soon as the others were out of earshot, Kim leaned over and said, 'I don't know what Tiffy's on, but if it comes in a bottle, I want some.'

'Probably just casino air and Flintstones vitamins,' Lucy replied.

'How old do you think she is?' asked Kim.

Lucy answered, 'I don't know, twelve? Twenty-seven? Ninety? It's so hard to tell now that they start with the Botox at puberty.'

Kim sighed. 'She'll probably never have a single wrinkle. *Anywhere.*'

Kim and Lucy entered the Cristallo Salon where the setup was almost complete. All it was missing were the fresh flowers and finishing details. Otherwise, it looked like a place to get married. The three hundred or so folding chairs were positioned in perfectly aligned rows, the chairs staggered from each other so that no one had to lean around a poufy hairdo for a view. The ceremony would take place at the front, up just two stairs. Easily manageable even in high heels and a train. It was a lovely space, regal and refined even with the roughly four thousand tons of crystal chandeliers hanging overhead.

Lucy watched from across the room as Tiffy shone her bright doe eyes at Chloe and Chandler, gesticulating wildly and making the couple laugh and bat their eyelashes at each other in adoration.

Lucy loved Chandler. He was bright, funny, and down-to-earth. Of course, Lucy couldn't help but notice that he was also crazy handsome with his sun-bleached hair and golden-hazel eyes. He had a sharp Henry Cavill jaw and a former lacrosse player's trim height and strength. (Listen, she was forty-something, not dead.) All of those things were great, especially for Chloe, but Lucy truly loved Chandler Heylen because he was completely besotted with her daughter. Whatever sappy vows he was going to recite at the ceremony would be one-hundred-percent sincere.

Now, who knew what might happen down the line. Things changed. People changed – sometimes not together. But right that minute, as Lucy saw Chandler kiss Chloe goodbye so that she could take her place *across the room*, Lucy was sure of Chloe's happiness. Chandler accepted Chloe for who she was, expected her only to be herself and nothing more. Chloe adored him, really deep-down loved him in that big, wonderful way that Lucy herself had always hoped for but had never managed to find.

Of course, Lucy's traitorous, sleep-deprived mind chose that moment to drift to Nicky.

Her feelings for him were becoming . . . complicated. She still felt the old anguish of 'The Breathing Room,' but since Nicky's revelation it was more like a tender, freshly healed scar. The damage was mostly repaired; only the ghost of it remained.

She could envision, with perfect clarity, the old notepad her parents always kept by the phone when she was in high school. Could picture it, discarded, yellowing with age, in the junk drawer in the kitchen. *Tell her Nicky called.*

The traces of bitterness and loss that had always hung like a filter over her memories was tempered by something even more dangerous, though – expansive, oppressive, fond feelings. Stubborn, inconvenient, *dangerous* things that made Lucy crave conversation with Nicky the way she'd craved chocolate when she was pregnant with Chloe. Missing his touch when he wasn't around with a desire that bordered on desperation. They were emotions that made her mind wander down impossible paths that involved more than either she or Nicky had to give.

It was difficult, but she pushed those feelings aside. They didn't matter. Anything beyond Sunday was nothing more than fantasy. Her wild week in Las Vegas notwithstanding, Lucy led a very conventional, manageable life. Rooted in reality. In her work and her students. She had a lawn that needed watering. A temporary hold on her mail that had to be picked up from the post office. Bills. Tenure. *Real* life. Chloe's destination wedding had turned into more of a vacation than Lucy had anticipated, but it was still that. Just like any other vacation Lucy had ever taken, there were still obligations waiting for her on the other side. Syllabi to finalize, meetings to schedule, advisees lining up to have their hands held. Vegas was a break from real life, not the start of a new one.

Luckily, one doesn't reach the age of forty without developing the ability to snuff out and bury hopes and dreams that have problematic consequences. Lucy had that particular routine down like the guy with the shovel and the extra-large trunk in a Scorsese movie. Impossible dreams, and their cousin's unbridled optimism, were privileges of youth.

Tiffy guided Kim to a seat in the bride's section, then worked her way through the rest of the family, placing

Devin, Sam, and James in the front row. Brandon slowly made his way toward Lucy at the back of the room.

He stood beside her and focused his attention on Chandler and the officiant, who were standing by for further instructions from Tiffy.

'Are your parents coming?' Brandon asked, stuffing his hands in his thousand-dollar pockets.

Lucy answered, 'My parents are in Bucharest . . . or Bratislava or some other European city that starts with a B. I sort of tuned out when they gave me some extremely lame excuse about non-refundable tickets a full nine months before the wedding.'

'Still not the sentimental types?' Brandon asked.

'Well, to be sentimental they'd have to be human, and I'm becoming less and less convinced that's the case.'

Tell her Nicky called.

Brandon only nodded. Lucy knew that as a man who had lost his own loving, caring parents many years before, Brandon couldn't understand her own. Truth was, Lucy couldn't either. But the Rollins family weirdness was a very old story that Brandon had been party to for as long as they'd been in each other's lives. The bar for the elder Rollinses' involvement in family matters was extremely low, and still they'd never managed to clear it.

Chloe and her entourage of bridesmaids joined Brandon and Lucy. Chloe carrying a bouquet of truly atrocious plastic flowers. Lucy could just make out a purple penis-pop tucked in behind a cluster of extremely unrealistic neon orange orchids. Somehow, though, the psychedelic color scheme was set off by Chloe's white Alexander McQueen suit so that the whole effect was the sort of garish favored by haute couture.

'You girls make this for her?' Lucy posed with a smile.

Alexis answered, 'We are dangerous with floral wire and a glue gun.'

Tiffy sauntered back up the aisle and directed Lucy and Brandon to a vestibule just outside the salon where the groomsmen awaited their bridesmaids. Tiffy lined them all up, giving firm but 'fantastic!' instructions.

Tiffy pushed a button on a Lusso-Resort-logo-emblazoned iPad and a string quartet's instrumental version of Bruno Mars's 'Marry You' filled the air. Lucy knew that on the day it would be performed by a live quartet that had a regular gig at The Venetian, but even the recorded version was lovely.

Lucy stood at the doors, awaiting her role at the head of the processional.

Tiffy whispered, 'Ready?'

'Yes,' Lucy replied.

'Fantastic!' Tiffy whisper-yelled, then pushed a button on the wall and the double doors to the salon opened simultaneously.

Something about the swelling strings, and the tune that Lucy knew by heart, started a rumble of nerves tickling her belly.

She stepped into the Cristallo Salon with Bruno Mars lyrics tripping through her brain in time with the instrumental score.

Lucy tried to remember Tiffy's instructions. 'Look up

not down at your feet. Keep your focus on the officiant at the front of the room.'

But Lucy couldn't, not when she'd spotted Nicky sitting in the front row between Jenna and Sam.

His smile was wide and open, and Lucy's stomach responded with a full flip. Olympic-level gymnastics. The excitement and nerves from the moment before morphed into something else. Something like exhilaration.

Nicky winked at her, and Lucy felt her face heat.

He wore another black button-down, this one short-sleeved, that showed off his tats, glistening like sugar-dusted candy in the crystal-refracted light.

Lucy felt her heart trip, skip a full beat.

When she reached the end of the aisle, Nicky rose to guide her to her seat.

'What are you doing here?' Lucy whispered.

'Chloe invited me,' he replied.

'When?' Lucy asked, confused.

'When she texted me the schedule.'

'You text with my daughter?' Lucy asked.

'Yup,' he replied into Lucy's ear, sending goose bumps down her neck. 'The tall one with the iPad sat me down here. I think she recognized me.'

'Famous-guy superpowers,' Lucy whispered back.

Their attention slid back to the aisle where the bridesmaids and groomsmen were finishing their paired walks to the front of the room.

Then, the music changed, and all assembled stood and faced the entry doors.

For her part, Lucy braced herself for the wave of emotions that always accompanied 'I Choose You' by Sara Bareilles. The string version, along with her daughter gliding down the aisle on Brandon's arm was just that much more devastating. Jesus, when Chloe had the wedding dress on, Lucy would be a mess.

Lucy felt Nicky's hand settle on her hip, holding her steady. With his other hand, he produced a silk handkerchief.

Good Lord, who is this man?

She looked up at him, tears making him a fuzzy kaleidoscopic version of himself. Lucy was sure that awe and wonder were smeared all over her face like cheap lipstick, but she couldn't help it. Couldn't have stopped it even if she'd wanted to.

When they were seated again, and Tiffy was back to pep-talking and commanding the wedding party like the world's prettiest brigadier general, Nicky leaned toward Lucy. He rested his left hand on her right knee, and Lucy felt it in her belly.

He touched his lips to her ear and said, 'Remind me again, what's the groom's name? Ross? Joey?'

Lucy chuckled quietly behind the handkerchief. 'Chandler,' she said.

'I was close,' he teased.

'You got the category right.'

'Does he have a brother named Ross? Sister named Joey?' Nicky teased.

'Monica,' Lucy replied.

'For real?'

'No.' Lucy smiled. 'His only brother's the best man. Mason.'

'Chandler and Mason,' Nicky said as though rolling the sounds around in his mouth. 'Sounds like a law firm.'

'Conner and Wade?' Lucy said with a wink, recalling his own son's names.

'Touché, Rollins.'

'Are either of your boys married?' Lucy asked.

'Nope. They're both a little more Tinder, a little less Match.com.'

She laughed. 'Gotcha.'

Lucy's brain proffered: *I can't wait to meet them*. Then she mentally punched her damn brain in the mouth. *Stop it*. She had to stop it.

Lucy focused her attention on Tiffy, and managed to make it through the rest of the rehearsal without any more daydreams about impossible things.

CHAPTER THIRTY

NICKY

Half of the Lusso's world-famous buffet room was occupied by Chloe's rehearsal dinner. The other half was populated entirely by octogenarians more interested in the all-you-can-eat Alaskan crab legs than the large group of partygoers.

Nicky enjoyed the high-low vibe of the female guests in their five-thousand-dollar outfits carrying plastic trays to vinyl-covered diner chairs more than he wanted to admit. It made him appreciate Chloe, and by extension Chandler, for their clearly chill, unpretentious way of walking through the world.

Chloe had caught him excitedly saying, 'The *buffet*?' as they approached the location. And she'd replied, 'When in Vegas, Nick. Better jump on those crab legs while you can!' The twinkle in those blue eyes of hers – Lucy's eyes – had his chest feeling heavy.

He spotted Brandon solicitously carrying a tray for his pregnant wife and his mind tumbled over itself wondering what might have been. What *could* have been if only he hadn't been such a fucking idiot when he was eighteen. Wondering if Chloe, or some other dazzling young woman, might have been *his* daughter. His and Lucy's.

It was amazing how much the glaring spotlight of truth had opened his eyes in the previous twenty-four hours. Lucy had lived inside him for so long; her memory cloistered deep. She had never been the subject for bandmate banter, or even the supposedly safe confines of any of his marriages. He had spoken to no one about 'The Breathing Room' or the real story of how he'd ended up in Seattle. Those thoughts and feelings had never been exposed to the light and examined. No second opinions or outside advice had ever informed his reflections on it.

Now, knowing Lucy's side of things, Nicky was seeing it all with new eyes. It was easy, ten . . . fifteen . . . twenty years away from it, to forget what life had been like in the late Nineties. Before cell phones and email. When the lucky few had pagers and answering machines. When phones were tied to places not people. A time when silence was the norm and people tended to fill it with conjecture and, more often than not, their own fears and self-doubt.

When Nicky left for Seattle, he was G-O-N-E gone. In the wind. What *had* he expected her to do? What would have happened if she'd shown up at Madison Square Garden trying to connect with him? Nothing, that's what. And fan mail? Jesus, who the fuck knew? Sometimes he would get stacks of promotional shit thrown at him to sign, but he never saw a request. Not once.

He could have tried harder. Tried to track down a phone number, any phone number to get to her. Written *her* a letter. Stopped at the goddamn beach on his way out West – *anything*. But the fact was, he'd just been a stupid fucking kid. He'd run, then been sucked into the riptide of fame and fortune, and had held on for dear life. His memories from huge swaths of the early 2000s were sleepy, hazy visions of tour buses and terrible hotels and poorly ventilated recording studios.

Oh, he had googled 'Lucy Rollins' beginning in, like, 2000 maybe? But almost no one had an online presence then. By the time they did, she was Lucy McManis. A name he couldn't have come up with if someone had put a gun to his head.

Nicky took a deep breath to shake himself out of the weeds. Intellectually, he knew that forgiving himself for being young and stupid was the best plan. No good could come out of 'what if.' 'What if' was a goddamn mind fuck and didn't resolve anything.

If he was going to convince Lucy that this thing between them was worth exploring for more than a few days, he had to get his head in the game. He had to stop beating himself up about the past and focus on the moment he was in. He was already running out of time.

*

Nicky's plate looked like the scene of a grizzly crab massacre. The pile was obscene. The guy behind the buffet, a crab-leg security professional, no doubt employed to keep little old ladies from stuffing their handbags with crustaceans, had given him at least twice the portion of everyone else. At Nicky's quizzical look, the guy had tugged at the neck of his chef's coat to reveal the top of a Super T-shirt. Occupational hazard.

Though he wasn't exactly sure how, Nicky found himself seated between Chandler's dad and someone called Aunt Glinda. The latter of whom was not, actually, a good witch. Aunt Glinda had felt him up pretty good while 'mistakenly' grabbing the napkin from Nicky's lap instead of her own. She was at least sixty, so old enough to know better, but fame did strange things to people. He doubted that Glinda went around groping random strangers on the regular. *Probably*.

Lucy was miles away; directly across from him, but the table between them was too wide for his liking.

'So, how long have you two known each other? A couple days or so?' Lucy's ex Devin asked, gesticulating wildly between them with a crab leg. The hint of a slur in his speech made all the little hairs on Nicky's neck stand on end.

'We knew each other in high school,' Nicky replied.

Devin's head turned to Lucy with the slight wobble of a man with several gallons of alcohol lubricating his movements. The look of unadulterated shock was probably down to the same condition.

Lucy's eyes drifted down to her plate. She took a hurried bite of cornbread, her sleek bob falling over her cheek like a curtain.

So, it seemed Nicky wasn't the only one who hadn't confessed the story of 'The Breathing Room' to a spouse.

'High school?' Devin repeated to Lucy's hair.

'Yep,' Nicky answered, tearing into the crab graveyard in front of him.

'Y-you,' Devin screeched as he continued to gape at Lucy. 'You knew him in *high school*? And didn't tell me? I talked about Super multiple . . . multiple. *Multiple* times. And you never thought to say "hey, funny fucking story, I know that dude?"'

'*Devin*,' Lucy soothed. 'This is probably not the best time—'

'When would be a good time?' he asked, tone oozing with sarcasm. He pulled up his arm and began tapping the screen of his smartwatch with the long pointy end of a crab leg. 'Here, let me pencil you in.'

'Devin,' Lucy tried again.

'No, no. No. I get it. I really fucking get it,' Devin grumbled, then seemed surprised to find a crab leg in his hand, giving the thing a look like it had just slapped his mother. 'You were always so . . . closed off. I mean, the sex was great . . .'

The word 'sex' had even the octogenarians across the room staring their way and turning up their hearing aids.

Devin continued, oblivious to the uncomfortable non-looks of everyone at their table, 'But you never really let me in.'

Nicky heard Lucy mumble, 'Really hitting the *This Is Your Life* highlights this week.'

'Devin,' Nicky growled. It was a tone so serious and menacing that everyone's eyes shot up. Nicky could feel their collective gaze on his skin. (Or maybe that was the rage?) 'You need to mind. Your. Mouth.' Nicky offered the drunk man his death stare. The one that had frightened paparazzi and made one obsessed fan piss his pants.

'You can't tell me what to do,' Devin said, shaking the crab leg at Nicky. 'You're fucking my wife.'

'*Ex*-wife,' Nicky said murderously.

'Oh-*kay*,' Kim said from down the table. She rose to her feet. 'I think it's nighty-night time for Devin.'

James appeared from somewhere and placed a hand on Devin's shoulder. 'I'll help,' he said brightly, as though to a child.

James, who was clearly stronger than his size would let on, lifted the muscle-bound Devin up by his armpits while Kim slowly peeled the man's fingers off the crab leg.

'All right, Dev,' Kim cooed as James nimbly maneuvered the stunned Devin to his feet. 'Is your little keycard in your pocket? Think you could get it for us?'

As Kim and James hustled Devin out of the room and the clinking of cutlery around the place resumed, Nicky saw Lucy mouth the words 'I'm sorry' to Chloe.

Chloe smiled serenely – earnestly – and mouthed back, 'It's okay.'

To the table (or really, to her cornbread) Lucy said, 'He's kind of a fitness nut. Doesn't drink much.'

It was clear enough to Nicky that Lucy was mortified. She wouldn't even look at him, even though he stared at her and sent her a bunch of really eloquent telepathic messages to get her to look up.

'Which one was that?' Chandler's dad mumbled at Nicky. 'The last one? Or the gay one?'

Nicky knew that Lucy had heard the man because he watched her shoulders fold in on themselves as though she could make herself disappear.

He wanted to punch Chandler's stupid dad in his stupid fucking mouth. But Nicky realized that, while satisfying, smashing the man's teeth into his colon would likely get Nicky disinvited to any future Heylen-McManis family gatherings real quick. So, instead, he slapped a smile on his face and replied, 'So, I hear you're from Iowa. What's *that* like?'

CHAPTER THIRTY-ONE

NICKY

Nicky tucked Lucy closer to his right side, snuggled in his bed, basking like a house cat in her warmth and nearness. He could feel every curve of her naked form and would happily hand over every single one of his Grammys to spend his life in that position.

'What's this one about?' she asked, lifting his left arm and pointing to the narwhal tattooed there.

'A bet with Hoop.'

'You lost?'

'Fuck no,' Nicky bellowed. 'I won. And now he can't ever get a narwhal tattoo *ever*.'

Lucy laughed. 'How about *this* one?' she said, pressing her finger into the ridge of muscle over his left hipbone in a way that made his cock twitch.

He moaned, and threw his head back enjoying the lick of tingles she'd sent to his middle. 'I don't know – what is it?'

'You don't know what you have permanently tattooed into your skin?'

'Maybe?' he answered, glancing down for a look.

'Nope,' she said, slapping her hand over the spot, her forearm dragging over what was rapidly becoming a chub situation. 'No cheating.'

With her arm putting pressure on his dick, his brain wasn't firing on all cylinders. He asked, 'Color or black?'

Lucy barely lifted her palm and leaned over him, bringing her head in close like she was peeking at a poker hand. Her warm exhaled breath skated across his cock. And, yep. Fully hard.

'Color. Also, don't think for a second I don't notice what's going on down here. It's not going to work. Guess.'

'Uh,' he said, trying not to focus on the fact that her breasts were rubbing on his thigh. 'Okay. It's the stylized "s" from the cover of the first Super album.'

'Correct!' she said, dropping a kiss to the head of his dick like a prize.

Lucy stretched back out, lifted her knee so that the smooth skin of her inner thigh slid against *ev-ery-thing*.

'How about the one on your back?' she asked softly.

'Which one?' He knew which one.

'The cassette tape.'

He made sure she was with him, focusing her blue eyes on his, so she wouldn't miss anything.

'I wanted to put it here,' he said, moving her hand from his waist to the left-center of his chest, right over his heart. 'But I knew that seeing it every day would be too hard. I put it back there so I could choose when I look at it. When I need it.'

Lucy's expression stumbled from amazed to confused to reverent in about ten seconds. Her mouth came down over his. Stole his breath and his thoughts and any lingering doubts he might have had about the two of them.

As she lifted up on all fours and straddled him, Nicky knew – *knew* like he knew his own fucking name – that he and Lucy were meant for each other.

Nicky understood that he would always be more fearless than she was. Maybe his disappearing act had made her careful and guarded. Maybe she was always that way. Didn't matter. It was how things were right then. Confident and intrepid were a way of life for him. Stripping away pretense and humility were the norm. Hell, baring his damn soul to the world was the first line of his fucking job description.

He just had to make her see what he saw in them.

That was it, he thought to himself as Lucy took all control and took him deep inside her.

It was the calming.
It was the fit.

CHAPTER THIRTY-TWO

LUCY

Lucy stepped into her suite with her mind still buzzing from Nicky's confession about the tattoo, and the orgasms that followed. As a person who hadn't felt strongly enough about anything to have it emblazoned permanently on her skin, the fact that he had her name on him felt significant. *Permanent* in a way that had nothing to do with the ink itself.

'Hi,' Chloe said, emerging from her room in a floral silk robe and wearing little moon-shaped sheet masks under her eyes. 'How are you?' she asked in a tone that Lucy recognized as deep concern. Lucy's guilt and shame from earlier in the evening flared right back up again.

'I'm good. I'm fine,' Lucy sighed.

'How's Nick? Still itching to go three rounds with Devin?'

'No, he's . . . *fine*.' Lucy inhaled deeply. 'I'm so sorry about all that, Clo,' she said, wrapping her daughter in a tight embrace. 'I guess I need to have a conversation with

Devin. He clearly has some unresolved feelings about the divorce. I just didn't know—'

'It's been almost two years, Mom. And he's a grown-up. I think it might just be that he's never seen you with someone else since. And so happy, too. That's on him, though. His shit to work out.'

'Maybe,' Lucy tried. 'But I could have done more. Noticed something. Been more considerate—'

'Uh, pretty sure *he* should have been more considerate tonight.'

'Yeah, but he was drunk,' Lucy said in a voice that she realized too late was actually quite small and sad.

'Unless somebody else forced his mouth open and tipped the bourbon in, I think that is *also* on him.'

Lucy huffed, 'Yeah.' She meant it, but someone needed to tell her guilty conscience.

'Okay,' Chloe said, her voice lighter. 'Enough of this heavy stuff.' She stepped out of Lucy's arms. 'The wedding stylist gave me this goop to put on my hair tonight. She told me to comb it through completely and wait thirty minutes before taking my shower. So, I need your help. We're on a deadline here, lady. The bride needs her beauty rest.'

'Lead on, Bridezilla!' Lucy teased.

*

Fifteen minutes later, Lucy was pretty sure she'd ruined her favorite sleep shirt, and that they'd dirtied every single towel in the suite.

'Is this just overpriced mayonnaise?' Lucy laughed as she combed through the great globs of white stuff in Chloe's hair and slapped them from the comb into the bathroom sink. 'I think this is just mayonnaise.'

'It does smell a little like a deli in here now.' Chloe laughed back.

'Is it thirty minutes from the time we put the goop in? Or thirty minutes from the time we've combed it out?' Lucy asked, flicking an errant blob of hair mask/mayonnaise from her hand.

'The directions were vague, at best. Let's go with from the time we put it in,' Chloe replied, wiping a smear of white stuff from her forehead. 'If this crap breaks me out on my wedding day, I'm going to sue.'

Lucy continued combing, and flicking goop mostly into the sink. (But also, the mirror, the counter, and a spot on the ceiling that would no doubt be the topic of much speculation by the cleaning crew.)

Lucy gazed at her daughter in the mirror and when she received a small smile back, Lucy decided to broach a subject that had been needling at her subconscious all night.

'Hey, Clo?'

'Yeah?'

'I'm sorry that your grandparents aren't here for your wedding. It's inexcusable and I'm sorry if it hurts you. They're—'

'I know who they are, Mom,' Chloe interrupted, still smiling. 'I know that they love me. In their way.'

Jesus, this girl is something. 'You are truly amazing,

Chloe.' Lucy beamed. 'You always meet people exactly where they are. No judgment. No pettiness.'

Chloe's eyes flicked down to her engagement ring and back again. 'I don't know about that. I try with Chandler's parents, but I just don't understand them. That said, I do know that they love him.'

'Like I said, *amazing*,' Lucy repeated.

'Just a good student, like someone else I know,' Chloe said pointedly to her mother, while dabbing a towel at her hairline. 'I read that *Love Languages* book in one of my psych classes. You know the one I mean?'

'Gary Chapman?'

'Yeah. Some of it seemed heavy-handed, like are there really only five love languages? That's a stretch, but I think the concept rings true.' Chloe's eyes caught Lucy's in the mirror. 'Daddy's love language is an AmEx Black Card. When he gives me money it's his way of trying to make me happy and safe.' She took a breath. 'Yours is more traditional – support, hugs and praise, kind words. Grandma and Grampa's is more subtle, sure, but when I get a postcard from them or a little gift from some crazy place they've traveled to, I know that they've been thinking about me and they're telling me that they love me. In *their* way. So, when they cross my mind, I'll text or send them a little something. I love them back in a language they understand. I get Daddy extravagant gifts. You, I call or hug.'

Lucy took Chloe's hand and smacked a kiss to it. 'I love you, Chloe.'

'I love you, too, Mom.'

Well, at least she'd gotten something right in her life. She didn't know how, because parenting had felt like decades adrift at sea, trying to keep her head above water. But clearly, she'd accidentally made some good choices where Chloe was concerned, because her daughter was fucking awesome.

God, Lucy was going to miss Chloe when she and Chandler were living in Boston. The empty nest bit sounded great, but also, maybe, a little bit heartbreaking.

Chloe squeezed her mother's hand and said, 'Hey, aren't you supposed to be giving *me* advice on the night before my wedding?'

Lucy couldn't help herself. 'When a man and a woman love each other very much, sometimes he puts his—'

'Not about the wedding night,' Chloe interrupted, rolling her eyes. 'About *marriage*.'

'Oh, God, Clo,' Lucy grumbled. 'You don't want my advice on that.'

'Why?'

'*Why?*' Lucy repeated indignantly. 'Because I'm clearly terrible at it. That's why.'

'Okay, even if that were true – which I'm not a hundred percent sure of, by the way – you could probably offer some advice on what *not* to do.'

Oh, boy. Could she. The problem there would be where to begin, and how many hours Chloe had to spare to hear it all.

Chloe asked, 'What's the most important thing? To do, or not to do. Your choice.'

'I mean, why not just ask me to solve poverty or racism or something easier instead?' Lucy tutted.

Their eyes connected in the bathroom mirror, Chloe's crinkled under-eye sheet masks clearly telling her to get over herself and get on with it.

Maybe Chloe really needed to hear something from Lucy, was nervous and worried about her future with Chandler and how to make it work. Shit.

'Um,' Lucy began, searching her mind for some sage words of wisdom. When none came, she said, 'I think listening is important.'

That was true. Okay, score one for Mom.

Lucy continued, 'Not just *hearing*, but listening. Without judgment or trying to come up with responses or retorts. Especially in a disagreement. Save the replies for after your brain has had time to process.

'In that same vein, you always hear "never go to bed angry." Well, that's a crock of shit. Sometimes if you don't go to bed angry you don't really give yourself time to think things through, to come at them from a different angle that's clearer in a new day. Sometimes trying not to go to bed angry just means that things aren't really settled, only glossed over. The compromises can make you resentful. And resentments grow over time.'

'This is good, Mom,' Chloe said with a smile.

'Thanks.'

'Anything else?'

Lucy inhaled deeply. Tried not to choke on the emotion that welled up. 'I just want you to be happy,' she said. 'Really, truly, bone-deep happy.'

'I am,' Chloe said. And Lucy believed her.

Lucy added, 'Just know that if that changes, for whatever reason, that it's a problem. Maybe not a terminal one – marriage counseling is a thing for a reason. But you shouldn't just live with it. For fear of failure or expectations or any other reason. Okay?'

'Okay.'

'Promise?'

'Yeah,' Chloe said, smiling at Lucy in the mirror. 'I promise.'

'Good,' Lucy said. 'Now, surely it's been thirty minutes?'

'Probably. Plus,' she added, bringing a strand of gloppy, white-painted hair to her nose. 'I think my mayonnaise is turning.' She sniffed again. 'God, do you think it's Miracle Whip?'

Chloe stood, headed to the adjoining section of the bathroom with the shower and toilet. Then she stopped. 'I just want you to know that I want you to be happy, too.'

'Thanks, Clo. I am.'

Chloe's gaze grew pointed, serious. 'With Nick, you are.'

Lucy sighed, trying to formulate a response that was at least part truth. 'I am. But another thing you should know is that sometimes that's not enough.'

'Explain that to me, Miss Bone-Deep Happiness,' Chloe said, cocking her head with attitude.

'Our lives are completely different. There's no path to even being on the same continent, Chloe. We had . . . have . . . *had* history that made this all a bit . . . *more* than what it would have been if we'd just met for the first time.'

'What kind of history?'

'The complicated kind. It was high school, but also not. And . . .' *Jesus, it's almost impossible to explain without actually explaining. What is going on with Nicky is so singular.* 'It doesn't matter. Just know that I am happy now. And I will be again, even if Nick Broome isn't in my life.'

Saying the words gave her a physical pain in her chest, sharp like a stab wound. *Oh God, this time it's really a heart attack, right?*

No, as she rubbed at the spot, the pain faded. What was left was an aching sort of void.

'I'm only dropping this because I am currently a ham salad,' Chloe said. 'Consider it to be continued.'

Chloe padded into the next room, and closed the door. A moment later, Lucy heard the shower running and began the arduous task of un-mayonnaise-ing the place.

As Lucy swiped at the greasy blobs, she mentally replayed her words to Chloe – about listening.

She had felt a shift between her and Nicky. From the uncomplicated fun of a short-term fling, to what felt like the building blocks of something more lasting. The elements were the same in a practical sense – the laughter, the sex, the talking – but entirely different in value and intent. Nicky didn't seem to simply listen to facts about Lucy and her life, he seemed to memorize and store them. Like he was laying them down as the first crucial course of bricks in a tower.

Given that Lucy's own approach was to kick down any stubborn bricks that happened to find themselves sticking inside her, the idea was terrifying. There was no future for them. There was only going back to their separate realities, which were so far removed from one another that it was laughable.

In a perfect world, could there be more with Nicky? Sure. Lucy wasn't an idiot. He was fucking incredible. If things were different, she would latch herself on to him like a koala, clinging to his chest forever. Probably. Maybe. But things *weren't* different. There was fantasy and then there was reality. She had made the distinction. Whatever they had between them wasn't going anywhere.

Also, she really was the absolute worst at relationships. Why would one with Nicky be any different? She made bad choices about men. Even if she did want to just throw caution to the wind and jump into something with him, it would probably go straight to hell in a handbasket anyway. Because her decisions about relationships and who to get into them with was obviously critically flawed. Exhibit C: Devin. Her judgment was completely untrustworthy.

Lucy knew, from hours of insomnia-fueled doomscrolling, that she had been married more times than the statistical American average. That had to mean she was also statistically crap at it, right?

Furthermore, maybe everything seemed so good between her and Nicky because they hadn't gotten to the part where she felt resentful about picking up his socks and he decided that grading papers at midnight was too much. They were in the honeymoon phase. She'd seen it enough to know the signs. When that passed, who was to say that things wouldn't be just as terrible as they had been with

Brandon? Or as awkward as with Sam? Or as one-sided as with Devin?

And, of course, all the conjecture was fantasy because she was gearing up for the tenure review that she'd been working toward her entire adult life and he was going to be *on another fucking continent*.

Lucy looked at herself in the mirror, rearranged her slimy, stained clothing and said, 'Get over it.'

The door to the shower room flew open, clanging against the wall so hard it made Lucy jump.

Lucy shrieked, 'What's wrong? Are you okay?'

Her daughter stood in the doorway holding a bath towel over her front, rivulets of white gloop streaming over her face and into her eyes.

'You're her, aren't you?' Chloe asked.

Lucy suddenly wondered if wedding stress could give a healthy twenty-one-year-old a stroke. She sputtered, 'Chloe, what are you talking about? Are you okay? Do you feel dizzy? Does one of your arms feel weak?'

'I'm fine,' Chloe grumbled, flicking watery white mess off her forehead. 'The love languages. It got me thinking. Nick Broome's is probably music, right? It's you! The *history*. The *complicated kind*. You're her! You're the "Breathing Room Girl"!'

Oh, shit.

CHAPTER THIRTY-THREE

NICKY

Nicky made his way down the hallway outside his suite, feeling every minute of the hours he should have been sleeping. He only ever felt his age in his knees. At some point maybe he could replace them with titanium and feel like he was twenty again. And now he needed to add knee-replacement fantasies to the ever-growing list of pathetic things his forties had done to him.

Nicky had left the room hours before, his notebook and acoustic guitar in his arms, racing down to meet the concierge. He'd needed a piano to make the music in his head arrange itself into something usable. Luckily, he was rich and famous with a very fine concierge at his beck and call. The man had found him an unused grand piano in one of the hotel's many nightclubs – mercifully closed.

As Nicky reached for his keycard, he heard a door down the hall click open. Hoping it was Lucy's, he waited to see who might emerge. The noise had come from her suite, but it was Chloe who stepped into the hall.

The hem of a long, flowing white nightgown peeked out from under a trench coat, fuzzy slippers on her feet. She closed the door sneakily, and backed away from it on tiptoe.

When Chloe looked up, she spotted Nicky immediately. Then tipped her head and rolled her eyes.

Busted.

She walked toward him, and Nicky teased, 'Where do you think you're going, young lady?'

'Cute,' Chloe replied. 'I'm going to see my fiancé.'

'Isn't that bad luck?'

'I'm not superstitious,' she said. 'And it's an evening wedding, as you well know. I can sleep in after I sneak back.'

'Got it all figured out, huh?'

Chloe nodded with a naughty gleam in her eye.

'All right, I guess.' Then, in a stern fatherly voice added, 'Don't do anything I wouldn't do.'

Chloe tutted. 'You're a rock star, Nick. What exactly might that be?'

'Oh, there's something. And it's real bad, kid.'

'I'll need diagrams on that sometime, but right now I'm off. Sleep well.'

'You, too, Chloe . . . eventually, I mean,' Nicky said with a wink.

Chloe walked on, and Nicky tapped the keycard to his door.

'Wait,' came Chloe's voice.

'What's up?'

She walked back to him and he flipped the bar lock on the door to keep it open.

'Look, it's probably not my business.' Chloe stuffed her hands in the pockets of her trench coat. 'But my mom, she can be . . . timid.'

Nicky's disbelief must have shown on his face because Chloe added, 'About certain things. About herself.'

'I don't—'

Chloe interrupted, 'One time, when I was about eight or nine, I was on this baseball team. Co-ed. We'd had a tough loss and after, as we were walking to the car, my mom and I saw one of my teammates crying. A kid named Jeffrey.'

Nicky had no idea where Chloe's story was headed, but he needed information on Lucy like he needed oxygen, so listened carefully.

Chloe continued, 'Jeffrey was walking with his dad, a complete troll, who said to Jeff, "Don't be a pussy. Quit crying."'

'Oh, boy,' Nicky grumbled.

'Yeah,' Chloe replied. 'So, without any hesitation, my mom goes right over to the troll and says, "Excuse me, what is your definition of pussy? Because I have one and I'm a fucking badass."'

'Jesus,' Nicky said, feeling the smile split his face.

'I know, right?' Chloe said with her own smile. 'Then she says to the troll, "Don't be a *dick*." She bent down to Jeffrey's height and said to him, "There's no shame in crying, Jeff. It shows you're human and you care." Jeff's dad was so stunned, he just stood there like a complete moron and watched us walk away.'

'Wow.'

'Needless to say, the troll avoided us from then on, and Jeff practically worshipped the ground my mother walked on. He ended up getting the last laugh on his dad, too. Mom helped him get into Yale where he and his boyfriend study dance.'

Nicky laughed.

'Yeah,' Chloe said. Then, she became more thoughtful, serious. 'Thing is, when it comes to others – me especially – she would go full ninja in a heartbeat. But when it comes to herself, she doesn't have the same sort of bravery. She would defend anyone. She sees the best in them and will bend over backward to make their dreams come true. But herself?' Chloe just shook her head. 'She's tough, but sometimes she aims all that badassery in the wrong direction. Know what I mean?'

It was Nicky's turn to nod. He understood. Completely.

Chloe added, 'I don't know what's going on with you two, but . . . just, maybe, don't give up on her.'

Nicky tried, 'I—'

Chloe stopped him with a hand to his arm. She said, 'No promises to me. Just wanted you to know.'

'Thanks, Chloe.'

'Anytime,' Chloe said over her shoulder as she walked away, her fuzzy slippers flip-flopping as she went.

CHAPTER THIRTY-FOUR

LUCY

Their suite had been transformed into a beauty salon with a side of charcuterie. A veritable battalion of eager experts had filed into the place shortly after noon, pulling giant hard-sided steel cases on wheels behind them. There were manicurists, makeup artists, and more hair stylists than seemed entirely safe. (So many hot tools! So many overloaded plugs!) One tiny older woman with a thick Russian accent was exclusively handling eyebrows, apparently.

Shortly after the beauty army had invaded, sliced meats and cheeses materialized. Men in white coats laid out massive wooden boards and champagne in deep ice buckets on the kitchen counter, before vanishing whence they came. Tiffy had followed behind, fussing over little arrangements of summer flowers that she'd placed on basically any surface that wasn't already covered in meat or curling utensils.

A wedding photographer was the *pièce de résistance*. She flitted around, clicking off hundreds of pictures of ladies who truly wished they could wait until *after* they'd been beautified to be memorialized for all time.

Lucy stood with her back against the living room wall, belly full of salami and brie, watching as a young person called Fire, with orange hair, neck tattoos, and a septum ring, arranged prim Mrs. Heylen's coif in a perfect copy of Betty White's curly gray/blonde helmet from *The Golden Girls*. The juxtaposition was riveting. Also, Lucy was beyond curious about Mrs. Heylen.

Chandler's mom was only two years older than Lucy and had gamely settled into a hairstyle that was favored by women Lucy's mother's age and older. Lucy had no desire to give up her Cool Chestnut Caramel, thank you very much. (Lucy's gray hairs could go straight to hell – if only the Church of Satan would return her calls.) But she did find it fascinating that some women just pointed themselves in the direction of whatever their age meant to them. Chandler's mom clearly believed midlife Betty White circa 1985–1992 was what her late forties required.

Lucy thought the process must go something like, 'Well, I'm a woman of a certain age now, better chop off all my hair and get a perm. Quick, QVC, send me the orthotic walking shoes! Also need a velour nightgown and a cardigan with cats embroidered on it, STAT!' Lucy couldn't imagine herself ever asking for a Betty White do; and embroidered cats had the ring of hair shirt to her. She wanted to age like Cindy Crawford or Bo Derek, dammit. If she was going down, she'd go down swinging, clutching an industrial-sized tub of Retin-A and a bottle of Clairol.

Lucy only looked away from Chandler's mom because she felt the weight of eyes upon her. Assessing, judgy, Lady Boss eyes. She found Chloe and Kim whispering conspiratorially and side-eyeing her from the spot where Kim was getting a blowout.

She knew what they were talking about. Now that they both knew her secret, they had to hash out all of 'The Breathing Room' details between them and compare notes. It wasn't surprising in the least, but it was uncomfortable.

Lucy pulled her phone from her back pocket and texted Kim.

Lucy: Could you two be *more* obvious?

KimmyR: Could you talk *more* like Chandler's namesake?

She was too old for the eye-rolling emoji, right?

Lucy: Knock it off, okay?

KimmyR: Fine. For now. TBC.

Lucy watched Kim gesture in her direction and whisper something else to Chloe. Then they both winked and waved at her.

This was why Lucy hadn't divulged the whole Nicky Broome melodrama to her daughter in the first place. As a blushing bride, Chloe had this air of hopeful romantic goodwill about her. It was a condition common to many blissfully happy coupled people. They feel compelled to spread their love and drag everyone around them into their state of blessed harmony. Lucy had seen it time and again during her various flirtations with singlehood. It was exasperating. Especially from her daughter. Particularly in relation to Nicky Broome.

'We're talking about it,' Chloe demanded as she sidled over to Lucy's hiding spot against the wall.

'No, we're not,' Lucy replied, trying to sound commanding and not petulant. Mostly failing.

'Look, you have to give me this. You've just completely reordered my entire childhood—'

'Hyperbole, much?'

'It's not hyperbole, Mom. It's fact. All those times you put earplugs in when I played Super—'

Lucy interrupted, 'Hey, I also did that with the Jonas Brothers.'

'Holy shit!' Chloe's eyes became saucers. 'Did you sleep with the Jonas Brothers?'

'No.'

Chloe clutched her chest. 'Jesus, you almost killed me on my wedding day. I actually saw my life flash before my eyes. Anyway, don't change the subject. You still switch the station anytime Super comes on. You can't convince me it's all in the past. Come on, you wandered into the suite last night all sex-drunk and goofy. From *his* room. He's coming to the wedding in a few hours. *With* you. He wrote the greatest love song ever about *you*.'

For me.

'Keep your voice down,' Lucy whisper-yelled. 'All of that is past tense, Chloe. This thing with Nicky and me is just temporary. A vacation thing. It already has an end date, remember? Now, as you were so kind to remind me, it's your wedding day. Can we please just enjoy it and focus on you and Chandler?'

Lucy was rapidly getting the same nagging feeling in her belly that she used to get when Chloe was little and begged for a second helping of ice cream, or a damn pony. A sense that the prodding would go on for an eternity unless she broke down and gave in – or Brandon did. Too bad for Chloe that Daddy's AmEx couldn't solve this one to her satisfaction.

Kim approached, hair gloriously smoothed to a high shine.

'She's being stubborn,' Chloe said to Kim.

'I'm shocked,' Kim deadpanned.

'It isn't stubbornness,' Lucy grumbled. She had to change tactics. Logic had never worked for farm animals and double dessert, but perhaps (if Lucy had earned any good karma in her life) it might sway Chloe this time. 'On Monday, he's leaving for Europe. For a full year of touring. A different city every . . . what was it, Kim?' Lucy asked her best friend. 'Two days?'

'Three,' Kim replied flatly.

Lucy turned back to Chloe. 'Tomorrow, I'm going back to Ohio where I begin a minimum of twelve months of interviews, meetings, evaluations, and general ass-kissing that I have been working toward for my entire professional life.'

Chloe inhaled deeply, sullen.

Lucy continued, 'Now you tell me how those two things are compatible, Chloe.'

'What about long distance?' Chloe asked.

'With a rock star? On tour? In Europe?' Kim interjected.

Chloe looked to Lucy. 'You don't think he would be faithful? Is that it?'

Lucy shrugged, but she knew. He would be faithful. Nicky was not that guy. Still. 'Even if he would, Chloe, think about it. We see each other for the first time in forever, have a lovely week together, and then aren't in the same room again for more than a year? Does that sound like the solid beginning to a relationship? To me, it doesn't sound like a relationship at all. It's . . . it's FaceTime pen pals. At best.'

Chloe groaned.

Yeah, welcome back to reality, kiddo. We've missed you here.

Lucy went on, 'And then, let's say that FaceTime pen pals is amazingly successful. The relationship survives, even thrives. Then what? Nicky moves to our tiny rural college town in Ohio?'

A sudden, intrusive vision of Nicky Broome sleepy and rumpled at her little breakfast table made her heart twist.

'He might,' Chloe exclaimed. 'Did you ask him?'

'No, I didn't,' Lucy replied. 'Because after this tour there will be another.'

'Six months in the US,' Kim threw in.

'Followed by an as-yet-unpublicized residency in Las Vegas that you can't tell anyone about,' Lucy added.

'Shit.' Chloe's shoulders sagged. 'Being an adult blows.'

Kim chimed in, 'Fucking sucks.'

'Yep,' Lucy agreed.

'I'm sorry, Mom.'

Lucy gripped her daughter's hand and squeezed. 'Nothing to be sorry about, Clo, it's just . . . well, life's a bitch and then you die.'

'Wow,' Chloe bellowed. 'That is *depressing*.'

'Wait, is that not a common saying anymore?' Lucy asked, genuinely shocked.

Chloe tutted. 'When was that ever a common saying?'

Lucy and Kim exchanged a look of shock.

'Uh, they made T-shirts,' Lucy said to Chloe.

'And bumper stickers,' added Kim.

Chloe griped, '*What?*'

Lucy couldn't believe it. 'It was practically GenX's motto.'

'The Nineties were a special, special time,' Kim mused, gazing wistfully out the window at the bright desert sky. She turned to Chloe. 'Doesn't your generation have a motto?'

Chloe looked at them both like they'd sprouted horns and fangs.

'Don't worry, be happy?' Lucy offered.

'No.' Kim shook her head. 'That was the Eighties.'

'Ah,' Lucy said. 'Yeah, that tracks.'

Chloe stared at them, mouth agape. 'This explains so, so much,' she said, gesturing between Kim and Lucy. 'Also, it's a miracle anyone in your generation made it out with their sanity.'

'But did we really though?' asked Kim.

'Sanity is so subjective,' Lucy quipped to Kim.

To which Kim quoted, '"Sanity is a little box. Insanity is everything."'

'Oh, that's good. Who said that?' Lucy asked.

'Charles Manson,' Kim replied matter-of-factly.

Chloe chuckled darkly. '*Aaaand* that's my cue.' She patted Lucy on the back. 'You two are twisted and not good for my mental health.'

Kim and Lucy nodded in agreement.

Chloe backed away. 'I'm going to go get my hair done now.'

'Love you, sweetheart,' cooed Lucy.

'Love you, too, you maniac,' Chloe replied.

Kim leaned into Lucy, resting her head on the other woman's shoulder as they observed the melee of beauty and wedding-day joy. 'These younglings don't know how good they've got it.'

'Nope.' Lucy sighed. 'Lucky them.'

CHAPTER THIRTY-FIVE

NICKY

Fancy weddings were nothing new for Nicky. He'd had two and a half of his own. Between the rest of the band there had been five more. (Or maybe it was six?) If he added in the other band-adjacent weddings of friends and colleagues over the years, the number was well into the double digits. Though, truthfully some of those hadn't been fancy, only expensive. The one with a village of overpriced yurts and another where the groom dropped in from a helicopter sprang to mind.

This one, though, felt different.

He was led to a spot in the front row, just as he had been at the rehearsal, seated between Brandon's wife, Jenna, and Lucy's ex-husband Sam. An open seat to his right was where Lucy would sit when she finally made it back to him.

Nicky hadn't slept well without Lucy wrapping her long limbs around him. Had he been so inclined, Nicky might have wondered at how quickly she had become essential to his life. Only days had passed since that first bumbling conversation surrounded by dick lollipops, but it hadn't felt fast to him. He wasn't in the beginning with Lucy, but the juicy heart-pounding middle of a story he'd waited twenty-eight long years to continue.

Devin had yet to make an appearance, but Nicky had already decided to simply ignore the man. He still wanted to put him in the ER for the way he'd treated Lucy, but wasn't about to ruin Chloe's wedding no matter how satisfying it would be.

The Cristallo Salon was filled with the smell of flowers and the liquid-soft sounds of a string quartet playing classical versions of modern songs. The bouncy chords of Maroon 5's 'Girls Like You' made Nicky wonder if they might play 'The Breathing Room' or if, perhaps, Lucy had barred it from the set list.

As the officiant took her place at the front of the room, the chirp of happy chatter dialed back to a quiet hum. Nicky felt, more than saw, Devin settle into his seat some ten feet away.

Chandler, beaming like a klieg light, walked up the aisle with his mother on his arm, depositing her on the groom's side of the room before taking his spot beside the officiant.

Moments later, the double doors at the back of the room opened. And Nicky stopped breathing.

The bright staccato swell of Bruno Mars from the violins played in time with his heart, pounding as it was at the sight of Lucy. She shined. Glowed. She was a pink, flickering light. He could feel her warmth in his chest as she smiled at him and took slow measured steps down the aisle. Her hair was pinned back on one side by a jeweled flower, the other side flowing in loose waves that begged for his fingers.

If only he was standing in Chandler's spot and Lucy was gliding toward *him* up there. Jesus, it was an ache. Deep in his belly.

Nicky had accepted that Lucy was wary of relationships in general after her three failed marriages. He also knew that she was unsure about the two of them. He wasn't. Not in the slightest. So, while he knew he shouldn't push her, God did he ever want to push. In that moment, he wanted to scoop her up and carry her over his shoulder straight to the nearest wedding chapel. Or maybe bump Chandler off the stage and take over right then and there.

Nicky offered Lucy his hand as she approached. Her hand in his felt so right he had to stop a moan from escaping his lips.

'You are beautiful,' he whispered as he guided her to her seat.

'Thank you,' she whispered back. Then: 'You look like a snack. Black tie suits you. Even if I can't see the tats.'

Lucy winked, a wicked gleam in her eye, and Nicky was done. Gone. He didn't want to be anywhere else on planet Earth. In the universe. He only wanted to be by Lucy's side. He knew right then, with his heart bursting open in his chest, that there would be no going back from this. Either he would be with Lucy for what was left of his life, or he would spend it pining for what might have been in a way that had been inconceivable when he was eighteen.

He wanted to shout this revelation to her, to the whole sequined and tuxedoed crowd. To the world. But it was time to stand for the bride.

As they got to their feet, Nicky tucked himself behind Lucy and placed a hand on her hip. She had already been snuffling quietly when the music changed, but when Chloe appeared at the end of the aisle, Nicky could feel Lucy's shoulders shake.

He produced another silk hankie (had run out that morning to the Lusso shops for a whole stack of them) and handed it to her.

She looked to him, her eyes misty and shining with an expression of such gratitude and love that it almost broke him. He wanted to squeeze her tight and make her say it. Make her admit how right they were together. Instead, he watched as she turned away and gazed at her daughter walking down the aisle on her father's arm.

'God, look at his *face*,' Lucy marveled, her eyes glancing to Chandler.

Nicky followed Lucy's gaze, and there was Chandler, looking like a man who was about to have every wish he'd ever made granted in a few minutes' time. Nicky was not jealous of much in life anymore, but he was sure as hell jealous of *that*.

Nicky barely registered the glittering white form that passed them, too focused on watching Lucy as her emotions played on her face. He saw pride, joy, humor and maybe just a touch of sadness, too. He was enthralled by them all.

For Nicky, the ceremony passed in a series of hand

squeezes and gentle swipes of his thumb on Lucy's neck. With all her focus on Chloe, Lucy didn't pay him a bit of attention. Nicky ate it up, loved every second of being there for Lucy as a strong, silent partner in her delight and bittersweet sorrow.

When Devin got up to do his reading, Nicky felt Lucy stiffen.

'Sonnet 116 by William Shakespeare,' Devin said into the mic. He cleared his throat and continued, 'Let me not to the marriage of true minds / Admit impediments. Love is not love / Which alters when it alteration finds, / Or bends with the remover to remove.'

Devin's amplified voice carried through the space, forceful and clear. 'O, no! It is an ever-fixed mark, / That looks on tempests and is never shaken.'

It was clearly supposed to be a heartwarming sentiment. Nicky could hear sniffles around the room. Poor Jenna was near sobbing. But Devin's voice was not in any way heartwarming. It was crestfallen. Bitter. Devin wasn't beaming at the happy couple. He was glaring. At Lucy.

Pointedly. Noticeably. Enough that heads began to turn their way.

'Shit,' Lucy whispered.

Devin went on, a noticeable haze of anger coloring his tone, 'It is the star to every wandering bark, / Whose worth's unknown, although his height be taken / Love's not Time's fool, though rosy lips and cheeks / Within his bending sickle's compass come . . .'

Nicky strengthened his grip on Lucy's hand. Silently telling her that it was all okay. That it would all be okay.

Devin's voice grew stronger as the reading went on. He never looked down at his paper. Like somehow, inexplicably, this slightly deranged Adidas-tracksuit-wearing jock had memorized Shakespeare just to have this very moment of retribution. *That fucking shithead.*

Devin bellowed, 'Love alters not with his brief hours and weeks, / But bears it out even to the edges of doom.'

Nicky squeezed her hand, again.

'Lucy,' he whispered. A plea.

Lucy looked down at their intertwined hands, and slowly peeled her fingers from his, placing them primly on her lap.

Devin boomed, 'If this be error and upon me prov'd, / I never writ nor no man ever lov'd.'

Lucy was physically inches away, but Nicky knew that she was already erecting a wall between them. Knowing her like he thought he did, the thing was bound to be damn near impenetrable by the time cocktails were served. So, Nicky did the only thing he could in the moment. He sighed. (Because screaming and smashing things were frowned upon at black-tie weddings.)

Vows were taken, kisses were had, and by the time the string quartet started up with a Taylor Swift song, Nicky's stomach was in knots.

He stood, and smiled, and clapped for the happy couple as they practically skipped back down the aisle. Then he watched Lucy's back as she followed Brandon and Jenna out of the room.

CHAPTER THIRTY-SIX

LUCY

Lucy's emotions were all over the place. She was ecstatic for Chloe and Chandler, beyond pissed at Devin, and sad. So unaccountably *sad* that she was convinced that she was a terrible person. She was wrung out. Exhausted.

Kim approached her in the vestibule outside the reception hall and Lucy all but collapsed into her hug.

Wedding guests streamed around them, happily chatting as they shuffled off to the rest of the evening's wedding events.

'Jesus,' Kim fussed. 'Are you okay?'

'No,' Lucy replied. 'I either want to dance with joy, curl up in the fetal position, or attack the top shelf of liquor at the reception. Maybe all three. Nicky was being really sweet in there. Considerate. Kind. And I don't know how to handle it. It's dumb. I'm dumb.'

'Take a breath,' Kim instructed.

Lucy, completely at a loss, did as she was told.

'Fucking Devin,' she mumbled as she exhaled.

'He's an idiot,' Kim added. 'His head is so far up his ass the man could do his own colonoscopy.'

A laugh escaped Lucy's mouth before she even knew it was coming. She tried to get a hold of herself, but failed. Only wheezing, 'That is so gross,' before her laughter pulled her under again.

Kim smiled at her warmly.

'I need to talk to him,' Lucy said finally.

'Yeah, you do.' Kim looked around. 'Hey, where's your rock star?'

'I don't know. Probably in the cocktail hour. Unless he's running for his life, as he should. I don't know what the fuck I'm doing with him, Kim.'

'*I* do,' she replied in her all-knowing Lady Boss tone.

'Don't,' Lucy snipped, pointing a finger at Kim. 'Just because we've developed this twisted psychic-friends thing over the last thirty-plus years doesn't mean you get to use it any damn time you please.'

'Of course it does,' Kim said flatly.

'You have to have permission to read my thoughts, witch,' Lucy (mostly) teased.

'As if,' Kim replied. 'Anyway, it doesn't take witchcraft to see what's going on with you, Luce. You're emoting like Daniel Day-Lewis with a camera pointed at him.'

'I'm a fucking mess.' Lucy sighed.

'Yeah,' Kim said, throwing her arm across Lucy's shoulders. 'But you're a beautiful mess, and I think he's up for it.'

'I can't, Kim.'

'Love him? Why the fuck not?'

'I don't know what I'm doing. What is even *happening*? Look at what happened with Devin. Like, what the fuck did I do to Devin? How did I screw that up so spectacularly?' Lucy roared, before silencing herself as she began to draw looks from Brandon's business associates passing by. She mumbled, 'I'm too old for this, Kim. Shouldn't I have some shit figured out by now?'

'Nobody has anything figured out, Lucy. Nobody. Anybody who says they do is a fucking liar. The best any of us can do is put one foot in front of the other and try to keep the collateral damage to a minimum.'

Lucy fumed, 'You are the worst at advice.'

'I'm *brilliant* at it,' she retorted with a lightness that made Lucy want to scream.

'You said he could be a nice distraction.'

'Oh, I think you're distracted.'

Lucy heard music strike up in the reception hall. 'Shit, I think I'm supposed to be announced or something.'

The two friends hugged each other fiercely, telling each other everything about how deep and true their love was, all without ever saying a word.

*

Lucy *was* announced. As were Jenna and Brandon, Mr. and Mrs. Heylen, and the newly minted McManis-Heylens. Chandler, prince that he was, had told Chloe – in no uncertain terms – that he never intended to take anything away from her, only add, so insisted that they share both of their names.

After the formalities had been observed and people were settling in for their trillion-course dinner, Lucy found Devin. At the damn bar.

Okay, time to pull up those big-girl pants.

'Have a second?' Lucy asked as he shoved a couple of bills into the tip jar.

Devin just grunted and followed her to an out-of-the-way nook where hotel staff buzzed by them, busy and unconcerned.

Lucy started, 'I wanted to say, I'm sorry.'

Devin just looked down at his highball glass, shuffling uncomfortably from one foot to the other in his stiff tuxedo and formal shoes.

She continued, 'I thought you were . . . that *we* were in an okay place after the divorce. And I guess I was wrong.'

Devin's only response was a grunt, just a single noise, but laced with so much meaning that it grated on Lucy's already frayed nerves.

'Devin,' she griped, 'you have to tell me what's going on with you so I can help.'

He looked up. 'You mean so you can get me off your conscience and get back to Nick-fucking-Broome? Or should I say, fucking Nick Broome?'

Lucy swallowed the curse that really, really wanted out. Instead, she said calmly, 'No, so that I can be a good friend to you and help you get out of whatever . . . *this* is. You don't drink, you don't make a scene, you're a truly decent human—'

'Just not *enough*,' he bit back.

Jesus. 'It isn't a contest between you, Dev. We were over a long time before I met Nicky again. You and I just didn't work.'

'You didn't *let* us work, Lucy. You never tried.'

Well, shit, she really didn't think that was true.

He went on, 'When things got hard, you just gave up. And I couldn't do it all myself, you know? If you weren't in it – which, I'm pretty sure you weren't from the beginning – but if you weren't in it, what could I do?'

Had she ever been in it?

Devin continued, 'We had fun, until we didn't. And then that was it.'

That was almost exactly how she'd described her relationship with Devin to Nicky. The unconscious echo sent a painful tingle between her shoulder blades.

He added, 'I thought there was something deeper between us, and you didn't. Which is fucking brutal when you realize it. Okay?'

Lucy looked in his eyes, could clearly read their sadness and disappointment. Realization began to dawn. 'I think—' *Shit*. 'I think, you're right.'

'I am?'

She really wished he wasn't but, 'Yeah,' Lucy replied. 'I wasn't in it. I was not a good partner and I didn't commit.'

'You didn't,' he repeated.

'No, and what's worse is that I was careless with your

feelings, Devin. That's what I'm really sorry for. Because I did . . . I *do* love you. Just . . . not in the way you need me to.'

Not like I feel for Nicky, her dumbass subconscious offered unhelpfully.

Lucy went on, 'I'm sorry we didn't work, Dev. I'm sorry that I hurt you. You have to believe; that was never my intention. I'm just . . . I'm just really fucking bad at relationships.'

I shouldn't get within a hundred miles of a relationship. Obviously, I'm toxic.

Devin stared at her, assessing, his eyebrows scrunching up in thought.

Lucy tried, 'I hope . . . I *know* that there is a woman out there who is looking for you, Dev. You are funny, sweet, and kind. You're a really good person.' She teased tentatively, 'When you're not on the sauce.'

He cringed. 'I *am* kind of a lightweight. Never shoulda said any of that shit the other night, Lucy. I'm sorry.'

'It's all right. I get it. Water under the bridge, okay?'

He nodded. Then said, 'I shouldn't let this shit still get to me—'

'No,' Lucy insisted. 'Don't apologize for your feelings. And don't beat yourself up for having them. Or for sharing them.' She smiled. 'Just maybe do it sober next time.'

'Yeah,' he replied, with another long look at his glass.

'Are you okay? I mean, I know that you will be okay. And I know that my apology doesn't really solve anything.' Lucy sighed. She wanted to touch his arm, comfort him, but knew it would be more helpful to her than him. 'In the long-term I know you'll be great. You know? You will. Right this minute though, are you okay?'

He nodded once, eyes still downcast, then took a deep breath and exhaled it roughly. 'Yeah,' he said finally.

Good. At least someone is. Lucy felt a headache coming on. A twist in her belly foreshadowed days of obsessing over all the ways she'd fucked things up. For Devin. For herself.

'Better get back out there,' he said, interrupting her existential meltdown.

This time, it was her turn to nod.

'See ya around, Lucy.'

'Yeah, Dev. See you around.'

Lucy watched Devin's retreating form as he was swallowed up by the crowd of mingling guests. She was so focused on him, and the ever-widening pit in her stomach, that she didn't notice her ex-husband Sam until he was right beside her.

'Hey,' he said, smoothing the facial hair that he'd insisted he hated until he married James who, apparently, loved it.

'Oh fuck,' Lucy grumbled. 'Do you have something to unburden yourself with, too? Go ahead. Tell me how I screwed everything up between *us*.'

'Wow,' Sam quipped with a smile, holding his hands up in surrender. 'I actually came over on the hunt for extra napkins.' He reached behind Lucy to a cart of silverware and straws and, yes, napkins.

'Shit, I'm sorry,' Lucy said.

'Everything okay?'

'Yeah, just . . . Devin.' And about a million other things. 'I'm a disaster.'

Sam smiled.

Stupid friendly Sam and his stupid friendly smile. Ugh.

'Hey,' he said, resting a hand on her shoulder. 'It's a wedding. What's a wedding without little disasters happening quietly in the background all over the place?' He waved the stack of napkins in his hand. 'I spilled red wine all over Aunt Glinda.'

Lucy cringed. 'Yikes.'

'Well, it only happened because she grabbed my ass as I was sitting down, so I think that's on her disaster count, not mine.'

A smile broke on Lucy's face before she could hold it back.

Gah! How did Sam always know how to do that?

He turned to go. Then, just as quickly, turned back.

'Hey, Luce?'

'Yeah?'

'You're not a disaster,' he said solemnly. 'You never were.' Sam exhaled heavily, like he was going to say something else, but changed his mind. 'You'll figure it out. You always do.'

Lucy truly hoped that was true but, just that second, she didn't really believe it.

'Yeah,' she whispered. 'Thanks.'

*

The dinner was delicious. And long. Lucy and Nicky sat beside each other making casual conversation with Chandler's parents and some Heylen cousins who'd traveled from Washington to be there. Oh, and Uncle Shane. (Who was, in fact, very nice. And a total silver fox.) Nicky had reminisced about Seattle with them and it had somehow made him feel even further away. His memories were sweet and warm and she had no part in them.

There were only inches between her and Nicky at the table, but the fact that they hadn't had a chance to discuss her pulling away from him during the ceremony made it feel like they were already in different time zones. He hadn't touched her once. Not so much as a graze of his thigh against hers. His absence was cold and painful, and she didn't know how to make it right. Or if she should.

Even if Lucy had been up to piling her dirty laundry on the table like a centerpiece and discussing it with all the Heylens around, she didn't know *what* to say to Nicky. She felt pretty good about where she'd left things with Devin, but that was just window dressing.

Had she ever really been in it *with any of her husbands? Had she been closed off her whole life? How was she supposed to move past that? Was there a hotline for emotionally unavailable forty-somethings she could call? Why had her internal dialogue turned into an opening of* Sex and the City *with all the dumb questions? Could Carrie Bradshaw please swoop in and solve all of her problems in thirty minutes (give or take a commercial break)?*

Lucy wanted to sleep for a year or two, and wake up

with an epiphany. Instead, though, she tried to listen to the speeches from Hannah, Mason, and Brandon. She smiled and clapped, acting the part she was meant to play. In truth, she was relieved when the superstar DJ they'd hired started up and the plates were cleared away.

Lucy ordered herself a vodka martini ('Just the idea of vermouth, please') and sucked it down hoping it could mute the churning of her mind for an hour or two.

She hadn't realized that she'd drifted back into thought until Nicky stood up and offered her his hand.

'Shall we?' he asked. He looked every bit like a hero from a black-and-white movie in his tuxedo. It threw his green eyes in sharp relief – the only color she could see – and it suddenly struck her that she'd gotten used to all his tattoos. A pure, vivid riot of colors was the norm around him.

Lucy recognized the crisp sound of Tom Odell and his piano. It was Chloe's first dance. And she was missing it.

She put her hand in Nicky's and he threaded his fingers through hers. Gave it one firm squeeze.

On the dance floor, Nicky folded her into his body, one arm fully wrapped around her back, his fingertips biting into her waist. One of her hands found the back of his neck, the other the solid curve of his shoulder. He rocked them back and forth, the music soothing like a lullaby, making Lucy's eyes droopy and her mind blissfully quiet.

As the song ended, Nicky buried his face in the tumble of waves at her cheek. She could feel him inhale deeply, the heat of his breath coasting over her bare shoulder as he exhaled. He pulled back, and their eyes connected. But it was only long enough for the beat of the next song to strike their ears.

The guitar was unmistakable, the drums quaked Lucy's heart as they always had. She and Nicky both looked over to the DJ booth in shock. There, they found Chloe sparkling like sunshine in her wedding gown. She winked at Nicky – at *Nicky* – before descending back down to the head table.

It was 'The Breathing Room.'

The hall went crazy as Nicky's voice blasted through the place. Eyes drifted his way. Cousin Whatever-His-Name-Was threw him a thumbs-up. Garbled, screamed lyrics pulsed around them as people sang along discordantly, bounced, and danced.

Sharp breaths, panted names
Beginnings and endings
Sometimes feel the same

But there would be no rocking out for Nicky and Lucy. Nicky held fast to Lucy's waist and swayed her back and forth on the slowest possible downbeat.

His lips found her ear and he whispered along with the lyrics, 'There with you, that was it . . . it was the calming . . . it was the fit . . . in the Breathing Room . . . you gave me breathing room.'

He was so close that Lucy could feel his heart pounding through the layers between them. Still, he guided her languidly, gripping her tight with the same strong fingers that had played 'The Breathing Room' a thousand times.

The DJ's lights blinked colors over their skin, discordant and as rapid as the blood whooshing through her veins. It made Lucy dizzy, unsteady.

Nicky's lips on her ear mumbled, 'Gasps, fiery and resounding . . . sated and restless, I cling . . . come undone, life changed . . . endings are beginnings . . . sometimes, they're the same.'

Lucy could feel the sorrow in his hushed tones. The low hum of grief was unmistakable as it rubbed up against the potency and energy of the version of his voice that suffused the air around them – the lush, hopeful timbre of a boy of twenty.

A knot formed in Lucy's throat. She wanted to scream it out. Rant before God and Uncle Shane about the unfairness of life, and time, and the baffling fragility of human hearts. She wanted to throw some rage at him. For making her feel sorry for him. She was the one who was left behind. She was the one who spent twenty-eight years with 'The Breathing Room' on her back. Instead, though, Lucy did what she had always done, she swallowed down her frustration and pretended like the world wasn't crashing down around her.

'There with you, that was it . . . you were the calming . . . you were the fit . . . Lucy.' The altered lyrics hit her like a blow. 'Lucy . . . Lucy . . . Everything for you. Anything for you.' There was no question in that final legendary line as it blew tenderly from his lips.

Nicky's eyes found Lucy's, his breath and hers growing ragged.

As the music around them swelled to its final triumphant conclusion, the room erupted again in applause. Lucy could feel the energy and bodies in the room all turn toward Nicky as the ovation dragged on.

He turned away from her and raised a single hand to the crowd in recognition of the admiration, dipping his head in a gesture of humble gratitude.

When a new song kicked up in the room, and the attention was once again on revelry and not Nicky, his hand slipped from her waist and found her hand.

Lucy allowed herself to be pulled away and off toward the exit. Looking back, she locked eyes with Chloe who was wrapped up in Chandler on the dance floor.

Her daughter gifted her a full-wattage Chloe smile, and a nod of her head.

'I love you,' Chloe mouthed.

Lucy blew her a kiss in response and followed Nicky out the door.

CHAPTER THIRTY-SEVEN

LUCY

They didn't speak a word on the trip through the Lusso, or on the elevator to the fortieth floor. Lucy could feel the quiet determination in Nicky's shoulders, set firm and square. She knew that the squeeze of his hand meant stop and go, that the rapid blink of his eyes was frustration at the glacial pace of the elevator. All the while, Lucy became angrier. Every calm, measured step Nicky took ratcheted up her rage. Her body was still, but inside she could feel her wrath coiling tighter.

How dare he make her feel things? How dare he take their benign casual arrangement and douse it in lighter fluid with his whispered lyrics? It was supposed to be easy this time. It wasn't supposed to hurt.

When the door to his suite had opened and closed again with a thunk, his mouth was on hers. He was gentle, tender. His lips grazed hers in soft caresses, his tongue playing carefully with hers in delicate tremors.

But Lucy didn't want him sweet and slow. She didn't

want to sit in every moment, wishing they weren't counting down to the end. Lucy didn't want to savor it. She wanted to burn. Even if it was only for a few blistering minutes. She had been a part of enough last times. She didn't want to feel it again. Not with him.

'No,' she said, backing out of his hold. 'What was that back there? Whispering to me. Singing to me.'

'I'm trying to say I'm sorry. For all of it. I'm sorr—'

'No!' Lucy shouted. 'You don't get to do that now. You don't get to be soft and sorry and decent.' *It'll be too hard to never see you again.* 'Fuck that.'

Lucy slipped out of her high heels and kicked them away, yanked the heavy jeweled flower from her hair. Heard it ping against the marble of the entryway. She grabbed Nicky's shoulders and turned him, slamming his back against the wall and attacking his mouth. Taking control.

She clawed at the side of her dress, beads popping as she jerked the zipper down. With her mouth still on his, she slipped her arms free and the heavy thing pooled on the floor with a rattle and hum.

Nicky pulled away, stared at her. His eyes took a leisurely trip over her collarbones and her bare breasts, down to the scrap of nude silk that was her only remaining piece of clothing.

His thumbs grazed the aching points of her nipples in long, deliberate strokes. A slinking, listless rebellion against her alacrity.

Nope.

Lucy tore at Nicky's tuxedo, peeling his jacket off and

dragging it roughly from his arms. She snatched his belt, unbuckling and pulling it free with an eager *thwack*. She tore at the button of his pants, then unzipped them with speed and thrust her hand inside, wrapping her fingers around his cock. She pulled once, twice, three times with a firm grip.

'*Fuck*,' he breathed, tipping his head back against the wall.

Nicky's left hand found the cuff of his right sleeve and he unbuttoned it slowly. He raised his arms and did the same again with the left. When his fingers moved unhurriedly to his bow tie, tugging it loose in what could only be described as slow-fucking-motion, Lucy was fully fed up with his insubordination.

She snatched the two halves of his shirt and pulled with every ounce of her strength. Buttons popped off in every direction. She snapped her teeth on his nipple, hard. Then laved it with her tongue when he hissed at the pleasure and pain of it.

'Behave,' she growled.

With both hands to his chest, Lucy pushed herself out of his hold and stepped away.

She sauntered toward the bedroom, only deviating from her quest long enough to slip her hands in the strings of her thong. She bent over at the waist, dragging the panties down her legs and kicking them away.

Lucy could feel Nicky stalking behind her, as though they had been connected by string and the thing was snapping taut.

When Nicky entered the room, Lucy circled to his

back and wrenched the shirt from his arms, scraping her fingernails across the tattoo of her name as she went. She dug in so hard that her freshly manicured tips left three sharp red lines in their wake.

She pushed Nicky roughly, turning him around and shoving him onto the bed with such force that the frame creaked when his back bounced onto the mattress.

Lucy tugged the shoes from his feet. Made quick work of his socks and pants and boxers until there was nothing but tattoos and skin on display. Until she could see his cock, rigid and weeping.

Lucy mounted the bed and prowled over him on hands and knees. He raised himself up on his elbows and put his hands over hers.

He breathed, '*Lou.*'

It came out sad and syrupy sweet. Her only response was a groan of frustration. She didn't want his endearments. She couldn't endure any more of his loving words. So, she shut him up with her mouth, smothering his tender moans with her prickly ones.

She pushed the nail of her index finger into his chest, right between the eyes of that California bear, forcing Nicky back where she wanted him – supine and at her mercy.

Lucy raked her teeth on his neck. Nipped at the ink on his chest. Ground her hips shamelessly into his until she couldn't stand it any longer.

Then, with a grasp and a stretch and a thrust, Lucy filled herself up with the heat and the strength of Nicky Broome until the softest part of her was no longer yielding but clasping. She dragged up and slammed down again with enough force to knock the breath from her lungs. She rolled her hips with him deep inside her, again and again, driving her clit into him so hard that it pinched with a sting that was both agony and bliss.

'*Lou*,' Nicky begged.

Lucy elongated her back, stretching till she thought her ribs might pop, and placed her nipple on his mouth. His lips closed around her, licking and sucking.

'Teeth,' she grunted.

When he nibbled, she clenched the muscles at her core and commanded, 'Harder.'

He complied, and she was so grateful for the pain that she moaned, wild and shrill. She felt herself grow even wetter, hotter.

Then, finally – *finally* – Nicky's hands slapped down on her ass, fingernails digging into her flesh. His hips thrust back against her hard and fast. The slap of sweat-soaked skin on skin filling what little space was left between them.

And Lucy was alive there, in that moment. Nothing but the heat and electricity between them. It was forever and it was fleeting. It was everything real and good and it couldn't last. Lucy held it back as long as she could. But eventually, their frisson became fission and their orgasms crackled along every bone like lightning caught on a wire. They were together in that. One last time. And it splintered what was left of Lucy's heart.

CHAPTER THIRTY-EIGHT

NICKY

Nicky was still panting, trying to come back down to earth from whatever the fuck *that* was. It hadn't been sex, not like any kind he'd ever had. It felt like his soul was trying to pry its way back into his body after being blasted out to space.

Lucy was splayed across his chest, her breath still coming as fast as his, even as he felt the tingle of the sweat between them drying in the frigid air. His mind remained foggy, his thoughts remote. It was only the thick, sticky evidence dripping down his cock as it softened, still inside her, that brought his thoughts close to some kind of clarity.

They lay there for what felt like forever.

Nicky could feel Lucy thinking.

It's past midnight now. Sunday.

There was no time left for caution or fear.

'You should come with me,' he whispered against the top of her head.

'What?' she mumbled groggily.

'You should come with me to Europe.'

He felt her muscles tense. All of them.

'What do you mean?' she asked again, her lips moving against his chest.

'You should get on the plane with me tomorrow and come with me to Europe for a year. And then the US. And then Las Vegas again. I want you to stay with me. To come with me. To be together.'

'Why don't you come with me back to Ohio?' He could hear the incredulity in her tone. Understood every beat and measure of it by heart.

'I would. If I could, Lou, I'd do it in a heartbeat.'

She raised herself up, rested an elbow on his chest and her chin in her hand so that she could look him in the eye. Her perfectly arched brows were all screwed up in confusion.

He continued, 'I've been over it nine thousand different ways. Unfortunately, Super is heavily committed. We've got eleven shows already sold out. That's something like five hundred thousand people give or take a rugby team.' He felt her wiggle against him, so he planted a hand on her back. 'We're scheduled for something like fifty-five shows in Europe alone. We've got maybe a thousand people relying on us for employment. Riggers, sound engineers, security, truckers, roadies, caterers. Another, God, maybe . . . three thousand locals who will work the shows when we come to town. All of these people would rather I didn't move to Ohio right this minute.'

'Holy shit,' she moaned as her forehead fell to his chest.

'We've got insurance, they'd cover some of it. The two

million or so we've already spent, maybe. But then, I could basically kiss any insurance on future tours goodbye. I'd be an untenable risk. Uninsurable.'

Lucy covered her face with one of her hands.

He had to finish, had to make her understand. 'Touring is the only way the band makes money now. There's no such thing as album sales anymore. Not really. But I don't even care about that. I'd rather be with you, but it's not just me. It's Gill and Hoop and Vinny's livelihoods, too. Plus, managers, agents, assistants—'

'I get it,' she said. Then mumbled, 'Impossible.' She lifted herself up and off him. It took every ounce of self-control he had not to pull her back down to him.

She sat next to him cross-legged and pulled the sheets up under her chin.

'My life is smaller,' she said. 'Easier to abandon.'

Fuck. 'No,' Nicky said firmly, sitting up to face her. 'No. That is not what this is about. This is about you and me, Lou. We are good together. Please tell me you see that.'

'I do,' she whimpered. 'Of course I do. But I can't just walk away from my *life*. I'm up for tenure. It's been the goal for a fucking decade. Longer. I've worked my ass off. Spent months of my best years writing incredibly boring fucking books and so many stupid articles I could paper the Lusso's lobby with them. I've sat through more committee meetings than is entirely safe. The State of California should slap a warning label on those things. Through three lousy marriages and Chloe's whole magnificent life I've been working for this.'

Nicky could only sigh and rub his unshaven jaw, hoping

that some miracle solution would present itself in the silence.

'Have you been happy, Lucy? Then? Now?'

'*Happy?*' she asked, her voice bordering on hysterical. 'Happiness is transient, Nicky. It's fickle and temporary.'

That might be the saddest thing Nicky had ever heard.

Nicky reached out for Lucy. Stroked a single finger on the outline of her thigh under the sheet. 'Let me tell you something. Since we've been together, I've been happier than I can ever remember being. In the whole of my life, Lucy. For a solid year I haven't written so much as a note, until you.'

Lucy shook her head. 'What are you talking about?'

'I had all these empty fucking notebooks. A goddamn beat-up Martin that I'd drag around from place to place waiting for my mind to start up again and it just . . . didn't. There was no music. Until you.'

'So what? I'm your *muse*?' she chided. 'My pussy is magic and the only way to keep your music engines going?'

'No, dammit,' Nicky growled. 'And I'm not going to let you do this.'

'Do what?'

'Push me away. Stop it. We've got enough shit going on here without adding that. Okay?'

Lucy's discomfort was palpable. A solid thing that had wrapped itself around her like the sheet she was clutching.

Nicky added, 'It's *me*. The happiness. The music. You make me happy. And that has led me back to something I lost.'

Lucy made no sound but that of her breathing, looking down at the crumpled sheets.

'Talk to me,' Nicky said. 'Just talk to me. We can figure it out.'

Her eyes snapped up. 'What is there to figure out? We've figured it out. You're going to Europe and I'm going to work. I can't be there. And you can't be here.' Lucy slid off the bed. Went to the closet and pulled one of the hotel bathrobes from a hanger.

'What are you doing?' Nicky asked, his heart rate spiking.

'It's Sunday,' she said softly. 'This was only supposed to last 'til Sunday.'

'Lucy,' Nicky begged. 'What do you want for the future? How does it look to you?'

Lucy exhaled roughly, slipped her feet into the hotel slippers.

'Forget the job for a minute,' Nicky added. 'Beyond the job. What do you want?'

Lucy stared at her feet, breathed out long and slow. 'I don't know.'

Nicky followed Lucy as she left the room. Watched as she gathered her things from the floor and headed for the door. He wanted to grab her. Hold her. But he knew that it would only be detrimental to his case in the long run.

She was so scared. So scared of everything.

'I'll see you later?' Nicky asked as her hand gripped the doorknob.

'Yeah,' she replied flatly.

Nicky could only watch Lucy walk away, and hope like hell it wouldn't be the last time he saw her face.

CHAPTER THIRTY-NINE

LUCY

It took about three seconds after the door to Nicky's suite closed for Lucy to realize that she didn't have her room key.

Three additional seconds passed and she realized that her phone and her keycard were both in the formal clutch she'd left at the table in the reception room.

It took five seconds more for Lucy to decide that she couldn't go back to Nicky's room and its guarantee of further conversation about unsolvable problems.

She padded down the corridor toward Kim's door and her final opportunity to avoid a humiliating trip to the hotel lobby in a bathrobe with sex hair.

The whole stupid situation made her feel even more out of control. She was clearly failing at her forties in much the same way she'd failed at her thirties. Shit, her twenties hadn't exactly been stellar either. But at least then she had the excuse of not being fully cooked. Lucy felt nothing like a grown-up as she slinked down the hall and knocked on Kim's door. She felt like a damn fool.

Lucy's knock was met with a loud clang and some grumbling.

Thank God.

Kim opened the door still in her gorgeous silk gown, mascara streaked under her eyes.

'Damn, you okay?' Lucy asked.

'Might have passed out on the couch,' Kim said, ushering Lucy in. 'At least, I think I started on the couch. Woke up on the floor.'

Lucy went straight to the kitchen and poured a glass of water, then headed for the bathroom where she found Kim's stash of pain relievers right where she knew they'd be.

When she got back to the living room, she found Kim sitting on the coffee table with her head in her hands.

'Here,' Lucy said, offering the Tylenol and water.

'Thanks.' Kim swallowed everything down and sighed. 'Don't think we're not getting into this whole situation,' Kim said, waving a hand at Lucy's bathrobe. 'Just give me a second for the room to stop spinning.'

'Did you have fun?' Lucy asked gently, settling herself on the couch.

'Obviously,' Kim quipped. 'But they have about three more hours in 'em down there. And don't even mention the after party. They'll be at it till dawn. If you tell anybody this, I'll deny it, but it turns out I'm too fucking old for an after party.'

'Your secret's safe with me.' Lucy's hand came to rest on Kim's knee. 'Think you need a trash can?'

'No,' Kim replied. 'It's not my stomach. It's my head. It'll pass.' Kim flopped herself around and sat next to Lucy on the sofa. 'Now, tell me.'

'Nicky asked me to go with him. On tour,' Lucy blurted.

'Wow.'

'Yeah. Fucking nuts, right? Can you imagine? Dropping out of your life completely and just following a guy around? On tour?'

'Yes, yes I can,' Kim said flatly.

'*What*?'

'I mean, I know where you're headed with this, because I know you so well it's fucking terrifying. Still, um, yep. I could totally see *myself* doing that. Any day. As a matter of fact, when you tell him no, why don't you go ahead and offer to send me in your place?'

That made Lucy's stomach churn. The idea of Kim and Nicky?

No. Nope. No, thank you.

'Kim, if one of my students came to me and said they were dropping out to follow their boyfriend on tour I would tell them that they were fucking nuts.'

Kim leaned back into the sofa and began running her hands through the tangles in her hair. 'Some nineteen-year-old dropping out of college to follow a stoner and his worthless friends in their garage band *would* be fucking nuts. If you'd take a second, you might realize that your situation is vastly different.'

Lucy tugged at the belt of her bathrobe, felt emboldened and steadied by the tight cinch at her waist. 'Is it, though? Kim, I consumed more Oprah Winfrey than grilled cheese growing up. I have seen the Barbie movie five times. I know my damn worth and the value of my dreams, dammit. I am liberated. I am a fucking feminist. I can't just walk away from my career – from everything I've ever worked for. For a *boy*!'

Kim sat up to her full Lady Boss stature, spine like a steel spike, golden eyes all business. 'Number one, Nick Broome is about the furthest thing from a *boy* I can imagine.' She locked her gaze on Lucy. 'Secondly, all of that – *all of it* – is fucking societal shit. Listen to yourself. Rewind and replay. None of those reasons have anything to do with you. With what *you* feel. Is Oprah going to sit at your desk in that sad little windowless office for the next twenty years? Is Barbie going to teach your classes? Will Gloria-goddamn-Steinem be coming to check on how well you've upheld the modern feminist ideal and reward you for it? We're not talking about you joining a damn polygamous cult here with husband-masters and a lifetime of servitude. We're talking about you choosing the life you want. Dreams can fucking change, Lucy. It's *allowed*.'

Lucy shook her head, but it didn't clear. It still felt like she'd been stuffed full of complicated thoughts and couldn't arrange them in any sort of coherent way. 'You don't know what it's like. It's so much.'

Kim closed her eyes and threw her head back. Exhaled in a dramatic huff. 'I do. I *do* know.' When her eyes peeled open again, she said, 'I left the firm. I'm leaving law *completely*. I fucking hate it. And I'm done.'

'What? When?' Lucy sputtered.

'Before I came out to Vegas,' Kim said sheepishly.

'Why didn't you tell me?'

'You had enough going on with the wedding and the panoply of ex-husbands.'

'*Kim*—'

'And, if I'm honest, I sort of thought you'd give me some version of that Oprah-feminist garbage and try to talk me out of it.'

Failure. It was the only word Lucy could form at that moment. She'd failed Devin. And Kim. She'd failed at casual. She'd failed at keeping her shit together. Lucy's tears started up, free and unrestrained. She didn't even try to hold them back.

'Kim, I'm so sorry. I would never—'

That wasn't true, Lucy realized. She probably would have given some dumb lecture. She was a college professor, after all; lectures were sort of her go-to.

Lucy started again, 'I'm sorry you felt you couldn't tell me. How do you feel about it? Do you feel good about it?'

That was the right thing to ask, right?

Kim's shoulders sagged a little. It made her look young and vulnerable. Lucy reached out and grabbed her best friend's hand. Kim said, 'It's scary as shit. But I feel great about it. I really do. I feel like a huge weight has lifted off my shoulders.'

Lucy bit back all the panicky questions that were begging to tip out of her gaping mouth. *What about money?*

Security? All that time you dedicated to your career? All that effort for what? To waste it? What about everything you sacrificed to get to this place? You're just going to throw it away?

She said none of it. Instead, Lucy asked, 'What are going to do now?'

'I don't know,' Kim replied, a huge grin spreading on her face. 'I have no fucking clue and it is *glorious*. I could do anything, Luce. Absolutely anything. I'm getting out of DC – that's for sure. I have plenty of savings. I'm just going to *be* for a while.'

'Wow,' Lucy breathed. That sounded terrifying.

'You could, too,' Kim said softly while squeezing Lucy's hand. 'Just *be*. With Nick Broome. If you wanted.'

'It's too hard, Kim. There are too many boulders in the way. It shouldn't be this hard if it's right. You know?'

'No, I don't. Who told you loving somebody would be easy? That's stupid. Wasn't that the theme of every single Nora Ephron movie? Who even are you?'

'This isn't a movie,' Lucy huffed, pulling her hand from Kim's, and cinching her belt again. She waited for the calm, steady feeling to follow, but it didn't.

A long moment of silence passed. It had weight and substance, like Lucy could feel Kim's thoughts stirring. Finally, Kim asked quietly, 'Did you ever think that maybe they were all too easy?'

'What do you mean? Who's *they*?'

Kim sighed. Gripped the back of her neck with a shaky hand. 'Your husbands, honey,' Kim said sweetly. 'Your marriages.' Lucy could tell that her friend was modulating her voice, trying to project calm. It pissed Lucy off.

'What is that supposed to mean?' Lucy protested.

Kim took a deep breath. A cleansing breath. And it made Lucy want to scream. Finally, Kim said, 'With Brandon you'd been dating forever. Living together in Manhattan. Where it was harder to be alone and, at the time, really scary. You were both in a weird place. And even though you had doubts you just went along. With what was easy and comfortable.'

Lucy shook her head, like her body was trying to spur a counter-argument. Her brain didn't get the message.

Kim went on, 'With Sam you were friends. Good friends. There weren't any arguments. It was relaxed, uncomplicated. But there was also no passion. No fire. It was safe. Easy.'

'Jesus, Kim,' Lucy griped.

Kim's hand rested on Lucy's arm before she continued, 'Then with Devin, it was *all* fire. He was there when you were lonely. He adored you, and the more difficult choice would have been to break it off when he wanted more. It would have been harder to say no when he asked you to marry him, even though deep down you knew that was probably the better course of action. It was easier to go along.' Kim sighed before adding, 'Be honest with yourself, Luce, if it had been you who was meant to do the asking, would you have proposed to any of them?'

Lucy's stomach lurched at that. If she could have found the power of speech, she might have told Kim to stop. But she didn't, so Kim carried on.

'You cared for Devin and wanted him to be happy. You gave that to him even though it didn't make *you* happy. You never got bitter about Sam – though you had every right to – because James made *him* happy.'

Lucy was stunned. Hurt and embarrassed and angry about a thousand other things she didn't have the strength or energy to put a name to.

'What the actual fuck, Kim?' Lucy spat. 'That's just fucking cruel—'

Kim's voice raised to match Lucy's. 'Go ahead and get angry. I can take it. Honestly, I'm glad you're pissed. I should have said something years ago. I was a fucking coward, okay? You have every right to be absolutely livid with me right now. But this right here,' Kim said, waving her hand between the two of them. '*This* is forever. If you wake up with a dead hooker in your bed, I'll be there with a shovel. You hear me? I love you, dammit.'

Lucy could only stare at the coffee table and sink under the weight of Kim's damning assessment of every adult relationship she'd ever had.

'Shit,' she muttered.

She felt Kim rise from the sofa. Felt a warm cozy blanket being wrapped around her shoulders. Heard Kim whisper, 'I'm sorry it took me so long, Lucy. I love you.' Felt a kiss being pressed to the top of her head. Saw the lights go off around her. Heard Kim's soft footsteps rise and fall and finally disappear entirely, leaving only cold, uncomfortable silence behind.

CHAPTER FORTY

NICKY

He had waited an excruciating number of hours. So many. But he was giving Lucy space. Knew she needed it.

Nicky hadn't really expected her to jump up and down on the bed and declare her undying love when he'd asked her to come with him to Europe. *Hoped*, but not expected.

Earlier, he'd clicked off his phone's shrieking reminder of the post-wedding brunch and had sat, dressed and vibrating with unspent energy, in his suite hoping (that fucking stupid hope again) that she would come knocking at the door.

She hadn't.

At two o'clock he couldn't take it anymore. Her flight was leaving at five.

Nicky rushed out of his suite, headed with strong, purposeful strides down the hall, only to see a rolling suitcase emerge from her door. Behind it, clutching the handle with white knuckles, was Lucy.

His heart kicked up at the sight of her, saw little white pops of light in his vision. She looked sad and tired. He wanted to wrap his arms around her and tell her everything was going to be all right.

'Hi,' he said.

'Hi,' she replied.

He muttered, 'How are you—' at exactly the same moment she said, 'I was just coming to—'

And they both laughed at the overlap.

'You first,' he said.

'I'm leaving . . . for the airport,' she said, looking everywhere but at him.

Nicky felt himself flinch at her words. They hit him right between his shoulder blades. Knocked the wind clear out of him.

Shit. That fucking hurt.

'So early?' he managed to choke out.

Her lips flickered in the sad imitation of a smile. Then it was gone. 'Flying commercial. Have to be there two hours ahead.'

Fuck he was an idiot. He'd been waiting all that time, and his twisted rich rock-star brain hadn't even contemplated the intricacies of commercial air travel as an issue.

Jesus. I should have gotten to her hours before. Now she's packed up. Already gone.

She stammered, 'I . . . I was just coming by to say – I can't. I can't go with you. It would be career suicide. To reject tenure. To quit. There's no going back once you start. It would mean starting over. Signing up for another six years of waiting and preparing somewhere else. I . . . I can't take that leap.' She moved back a step. Her voice became impossibly smaller, weaker. Not her. 'I don't know how.'

Nicky tried to regain the power of speech. Tried to remember how to breathe, the magic words to keep his heart beating.

Lucy was faster. 'So I guess this is—'

Before another word could leave her mouth, Nicky slammed his lips to hers. He knew what she was going to say. He knew her next word was 'goodbye' and he couldn't bear it.

Nicky's tongue found hers and he moaned, the first wave of sorrow gripping his throat and making it hard for him to breathe. Still, he tried to tell her without words how much he loved her and wanted her to stay with him. He *tried*. Until he felt her tears on his cheek.

He pulled back and rested his forehead on hers, gasped past the knot in his throat.

'It was good to see you, Nicky Broome,' she whispered.

He croaked, 'It was good to see you, Lucy Rollins.'

She brought her hand to his jaw. He watched her blue eyes flick over his face. Memorizing, he realized.

Fuck.

Lucy took one step, then another. All the way down the gold corridor to the private elevator. It opened instantly at her touch and she disappeared behind the sliding doors.

She didn't look back. Not once.

CHAPTER FORTY-ONE

LUCY

There was a heatwave in Ohio. It seemed like there was always a heatwave now. How could they continue to call it a heatwave when one came right on the heels of another with only a day or two in between when the temperature dipped below ninety? Shouldn't they call them cool patches instead?

It was a trivial train of thought, but a nice break from the 24/7 Nicky show that seemed to be Lucy's new normal.

She wondered where he was, what he was doing. In weak, quiet moments, she looked up his tour schedule and his likely time zone. She did pointless math to determine if he was asleep, or eating breakfast, or on stage somewhere. She missed his face. His tattoos. His laugh. It was an ache, a deeply hollow sensation like something inside her had been carved away.

It had only been two weeks since Vegas, but those fourteen days had dragged. Lucy kept telling herself that the feelings of loss and grief would pass eventually. It would just take time. Meanwhile, she had to go on with her life.

She had gone through all the mail that had accumulated while she was away. She'd answered all the emails sent to her. She put the trash in front of the house for pickup. Went to yoga class and the grocery store. And it had all felt so dim, a sad gray imitation of her life before.

Lucy didn't allow herself to wallow in it, though. She had requests for external review to write. A committee meeting to prepare for. Things to be approved and signed. Class materials to finalize. She was busy. And bored. She was back on campus. And lonely.

An empty nest had sounded so liberating. The house all to herself. Chloe wouldn't drop by with friends unannounced while Lucy was wandering around the house in her bra and panties. Chandler wouldn't 'accidentally' eat the entire contents of her fridge. Her time was her own. She was free. It felt like a suit that was too small, too close and confining. But eventually she'd get her bearings and it would all be fine. It would be *fine*.

Lucy walked to her office. Up the small hill from her home and down again into her beloved little university town. The humidity of the summer morning pressed in on her from all sides, so she stopped to grab an iced coffee from Starbucks. She sipped it as she meandered through the tree-lined quad at the heart of campus.

It was the long way to work. She could have taken her car. It would have been more comfortable, but also faster. Walking helped fill the hours. *And it's good exercise*, she reminded herself for the three-hundredth time. *Good. Exercise.*

Lucy walked up the cracked stone steps to her office building, a stately brick structure built in 1882. She pulled open the enormous wooden door and waited for the charm of Crestwell Hall to envelop her in its warm embrace. All she could see, though, were the yellowing marble tiles and the paint chipping from the baseboards.

The wooden steps up to her third-floor office were worn with age. Their smooth undulations had always been a comfort, a physical reminder of the many thousands of feet that had tread the path to education and enlightenment over hundreds of years. This day, though, with her sweaty thighs rubbing together as she ascended, they only seemed troublesome and dangerous. She told herself that the feeling was also temporary, a consequence of having been lately in Las Vegas. That was it. That was all. *Everything in Las Vegas is so new and fresh and glossed to a high sheen. It's only the juxtaposition. That's all.*

Lucy unlocked her office door and took a deep breath, inhaling the scent of books and wood polish. She didn't have a window. Which was a shame. When she made full tenure, she'd request a different office. She couldn't immediately think of one that would be open. All the other tenured professors had claimed them already over the years. But one of them would probably die at some point. Eventually she'd get a window.

She sat in her specially ordered ergonomic chair behind the enormous wooden desk that was slightly too big for the space and flipped open her laptop. She slung her canvas work bag emblazoned with a UFO and 'Get in, Loser,' a birthday present from Chloe. She flicked on the desk lamp and tried to find the right words to self-motivate.

Lucy reminded herself that she was good at her job. It had value. It made sense. Once she got back into the rhythm it would be good again. She was throwing herself back into her goal and it was a good thing. Maybe, eventually, she'd figure out how to not be terrible at relationships. In the meantime, there was work to be done. There were things to accomplish.

Lucy sipped her iced coffee and checked the email that she'd already gone over while she ate breakfast at her kitchen table.

'Knock, knock,' said a female voice along with a gentle tap at the doorframe.

A messy topknot of blonde curls peeked through the partially open office door.

'Olivia!' Lucy trilled. 'Good to see you.'

'Hi, Dr. McManis,' the young woman said as she entered the room.

'How many times do I have to tell you to call me Lucy?' she joked.

'How many times do I have to tell you that there *aren't* enough times to get me to do that?' Olivia quipped back.

Lucy chuckled. 'Fine. Have a seat. How's your summer been?'

Olivia slipped the backpack off her shoulders and placed it at her feet as she sat down in the chair on the opposite side of the desk. 'It's been good,' she said. 'Really good.'

'Get through that comm symposium, okay?'

'Yeah, it was interesting. A nice break from summer classes.'

'Good.' Lucy beamed.

Olivia was one of Lucy's special students. A twenty-year-old young woman who was majoring in American Cultural Studies and had shown an interest in pursuing academia from the first class she'd taken from Lucy her freshman year. Lucy was her academic advisor, but also (Lucy hoped) something of a friend. Which is why she felt comfortable asking, 'Are you okay?'

'Yeah,' Olivia replied weakly, looking at the coffee mug of pens on Lucy's desk.

'Are you sure?'

'Yeah,' she repeated. 'It's just . . . I wanted to talk to you about something.'

Olivia finally looked up and Lucy could see that she was nervous, maybe even a bit anxious.

'Sure, what's up?'

'Well, you know that my minor is Art History?'

'Yeah,' Lucy replied.

'Well, I've been getting more involved with the art restoration side of things lately. Aiming more toward conservation. The physical, practical side of art history rather than the more theoretical, academic side. And I realized recently that I really love it. I kind of have a mind for the chemistry and mechanics of it and I just . . . I love it.'

Lucy could sense where the conversation was heading, had heard it before from other students over the years.

Olivia continued, 'So, I'm changing majors.'

Lucy opened her mouth to offer words of encouragement, but Olivia spoke first.

She continued, 'It's just that . . . I mean, I also love American Cultural Studies and I'm already deep in the major at this point. But I think if I switch this semester, I can probably finish college in a total of five years. I'd really rather not bankrupt my parents or finish under a heap of debt. If I let it go any longer . . .'

'I understand,' Lucy said.

'You do?'

'Of course. You don't owe me any explanations, Olivia. I'm glad you found something that you feel good about. It's the perfect time to make the switch.'

Olivia visibly relaxed, her shoulders settling lower. 'I was just feeling pot committed, you know? Like maybe I shouldn't throw away all of this work in ACS and take the extra year.'

'I'm sorry,' Lucy interrupted. 'Pot committed?'

'Oh, yeah. Sorry. My dad is big into poker. He's a contractor, but his hobby is cards. Drags us all to Vegas twice a year, the whole thing.'

At the mention of Vegas, Lucy felt the air in the room shimmer. A tingle up her spine had her leaning forward in her seat. Like it was destiny or fate or some other hokey shit she normally laughed off, but couldn't ignore this time. She put her hands flat on the desk to steady herself.

Oliva went on, 'In poker, pot committed is basically when you've bet into a hand round after round, but then when it comes time for the last cards to be turned over –

even though it seems like you're probably going to lose – you bet in anyway. Because all of your money is in there, right? So, if there's even a tiny chance that you could win, it would be better to stick some more cash in there and see it through to the finish than it would be to fold. But the chances are slim. You almost always lose.'

'Pot committed,' Lucy whispered.

Olivia nodded. 'Yeah, um, I realized that I was starting to think of my life that way. Which is beyond ridiculous.' The young woman became more animated, punctuating her words with sweeping movements of her arms. 'I can't stay on this path just because I've accidentally overplayed my hand. It's not cards, it's my *life*. I want to enjoy it. I actually considered being miserable for my whole life because I didn't want to commit to one extra year of college. Can you believe that?'

Lucy's thoughts and feelings shuffled and rearranged themselves. Her stomach flipped with excitement – fucking *epiphany*. Lucy muttered, sort of at Olivia, 'You've sacrificed. Given so much to this thing. This *goal*. But what would be the greater waste?' Lucy was so far on the edge of her seat, the rolling chair almost slipped out from under her. 'To be miserable and achieve it? Or shift gears with the possibility of some inconvenient consequences for the chance to be truly happy?'

'Exactly,' Olivia said. 'That's what it's about after all, right?'

Lucy looked up at the ceiling in astonishment and chuckled. 'It is.' She looked down at Olivia. 'Sometimes you just have to take the leap.'

'Yeah.'

Lucy griped, 'It's fucking terrifying though, isn't it?'

Olivia laughed. 'Yeah.'

Lucy stood, suddenly vibrating with the need to move. 'Can I hug you, Olivia?'

Olivia looked momentarily stunned, then stood. 'Sure!'

Lucy wrapped her student in her arms and squeezed. 'You're going to do great things, Olivia. I know it.'

'Thank you, Dr. McManis,' Olivia sighed, melting into the hug.

Lucy took a step back, held Olivia by her shoulders. 'You stay in touch, okay? Here, let me give you my personal email.' Lucy grabbed a piece of paper and jotted down her address. 'Reach out anytime. If you're feeling frustrated or you have some great news. All right?'

'Sure. Of course,' Olivia said, pocketing the paper and retrieving her backpack.

Olivia waved goodbye as she slipped through the office door.

Lucy took a look around her. Surveyed the dusty shelves of books, her desk, the careworn carpet, the windowless walls with their framed degrees.

'Oh my God,' she bellowed to the room, to herself, to the damn *universe*. So much education in her life, and still dumb as a bag of rocks.

Lucy could almost see a bright, shining field of stars erupt before her eyes. It was either a life-changing flash of insight, or a dire medical emergency. At her age, it was difficult to tell.

CHAPTER FORTY-TWO

LUCY

The thing they don't tell you about making a grand gesture is that it is fucking *excruciating*. In the movies there's a decision, and a plane ride that takes approximately three seconds, and *boom* – happily ever after. Easy.

In real life, apparently, it's seven full days of agony.

Case in point: Lucy stood at the door of her neighbor, Oumarou, beside her other neighbor Carl, a slender man in a Bengals sweatshirt and flip-flops, whom she'd dragged from an apparently riveting documentary on Tudor England.

'So, *then*,' Carl said, jabbering away as he had for five minutes, 'the last one, Catherine Parr, enters the picture—'

'Hello, neighbors!' said Oumarou, opening the door on his tidy Midwestern bungalow. His wife, Pauline, shuffled in behind him carrying their baby daughter. Lucy resisted the urge to reach out and grab little Marthe for the baby-cuddle time she usually enjoyed when hanging out next door. Unfortunately, Lucy didn't have the time to indulge.

'Are you two still interested in getting a car?' Lucy asked.

'We are,' Pauline replied. 'But the prices are still too high.'

Lucy beamed. 'Well, do I have a deal for you! I will sell you my Subaru for one dollar.'

'What?' asked Oumarou, shocked. 'No, that is too generous.'

'Well, look,' Lucy said, 'it has seventy-eight thousand miles on it and there's something squidgy going on with the emergency brake. However, it also has a new set of tires and a full tank of gas.'

'We'll take it!' chirped Pauline.

'Pauline!' Oumarou protested.

A spate of rapid-fire French ensued. While Lucy was extremely bad at French, she could tell by the hand motions and general air of exasperation that Pauline was winning and Oumarou was deeply in love with his wife.

'Are you escaping from the law?' Oumarou asked Lucy.

'No, I am running away to be with the man I love.'

'Carl?' Pauline gasped.

'*Not* Carl,' Lucy said, absolutely not laughing. 'Carl is here because he's a notary. For the car title. To make it official.'

Carl held his hand up showing the couple his very official notary stamp thingy that looked like it could have been purchased at Staples.

'We will take it,' Oumarou said finally.

Five minutes and four-quarters later, Oumarou and Pauline were the proud owners of an eight-year-old Subaru hatchback and Lucy was one step closer to the future.

Lucy was clearly too practical for her own good. She couldn't just hop on a plane, damn the consequences. She had to carefully dismantle her life first. She had to be sure her students would be in good hands for the fall semester. She had to write a letter of resignation and formally withdraw from the tenure review process. Then, when that was done, she had to spend an enormous chunk of her life savings on a last-minute, one-way ticket to Monaco. As one does.

The internal struggle was a whole other animal. She could have texted or called Nicky at any point. Typed something like, 'Hey, remember that invitation? Uh, quitting my whole fucking life over here. Still into that?' But she didn't. She couldn't. She wanted to *show* Nicky that she was *in it*, that she was leaping. She needed to feel it. For her own sanity. Lucy had to experience every brave step, if giving up on everything she'd ever worked for could be considered brave and not colossally stupid.

What's more, Lucy wanted to be there to witness Nicky's reaction, to see with her own eyes that she hadn't irreparably and terminally screwed up what they had because of her lifelong reliance on the safety of inertia. It couldn't be easy. She wouldn't let it be easy. For all those years Nicky had needed her to *want* to be found. It was beyond time for Lucy to prove exactly how much she wanted it – by leaping headfirst into the unknown and hoping that she wouldn't fall flat on her face.

Lucy made one last tour of her home. The dusty corners she hadn't had time to clean, the bathroom faucet that dripped and needed mending.

She passed Chloe's childhood bedroom and couldn't resist peeking in. Chloe wasn't there, of course, she was in Boston. All she'd left behind were dog-eared Taylor Swift posters and a bunch of boxes that probably wouldn't get opened again for a decade. There were memories, too. Sweet ones. Maybe bittersweet since the place they all happened would very likely live only in Lucy's memory from then on.

Still, Lucy trudged forward. Past the sofa she'd spent hours on, past the front door she'd painted blue after her last divorce. She locked the house up tight and rolled her suitcase down the driveway that Chloe had turned into a gruesome chalk-art masterpiece every Halloween.

Lucy knew that the little tug she felt in her chest when she got in the Uber wasn't fatal. It was only the evidence of an ending. That her choice meant something dear and true.

*

In further proof that life is not like the movies, Lucy's seven days of craziness were followed by two hours of drinking terrible coffee and being fondled by the TSA, ninety minutes of layover in New York, another ninety minutes in Paris, and thirteen total hours in the air. This was followed by a car ride from Nice with a driver who really, really loved French rap. Every single moment was spent oozing excitement, doubt, and fear in equal measures.

By the time Lucy's taxi pulled up to the exquisite Hôtel de Paris Monte-Carlo at 5 p.m. the day after she'd walked out of her living room in Ohio, she was shaking with the nerves she'd been desperately trying to hold up over her head like a boom box blaring Peter Gabriel.

The surroundings didn't help. The hotel was intimidating. Grand on a scale that made Lucy's palms sweat. Luxurious as a fairy tale. Or an Audrey Hepburn movie. Maybe a fairy-tale Audrey Hepburn movie. Golden, Cote d'Azur twilight streamed in from an extravagant domed skylight. A bronze statue of Louis the XIV on horseback stood sentry at one end of the marbled hall. Its bent knee was rubbed shiny and bright by gamblers hoping for a mystical edge on the casino. She knew this because, ever the researcher, Lucy had downloaded a traveler's guide on her Kindle with the hope that it would make her feel more prepared for what lay ahead. (Spoiler, it did not.)

Lucy wheeled her bag to the sculpture of Louis and ran her clammy fingers along the smooth bronze of the horse's knee. Superstitions weren't usually part of Lucy's repertoire, but at this point she'd try anything that might put luck on her side. She was all-in on the biggest gamble of her life; she'd take any edge she could get.

Lucy checked her phone. There was a text from Kim.

KimmyR: I think you're there by now. Don't text me. Just go get him. You're doing great. It will all be GREAT. I miss you! I love you!

Lucy tried to smile, then dug through her old messages for Chloe's text.

Chloe had reached out to Nicky with some excuse about post-wedding thank-you notes to get his location. He'd been forthcoming and asked about her honeymoon. Chloe had pasted their whole conversation into their long mother-daughter thread, and his interest and sweetness had felt like nails being driven into Lucy's heart.

God, she hoped he would forgive her. If he didn't . . . well, if he didn't, she would deal with it. Probably. She might deal with it by curling up in the fetal position under the ginormous floral arrangement in the lobby of the Hôtel de Paris Monte-Carlo, but she would deal with it. So, that was something. A backup plan.

She approached the reception attendant.

'How may I be of service to you, *madame*?' the silver-haired man said in a thick French accent.

'I am joining a friend,' she said, uttering the lines she had rehearsed in her head somewhere over the Atlantic. Lucy did her best to project confidence as she pressed on, 'He's staying in the Garnier Suite.'

The man was silent, but perused her in a way that made it perfectly clear that he knew exactly who was staying in the Garnier Suite. The man scrutinized her as though strange women trying to get into the Garnier Suite was a regular occurrence. Lucy's heart vanished into a black hole.

'Your name, *madame*?'

'Rollins,' Lucy offered.

The man picked up the house phone, dialing a string of numbers. She caught a heavily accented 'Rollins' and a couple of 'ouis.'

'One moment, please,' the attendant said before disappearing through a door behind the desk.

Lucy was half convinced they thought she was a stalker and she was about to be escorted off to some Monte-Carlo jail cell when the older man arrived with a young woman in tow.

'Please, follow me,' he said to Lucy.

Here it comes. If the jails in Monte-Carlo are even a tenth as nice as the hotels I'll be fine. I'll call Kim and try again tomorrow.

But the hotel employee didn't veer off for the exit, instead he moved further into the hotel to a discreetly placed elevator. He pulled out a keycard, attached to his sport coat by a lanyard, and waved it in front of a keypad.

'Bonsoir, Madame Rollins,' he said with a bow as the elevator doors opened.

He pressed the button for the second floor and waited for the doors to close between them.

When the doors opened again, Lucy was greeted by a smiling semi-familiar face. 'Hello, Lucy,' he said in a distinctly American accent. 'I'm Jacob, we met in Las Vegas?'

Lucy's jet-lagged brain clicked slowly, but finally placed the man. From the Scala Theater, in another hotel some five thousand miles away. On a different continent. A lifetime ago.

Behind Jacob was a very large black man with muscles stacked on top of his muscles, all of them squeezed into a smart black suit and thin black tie. Lucy noticed an earpiece curled around his ear.

Jesus. Security.

'Right this way,' Jacob said, taking off down the hall.

She followed Jacob, the suited giant, and his muscles.

By the time Jacob stopped at a door, Lucy was overcome by a sensation that was alarmingly similar to the one and only time she'd done 'shrooms in college. She felt woozy and like her bones were made of jelly.

Jacob knocked on the door before Lucy could stop him. To collect herself. To take a breath.

Lucy heard the lock click open and half expected to see another brawny bodyguard. Instead, it was Nicky.

Shock was the only thing she could read from his expression. Shock and maybe a little confusion. He was scruffy, like he hadn't shaved in a couple of days. The black T-shirt she'd worn in Vegas hung off his strong shoulders and highlighted the brash color of his tattooed arms.

Nicky nodded to the men behind her.

Jacob and the giant shuffled off.

Lucy dropped the handle of her suitcase and rubbed her hands roughly on her pants.

She blurted, 'I fucked up.' *Not* the words she had rehearsed in her head over the Atlantic. Still, she held his gaze, willing him to understand.

Nicky opened the door completely, stood aside to let her pass. Lucy was briefly spellbound by the amber and lavender show of sunset over the Mediterranean through the suite's windows, then by Nicky who was rolling her suitcase into the room and shutting the door.

Lucy tried, 'I was scared. I was closed off. I was . . . I was pot committed. Do you know what that means?'

Nicky nodded.

'My career is the only thing I've ever really invested in, I think. Other than Chloe. A lifeline. A crutch, maybe? Safe and steady. Being on campus, with its permanence and its rules. The seasons and semesters. It was where I was happiest. *Was*. Past tense. Because now, I know I am happiest when I'm with you. That I will be the happiest I have ever been with *you*. Wherever that is.'

Nicky stepped closer, further into the room, but remained terrifyingly silent. He leaned his back against the white-paneled walls of the living area and looked at his feet.

She blubbered, 'I was scared. I was stuck. I think . . .' Lucy was floundering. Lost. 'I think that night at the beach was pivotal for me, too. But instead of making me free, it might have . . . it might have made me careful. Too careful. I'm not saying it's your fault. I'm only saying, I couldn't leap. I trained myself not to.'

Nicky was still studying the carpet. She was screwing this up.

'I quit my job,' she said.

At that, Nicky looked up.

She pressed on, 'I set a match to nearly every professional bridge I've ever built.' She chewed at her lip, racking her brain for any scrap of evidence that might keep him looking at her. 'I, um, got a real estate agent. She's putting my house on the market on Monday. I sold my car. For one dollar to the grad students that live next door to me. They're from Cameroon. They have a baby named Marthe who still has that delicious new baby smell.'

What the fuck was she saying? Why didn't she know what the fuck to say? She had been giving lectures for most of her adult life. She knew how to speak! *Where is that Badass Bitch when I need her?*

She went on, 'I emptied my cupboards and returned my cable boxes. I flew here on a one-way ticket. No return.' Lucy thought her heart was going to crack open. She pressed her fingers to her tired eyes and felt two-day-old mascara crumbling beneath them.

Lucy said, 'I love you, Nicky.' She stared into those loden green eyes of his and repeated, 'I love you in a way that is terrifying and shocking and like nothing I've ever felt before.' She took a deep breath. 'I'm leaping now. Upside down and backwards probably, judging by the look on your face. But I'm doing it. I came here because I love you and I don't want to spend the *next* twenty-eight years regretting you. If you . . . if you still want me.'

Nicky took three great strides toward her. He wrapped his arms under hers and around her back, lifting her feet from the ground. When his mouth came to hers, Lucy finally exhaled. He breathed her in and swallowed her down, kissing her so hard that her body went limp under the weight of her relief and gratitude.

His grip around her tightened. 'I've got you, Lou,' he said. 'I love you. I've got you.'

He steadied his gaze on hers. 'Now we're even, okay? I disappeared once. You disappeared once. Even. But that's it. Next time you feel like running, you talk to me.'

'I won't run,' Lucy insisted.

'It might not be that simple. I hope it is, but just promise me that we can do this together.'

'I promise.'

Nicky lifted Lucy up and carried her into a nearby bedroom. He placed her gently on the crisp white linens and began undressing her. First her shoes. Then her socks. The rumpled cardigan she'd put on in Ohio.

'How long were you on a plane, baby?' he asked, laying the dirty cardigan carefully over a chair.

'Thirteen hours plus layovers,' she replied.

'Shit,' he mumbled.

'I really need a shower, Nicky,' she said, suddenly realizing where all the clothing removal was headed when she spotted the outline of a suspicious bulge in his sweatpants.

'I don't care if you don't, Lou,' he said, pausing with his hand at the button of her pants.

'Go on then.' She smiled. When Nicky smiled back, Lucy knew that whatever might come next, for a dozen years or a hundred, or five minutes it would be worth it. Whatever she had to give up was nothing compared to what she would get back.

'You quit your job, Lou? Really? For me?' he asked, pulling her pants and underwear down in one go.

'Well, for *me*. To be with you. You were right – I wasn't happy. I hadn't been for a while. Maybe you'll turn out to be my toupee, or my Margaritaville,' she said, referencing their conversation on the balcony of the Lusso. 'But I know I was stuck . . . personally, professionally. All of it. Now I'm free to do what I want.'

'With me,' Nicky added.

'With you.'

'I think I'd rather be the Porsche.'

He hopped on the bed beside her.

She laughed. 'Like a classic model with a few miles under the hood?' she teased.

'Like a finely tuned, world-class machine. With power and speed.'

'Oh, right. Of course.'

'I love you,' he said against her lips, pulling her shirt over her head.

'Say it again,' she begged.

'I love you,' he whispered in her ear.

'I love you, too,' she said, trying to hold herself together and not weep with pure relief.

'I missed you,' he said.

'God, Nicky, I missed you so fucking much I don't even know how to describe it. It felt like the whole world was a different place without you in it. I was lost.'

Lucy arched her back just long enough for Nicky to unhook her bra and fling it in the direction of her cardigan.

'I'm here now. You're here now. I can't fucking believe you're in Monaco.'

'I can't believe I'm naked and you still have all your clothes on,' Lucy said, making a pointed glance down his still fully dressed frame.

'*Shit*,' he said as though just realizing he was the only one in the room with clothes on.

The bed was a flurry of motion, T-shirt, pants, boxers, and socks tossed haphazardly around the place.

When Nicky finally settled again, he put the full weight of himself – skin to skin – against her. Brought his soft lips to her ear.

'I love you,' he murmured.

Lucy felt her entire body relax, the tension of days – weeks – melting into the mattress beneath her. She carded her fingernails through his soft brown waves and replied, 'I love you.'

Nicky slowly brought his lips to one cheek, then the other. He touched their noses together and exhaled, long and slow as if he'd been holding his breath and was finally able to release it. When she brought her teeth to his lower lip, his hips jerked and she could feel the hot length of him pressing on her hip.

She said, 'I'm not going to be much help to you right now, but I want you close. Please.'

Nicky pushed up on one arm, trailed the other lazily over her breast. His calloused fingers lifted goose bumps on her exposed skin as he gently stroked her waist, then her thigh.

When his fingers found her wet, needy core she gasped, '*Nicky.*'

'God, I want to hear that forever.'

'Okay,' Lucy mumbled, losing herself in his touch.

'Everything. Always,' he whispered, rising up and slotting himself between her welcoming thighs.

When he slid slowly inside her, Lucy was struck by the sudden thought that they were made for each other. It was astounding, really, that they had found one another at that dumb party a million years before. That they had found each other a second time was nothing short of miraculous. She resolved never to tempt fate again. Another miracle would be asking too much of the universe.

Time lost all of its meaning and power as Nicky kissed her, held her, worked himself inside her. She chanted his name like a prayer. Into his mouth, his ear, the soft curve of his neck that perpetually smelled like clean ocean air and sunshine.

'*Nicky*, please,' she begged when the exhaustion and pleasure had become overwhelming.

He gently brought them both to their sides, his arm tucked under her neck. Her lips found his as he lifted her knee and hooked it over his hip.

She gasped at the friction. At the perfection. Then, Lucy came apart. She pressed her hands on the firm swell of his ass to push him deep and hold him there as the muscles inside her grasped and squeezed at him. She held him close until she could feel the pulse of him inside her and was deafened by his groans and her name breathed out like a sigh when he stilled.

Endings are beginnings. Sometimes, they're the same.

CHAPTER FORTY-THREE

LUCY

Lucy was running late. She'd bumped into Tiffy outside the Scala Theater and had been cajoled into giving a 'fantastic!' update on Chloe and Chandler that had screwed up her schedule.

Super was finally finishing their residency – which had been extended once, then twice. Tonight was the band's final show after approximately seven hundred years on tour. The residency at the Lusso was designed as a break from the grind of the road, but three shows a week hadn't felt like a break from anything for any of them. Even Lucy, who did nothing but watch every performance from the wings like the number-one groupie she was, felt like she could use a few months off.

Lucy had long since memorized Super's entire catalog forward and back. She still cried every time she heard 'The Breathing Room,' but for different reasons than all those years before.

Lucy stood in front of the bathroom mirror, in suite 4023, their home away from . . . well, the other twelve thousand hotel rooms they'd lived in. She inspected her look against a picture of Madonna on her phone.

Close enough.

The final show at the Lusso happened to land on Halloween, so the band decided to make it a party and give it a theme – Eighties Night. Lucy was dressed as circa-1984 Madonna in all of her MTV VMAs 'Like a Virgin' glory. She slipped on a pair of white lace opera gloves and bedazzled her wrist with as many diamond bangles as the costume shop on Charleston had to spare.

She rushed out of the suite, passing Nicky's bandmate Hooper in the hall.

'Madonna,' he said, by way of a greeting.

'Rick,' she replied flatly. Hoop was supposed to be Rick Astley from his most famous video, but something about the combo of the tats crawling up his neck, the scraggly man bun, and the long camel raincoat made him look more like a subway flasher.

Hope no one tells him before I have the chance. She loved giving that guy shit almost as much as Nicky did.

Lucy was spit out by the Penthouse Tower elevator into the lobby and raced past the check-in, waving to the now familiar crew stationed there.

Then she thought of something. 'Oh, Wanda,' she shouted to the woman behind the desk. 'Remind your son to email me that admissions essay, okay?' Wanda's son wanted to get into UCLA and Lucy had enthusiastically promised to help.

'Will do, Lucy,' Wanda called back. 'Thank you!'

Lucy spun herself through the revolving doors. Instead of their usual black SUV, she found their driver, Sonny, standing beside a Rolls-Royce.

'What is this?' Lucy asked Sonny as he opened the rear door for her.

'The Range Rover is being detailed. And Nick thought this was more on-theme.'

'Oh, shit,' she exclaimed, after her mind caught up. It was a convertible, but the soft top was up. 'It's the car from *Sixteen Candles*, isn't it?'

'Same model,' Sonny replied.

'Cool,' she said. 'Thanks, Sonny,' she trilled as she slipped into the back.

'My pleasure, Miss Ciccone,' he replied, using Madonna's real last name.

'Nice,' Lucy replied with a fist bump.

Lucy plopped herself in the back seat and took a deep, cleansing breath.

Phew. Made it.

The car started up and headed off into Las Vegas.

'Oh, hi!' she said to Nicky as he scooted closer to her. She bussed a quick smooch on his cheek, then wiped the red lipstick off with her thumb. She asked, 'How was your day?'

'Good,' he replied dully, before sitting back in the seat. His eyes were focused on the rearview mirror, and he was suspiciously quiet.

She asked, 'What's up? Something happen with Wade?'

A ton of family was in town for the final Super show,

including Nicky's sons. Nicky and Wade had gone out golfing. Nicky really only enjoyed golf when he was playing with Alice Cooper. Maybe that was it?

'Nope,' Nicky said. 'All good.'

'Hey,' Lucy said. She felt Nicky jolt beside her, but decided to ignore it. 'Can I be the one to tell Hooper that he looks nothing like Rick Astley and everything like a dirty old man who likes to expose his junk to unsuspecting ladies on the subway?'

Nicky laughed, but didn't look at her. 'Sure,' he said.

'Good, thanks,' Lucy said. 'Where are we going for dinner? Think I'm underdressed?' she joked, waving a hand to indicate her lace-covered bodice.

'Um, about that,' Nicky drawled.

Lucy followed Nicky's gaze through the window and yelled, 'What the hell?'

Outside the Rolls-Royce, past a tidy sidewalk and a couple of potted cactus plants, was a sturdy square office building. Not a restaurant. Big cursive letters over the door spelled out, *Marriage License Bureau.*

Nicky turned toward her, and she noticed that he was wearing a black tuxedo T-shirt.

Oh shit.

Lucy carped, 'I thought you were going to be Spicoli.'

'I said a character from *Fast Times*,' he retorted. 'You *assumed* Spicoli.'

'Holy shit,' Lucy said, the fist rays of enlightenment dawning. 'I'm a . . . *bride* and you're . . .'

'A groom, yeah.'

Nicky smiled his soft, pleading smile. The one that Lucy knew, after all their time together, was the prelude to him asking for something. It was usually something kinky, but this felt different.

He took her hands in his, focused those damn irresistible green eyes on her. 'Lou, I know you said you would only get married again if it was accidentally, but it turns out that's not actually legal outside terrible Nineties sitcoms. And, fuck do I want it to be legal, baby.' He reached into the pocket of his jeans and pulled out a slip of paper. 'I got Chloe to help me fill out the forms online. All we have to do is hand them this piece of paper.'

Nicky turned one of her hands over and rested the narrow sheet on her palm, their names and a string of numbers and letters typed on it.

Nicky continued, 'All *you* have to do is say yes and go in there with me and hand over this piece of paper. They'll give us a license and we'll go down to the drive-thru at the Little White Wedding Chapel.'

'Just like Elvis and Priscilla,' Lucy said dumbly, because her addled brain was not functioning properly.

'Yep, except I don't think that was a drive-thru. And I'm pretty sure it was at the old Aladdin Casino. And I don't plan on dying on a toilet. But otherwise, yeah, just like that.'

Lucy was stunned. Surprised, but not angry. Just shocked really.

Nicky reached into the pocket of his khaki pants and pulled out a black velvet box. He opened it to reveal three rings. Two wedding bands and an enormous diamond solitaire that glimmered even in the dim car light.

Lucy chuckled. 'Wow. You know when they say an engagement ring should cost two months' salary, I don't think it counts for rock stars on tour.'

Nicky smiled. 'Worth it.'

Lucy fondled the rings lightly with her fingertips, then tugged the engagement ring from its velvet recess. Inside the band she noticed etching. Writing. It said, *There with you, that was it*.

She looked up to Nicky with watery eyes, questioning.

He answered her by pulling the two platinum bands from the box and placing them carefully on top of the paper in her palm. Inside the larger ring was etched *Everything from you*. And in the smaller, was *Anything for you*. No question mark.

'Yes,' Lucy breathed.

'Yeah?' Nicky asked, as though he had really been unsure of her answer. *This fucking guy*.

'Of course,' Lucy replied. 'You're it for me, Broome.'

'You mean it?'

'I would accidentally marry you any day.'

In a flash, Lucy had an engagement ring on her finger, and Sonny was opening the back door for them.

Within thirty minutes, the top was down on the Rolls and they were in a carport with blinking twinkly lights and cherubs staring down at them.

A very nice man in blue suede shoes (who was not Elvis) said, 'Do you, Nicholas Trent Broome, take this woman, Lucy Diane McManis, to be your lawfully wedded wife?'

And he did.

And then she did.

They slipped rings on each other's fingers and when the man who was not Elvis said, 'You may kiss the bride,' The Crystals 'Then He Kissed Me' bubbled from the car's speakers.

And Nicky kissed her. Long and slow, and with far too much tongue for the number of witnesses present (three).

Their wedding dinner was drive-thru Jack in the Box in the back of the convertible right under the blazing neon of the Welcome to Las Vegas sign in the cool desert night air. It was, without a doubt, the best wedding Lucy had ever had.

It was sure as hell going to be the last.

ENCORE

NICKY

Lucy guided the Jeep to the curb on Stockley Street, right in front of the old house. It looked like it needed new siding and probably a new roof, but Nicky would have recognized it anywhere. The image of it had lived in his memory like one of the seven wonders of the world. He could remember the feeling of joy in his belly as he'd glanced at it in his rearview mirror, headed back to Dover to load up his shit and spend the summer with Lucy. And he could easily recall the despair when he'd driven by it in Super's first beat-up old tour van.

The Jeep they were in now was a hell of a lot nicer than either of those cars, and a whole lot of years had passed. But he and Lucy were finally getting their summer at the beach.

'There it is,' Nicky said as Lucy put the car in park.
'Yep, there it is,' she parroted. 'Hey, Nicky?'
'Yeah?'

'I didn't get us an Airbnb on Silver Lake.'

'No?'

She brushed her windswept bangs from her eyelashes and tucked her hair behind her ear. 'Remember how you told me that I should spend some of your money—'

'*Our* money,' he corrected.

'Right, our money.'

He noticed then that Lucy seemed a little nervous.

'Did you?' he asked. 'You don't have to feel bad about it, Lou.'

'I bought *you* something,' she said.

She reached into the pocket of her jacket and pulled out a Philadelphia Eagles keychain. She shook it between them, the three keys there jangling like bells.

He was utterly fucking speechless, could feel his eyes bugging out of his head.

Nicky snatched the keys from her hand. 'Are you serious?' he screamed, about to jump out of his skin with excitement.

'Look, I paid too much,' she said as he whipped the car door open. Somewhere behind him she shouted, 'Kim acted as her dad's broker and I'm not entirely sure if that helped us or made it ten times worse. But it's ours, either way.'

Nicky raced to the back door of the house on Stockley Street, fumbled with the keys until he found one that fit into the lock.

'Oh, my God, it's the same! It's almost exactly the same!' he yelped.

He ran through the living room and opened the door to

the front porch. The cushions were different but . . . 'Is that the same fucking porch furniture?' he yelled out to Lucy.

She stepped out from the house. 'Probably.'

'And we get to live here together, alone all summer?' he exclaimed.

'I mean, all the kids are coming in July. But I rented them a house down the block. We can live here as long as we want.'

'We'll get a boom box off eBay, okay? Put it right there in the corner.' He felt like he was bouncing on marshmallows, like his damn chest was full of bubbles. It was ridiculous.

Lucy laughed. 'I mean, I thought we should probably get a dumpster and have everything hauled away.'

'No. Nope,' Nicky griped. 'Veto.'

He raced to Lucy and held her tight. Pressed a kiss to her temple and tried not to cry.

'Best present ever, Lou,' he said when her eyes locked on his.

'Yeah?'

'Yeah.'

He said, 'Some superfan is making a museum out of my old apartment in Seattle. Did you know that?'

'No, I didn't.'

'Closing off the room I slept in behind velvet ropes and using old pictures to recreate it. My lumpy-ass mattress on the floor and the dresser I used to prop my guitar on in the corner. Making it a shrine.'

'Because that's where you wrote "The Breathing Room,"' she said matter-of-factly.

'Because they think it *is* the Breathing Room, Lou.'

Nicky laced his fingers in Lucy's and pulled her through the living room, past the bathroom (that he might be willing to have gutted) and down the hall.

And then, there they were. Together. In the Breathing Room.

Fucking finally.

'Better late than never,' he roared, flinging himself on the bed, not caring one bit that he was acting like a kid on Christmas. 'Why do you still have clothes on?' he quipped to Lucy.

She laughed, a sound better than any song he'd ever written. He wanted to hear it every fucking day for the rest of his life.

'Slow your roll there, big guy,' she griped playfully.

Lucy pulled her phone from the back of her jeans and fumbled around clicking apps.

He was about to get up and drag her into the double bed that was way smaller than he remembered when the first heavy growls of 'Speedy Marie' came out of her phone.

'*Jesus*,' he said, lying back and letting thirty years or so melt away.

Just when he thought he couldn't get any happier, Lucy nestled herself next to him. Found her favorite spot with her head on his shoulder and her leg draped over his thigh.

'I fucking love you, Lucy Broome.'

'I fucking love you more, Nicky Broome.'

ACKNOWLEDGMENTS

While writing a novel takes place in isolation, publishing a book most definitely does not.

First, a mere thank you cannot express the depth of gratitude I feel for my amazing agent, Judith Murray. Your enthusiasm, humor, and kindness are outmatched only by your business savvy and publishing chops. I feel so lucky to have you at my side as I kick off this new chapter of my career.

Thank you also to the rest of the team at Greene & Heaton Literary Agency, especially Mia Dakin, who endures my rambling emails and time zone confusion with patience and grace.

The team at HQ has been so lovely and supportive. Kate Byrne, you are a spectacular editor and I suspect that you might love Nicky Broome even more than I do, which is the stuff author dreams are made of.

On the home front, my parents Randy and Shawn Morris are the very foundation of my support system. You know how much I love you, but look! Here it is in print to prove it! My sisters Mary Morris Turocy and Katie Smith and their families are the best cheerleaders. Mary, who is almost as obsessed with romance as I am, is also a world-class beta reader. Thank you.

It was easy to write Kim and Lucy's relationship only because (for forty-plus years!) Jen Dorre and Sarah Castellano have demonstrated what true, deep, unrelenting friendship looks like. Thank you for your unwavering encouragement and for quality answers to questions that begin with 'Am I crazy?' I hope you know that I love you both beyond words. And I always have my shovel.

Finally, thank you to my calm, steady, tolerant husband Tony, and my glorious boys, E & M. You two march through the world with such astounding bravery and determination. Your stellar example gave me the courage to write more books. I love you.

EXTRAS

Kitty

'Wild Horses' – The Sundays, *Blind*
'When the Sun Hits' – Slowdive, *Souvlaki*
'Black' – Pearl Jam, *Ten*
'Sugar Kane' – Sonic Youth, *Dirty*
'Black Dog' – Led Zeppelin, *Mothership*
'Bad for the Soul' – Brad, *Shame*
'Slide Away' – The Verve, *A Storm in Heaven*
'Lover, You Should Have Come Over' – Jeff Buckley, *Live at Sin*-é
'Little Wing' – Stevie Ray Vaughan, *Couldn't Stand the Weather*
'Sweet Jane' – Cowboy Junkies, *The Trinity Session*
'The Day I Tried to Live' – Soundgarden, *Superunknown*
'Yellow Ledbetter' – Pearl Jam, B-Side Single of 'Jeremy'
'Ecstasy' – PJ Harvey, *Rid of Me*
'Butterfly McQueen' – The Boo Radleys, *Giant Steps*
'Gentlemen' – Afghan Whigs, *Gentlemen*
'Fade into You' – Mazzy Star, *So Tonight That I Might See*
'Creep' – Radiohead, *Pablo Honey*

Lucy's Make-out Mix

'Speedy Marie' – Frank Black, *Teenager of the Year*
'Summer Babe' – Pavement, *Westing (by Musket and Sextant)*
'Cherry Bomb' – The Runaways, *The Runaways*
'The Lemon Song' – Led Zeppelin, *Led Zeppelin II*
'Soon' – My Bloody Valentine, *Loveless*
'Close to Me' – The Cure, *The Head on the Door*
'Stutter' – Elastica, *Elastica*
'Cannonball' – The Breeders, *Last Splash*
'Rebel Girl' – Bikini Kill, *Yeah Yeah Yeah Yeah*
'Bad Girl' – New York Dolls, *New York Dolls*
'Seether' – Veruca Salt, *American Thighs*
'Supernova' – Liz Phair, *Whip-Smart*
'Laid' – James, *Laid*
'Here Comes Your Man' – Pixies, *Doolittle*
'Just Like Heaven' – The Cure, *Kiss Me, Kiss Me, Kiss Me*
'Birthday' – The Sugarcubes, *Life's Too Good*
'Here's Where the Story Ends' – The Sundays, *Reading, Writing & Arithmetic*

Lou

'Interstate Love Song' – Stone Temple Pilots, *Purple*
'Lover, You Should Have Come Over' – Jeff Buckley, *Grace*
'Doesn't Remind Me' – Audioslave, *Out of Exile*
'You've Got a Killer Scene There, Man' – Queens of the Stone Age, *Lullabies to Paralyze*

'Fucked My Way to the Top' – Lana Del Rey, *Ultraviolence*
'Love Spreads' – The Stone Roses, *Second Coming*
'Everlong' – Foo Fighters, *The Colour and the Shape*
'Elderly Woman Behind the Counter in a Small Town' – Pearl Jam, *Vs.*
'Death by Rock and Roll' – The Pretty Reckless, *Death by Rock and Roll*
'Woman' – Wolfmother, *Wolfmother*
'Chelsea Dagger' – The Fratellis, *Costello Music*
'Thunderstruck' – AC/DC, *The Razors Edge*
'505' – Arctic Monkeys, *Favourite Worst Nightmare*
'All Right Now' – Free, *Fire and Water*
'Save It for Later' – Eddie Vedder, *Save It for Later* (Single)

Rehoboth Mix

'Sweetness' – Jimmy Eat World, *Bleed American*
'Such Great Heights' – The Postal Service, *Give Up*
'Here Comes Your Man' – Pixies, *Doolittle*
'High and Dry' – Radiohead, *The Bends*
'Follow Me Down' – The Pretty Reckless, *Going to Hell*
'Hate to Say I Told You So' – The Hives, *Veni Vidi Vicious*
'Doesn't Remind Me of Anything' – Audioslave, *Out of Exile*
'He Can Only Hold Her' – Amy Winehouse, *Back to Black*
'Use Me' – Bill Withers, *Still Bill*
'Everlong' – Foo Fighters, *The Colour and the Shape*
'Radiation Vibe' – Fountains of Wayne, *Fountains of Wayne*

'All My Ghosts' – Lizzy McAlpine, *five seconds flat*
'Wild Child' – The Black Keys, *Dropout Boogie*
'Blame Brett' – The Beaches, *Blame My Ex*
'Wet Dream' – Wet Leg, *Wet Leg*
'Got You (Where I Want You)' – The Flys, *Holiday Man*
'Bros' – Wolf Alice, *My Love Is Cool*
'Jealous Guy' – Donny Hathaway, *Live*
'It's Oh So Quiet' – Björk, *Post*
'Lightning of July' – Baird, *BIRDSONGS, Vol. 3*
'Maps' – Yeah, Yeah, Yeahs, *Fever to Tell*

Dear Reader,
We hope you enjoyed reading this book. If you did, we'd be so appreciative if you left a review. It really helps us and the author to bring more books like this to you.

Here at HQ Digital we are dedicated to publishing fiction that will keep you turning the pages into the early hours. Don't want to miss a thing? To find out more about our books, promotions, discover exclusive content and enter competitions you can keep in touch in the following ways:

JOIN OUR COMMUNITY:
Sign up to our new email newsletter: http://smarturl.it/SignUpHQ
Read our new blog www.hqstories.co.uk

𝕏 https://twitter.com/HQStories
f www.facebook.com/HQStories

BUDDING WRITER?
We're also looking for authors to join the HQ Digital family!
Find out more here:

https://www.hqstories.co.uk/want-to-write-for-us/

Thanks for reading, from the HQ Digital team